Massacre
at Sirte

PIERCE KELLEY

MASSACRE AT SIRTE

iUniverse books may be ordered through booksellers or by contacting:

iUniverse
1663 Liberty Drive
Bloomington, IN 47403
www.iuniverse.com
1-800-Authors (1-800-288-4677)

ISBN: 978-1-4917-9655-9 (sc)
ISBN: 978-1-4917-9657-3 (hc)
ISBN: 978-1-4917-9656-6 (e)

Library of Congress Control Number: 2016909577

Print information available on the last page.

iUniverse rev. date: 11/29/2016

Massacre
at Sirte

OTHER WORKS BY PIERCE KELLEY

To Valhalla (iUniverse, 2015)

A Deadly Legacy (iUniverse, 2013)

Roxy Blues (iUniverse, 2012)

Father, I Must Go (iUniverse, 2011)

Thousand Yard Stare (iUniverse, 2010)

Kennedy Homes: An American Tragedy (iUniverse, 2009)

A Foreseeable Risk (iUniverse, 2009)

Asleep at the Wheel (iUniverse, 2009)

A Tinker's Damn! (iUniverse, 2008)

Bocas del Toro (iUniverse, 2007)

A Plenary Indulgence (iUniverse, 2007)

Pieces to the Puzzle (iUniverse, 2007)

Introducing Children to the Game of Tennis (iUniverse, 2007)

A Very Fine Line (iUniverse, 2006)

Fistfight at the L and M Saloon (iUniverse, 2006)

Civil Litigation: A Case Study (Pearson Publications, 2001)

The Parent's Guide to Coaching Tennis (F &W Publications, 1995)

A Parent's Guide to Coaching Tennis (Betterway Publications, 1991)

ABOUT THE COVER ART

Front Cover

The artwork on the front cover was created by Tony Rezk, an artist who lives in Alexandria, Virginia. It depicts the twenty-one men who were put to death by Islamic extremists in Sirte, Libya, last year. Those men have been declared martyrs by both the Coptic Church and the Roman Catholic Church.

Mr. Rezk was born in Egypt, and he is a Copt. He uses a computer to create his art, which is called digital iconography. He characterizes the icons he creates as "windows to heaven" that tell a story and have theological implications.

Further biographic information may be found at National Review Online. He was interviewed by Kathryn Jean Lopez, a senior fellow at the National Review Institute, in February 2015, and a copy of that interview may be found at their website. He also writes a blog called *Contra Mundum*, which is Latin for "against the world."

Back Cover

The photograph on the back cover pictures St. Mark's Coptic Church in Cairo, Egypt. It is the mother church of the Coptic Christians. The original Coptic Church, established by St. Mark in the first century, is in Alexandria.

This book is dedicated to the twenty-one Coptic Christians who were beheaded in Sirte, Libya, in February of 2015 by members of ISIS and to all others who have been killed by terrorists in recent years because of their religious beliefs. The names of those twenty-one men are as follows:

- Milad Makeen Zaky
- Abanub Ayad Atiya
- Maged Soliman Shehata
- Youssef Shukry Younan
- Kirollos Boshra Fawzy
- Bishoy Astafanous Kamel
- Samuel Astafanous Kamel
- Malak Ibrahim Sinyout
- Tawadros Youssef Tawadros
- Gerges Milad Sinyout
- Mina Fayez Aziz
- Hany Abdel Mesih Salib
- Samuel Alham Wilson
- Ezzat Boshra Naseef
- Luka Nagaty Anis
- Gaber Mounir Adly
- Essam Baddar Samir
- Malak Farag Abrahim
- Sameh Salah Farouk
- Gerges Samir Megally
- Mathew Ayairga

DISCLAIMER

This is a work of fiction. It is, however, based upon what actually happened in Sirte, Libya, in February of 2015 to twenty-one Coptic Christians who were beheaded by Muslim extremists. That is fact, not fiction. There were no survivors, so no one knows what actually took place after the men were captured and before they were killed.

I have taken the liberty of creating the characters and the dialogue in order to tell the story of what happened to those men so that the world may remember what took place last year and what is continuing to occur in that part of the world to this day. Any resemblance to the actual people involved in that horrific incident is purely coincidental and completely unintentional.

The names of the people in this book are entirely fictitious. I used names that I believe are traditional ones in the Coptic community. No disrespect is intended to anyone, especially the families and friends of those who were killed. The topics of conversation among the men on the night before they were to be killed are entirely imagined, but we can be reasonably certain they did not include a discussion of the history of the Coptic religion, of Islam, or of any other such intellectual topics.

There were no college professors, church deacons, or successful businessmen among those twenty-one men, as there are in this book. They were simple men. All were ardent Coptic Christians. There was no Muslim in the group, as there is in this book. More than likely, they said prayers and sang spiritual songs. These were deeply religious men.

I am concerned that the portion of dialogue in which the men question their faith may be offensive to some. As an author, especially one who writes novels, I am a storyteller seeking to tell a tale that captures the imaginations of readers. I am keenly aware of the fact that all Copts suffered an enormous loss as a result of this incident, and no disrespect is intended to anyone. I purposely created conflict between the men regarding their beliefs in order to present different points of view, while knowing full well that such conflict more than likely didn't exist between those men. Please keep that in mind.

Many of the problems that exist in the Middle East today are at least fifteen hundred years in the making, dating back to when Mohammad established the Islamic religion, and some of the problems date back to the time when Christ walked the earth. The Coptic Church was created in Alexandria, Egypt, by St. Mark several years after Christ was crucified, and it has been in existence ever since. The Copts have endured nearly two thousand years of trials and tribulations, and they will endure this most recent tragedy as they have all others.

It is my hope that I have told a story that helps readers better understand the problems that exist in the Middle East and the world, based upon the differing religious beliefs of Christians, Muslims, and Jews. Moreover, I hope that I have fairly portrayed the Copts and their religion. I confess that I knew little about them prior to embarking upon this journey, and I could not be more impressed by what I have learned of them and the strength of their faith. Martyrdom is now and has always been an unwanted, but integral, part of their church.

I offer no solutions to the problems. However, we, as members of the human race, must find solutions to those problems, or else incidents like that which took place in Sirte last year will continue to occur. I hope you will find this book engaging and informative, but I ask you to remember as you read it that it is a work of fiction, though it is factually accurate in many respects.

ACKNOWLEDGMENTS

I thank those who have supported and encouraged me on this and other projects. I wish to specifically thank Paul Sullivan, Dennis Geagan, and Tug Miller, who have read drafts and offered their insights into this and other books. I also thank Sarah Disbrow, manager of the editorial consultation department within iUniverse, for her assistance with this project.

—Pierce Kelley

Those who cannot remember the past are condemned to repeat it.

—George Santayana

PROLOGUE

When Colonel Muammar Khaddafi was deposed and killed in 2011, after more than forty years of rule, a number of factions vied for control of Libya. Within a few years, some Islamic terrorist organizations, such as al-Qaeda of the Arabian Peninsula and ISIS, the Islamic State of Iraq and Syria, were among those groups.

At the beginning of 2015, ISIS actively began a military campaign to take over the city of Sirte, located on the Mediterranean Sea. It was a desirable target because of the lucrative oil business conducted there. The Libyan Army was as divided as the rest of the country, and it offered little resistance. The city and its inhabitants were in grave danger.

Despite the political instability and pervasive life-threatening situation, people in Sirte did their best to continue with their lives by caring for their families and conducting business as well as possible under the circumstances. Among their first challenges, after Khaddafi was gone, was the rebuilding of their homes and places of work.

After years of a destructive civil war, there was much need to repair a damaged infrastructure. Jobs in the construction industry were plentiful, and the pay was good. Many people came to Libya from neighboring countries to perform that work out of a desperate need for the money, knowing full well the risks of doing so.

With that as background, on a Friday afternoon, just past noon, in February of 2015, as twenty-one men—twenty of whom were from Egypt, and all of whom were Coptic Christians—were busily working at a construction site in the outskirts of Sirte, a young boy shouted out a warning.

CHAPTER 1

Captured

"Here they come! Hide!"

All of us stopped what we were doing and ran. We all knew who was coming. We were immediately afraid for our lives and safety.

We didn't want to be there. None of us did. I was with two of my older brothers, and though I was only sixteen, I looked much younger. My brothers were in their early twenties. Our father had been begging us to come home for weeks. We had been hearing the sounds of gunfire for days, and it had become louder and more frequent of late.

Though we knew the fighting was getting closer, we thought we had time. It was a Friday, and my brothers and all the other men we were with had decided to stay one more day to get our last paycheck before leaving. We were always paid on Saturdays.

Sirte had been the site of many battles since the people of Libya rose up against Khaddafi. It was where he had been born, and it was where he died in October of 2011. The city and its inhabitants had remained loyal to him to the end. It was his final stronghold.

After his death, the rebels mutilated his body and hung him in effigy for the world to see. The city was in shambles. Most buildings had been damaged or destroyed, many as a result of bombings from Western powers who wanted to see Khaddafi dead, including the United States. Within six months of his death, however, more than sixty thousand of the city's eighty thousand inhabitants were back in their homes, despite the devastation, after having been driven from Sirte while the most intense fighting and bombings were going on.

There was much work to be done to rebuild the city, so jobs were plentiful and the money was good—so good that it was hard for us to resist. Many of us in Egypt were desperate for work—especially in our little village of al-Aour. Things had been better for us since the army ousted Mohammad Morsi and his Muslim Brotherhood in July of 2013, but things weren't good. Christians had suffered much discrimination during the days when Morsi was in power, and it would take time to reverse that. It was nearly impossible to find a job, let alone a good-paying job, and our family badly needed the money.

After Khaddafi took control over Libya in 1969, he spent a fortune to turn what had been a small village into a large, prosperous city. He wanted to see an international airport built there, and he had plans to make it a center for a united Africa. Oil exploration in the country had been fruitful, and that brought more jobs, and money, to the area. Much more work was available in Sirte than there were people to do the work, and employers were paying top dollar to get good workers.

Four years later, when we were there, the country was still in turmoil, and Islamic terrorists bent on gaining control of the country were wreaking havoc throughout all of Libya. There was a weak central government and a weak military. No one like Khaddafi had emerged to lead the country as he had, and one wasn't likely to emerge for some time to come.

He had been a strong leader for more than forty years. Most called him a dictator. He had tolerated no dissent. There was little the new leaders could do to defend themselves against the attacks, and they were focusing their efforts on the larger urban areas, such as Tripoli, the capitol city, and Benghazi.

We had heard reports that the terrorists had taken control of cities not far from where we were working, and we had been told they were headed our way. We knew it was dangerous to be where we were, and we were in fear that this day would come. We took the risk because we were in such desperate need for the money.

Also, we were working for a Chinese company, the China Railway Construction Corporation, not for anyone affiliated with the government or anyone with political connections. It had won a $2.5-billion bid to construct a railway from east to west across Libya, ending in Sirte. We decided to go to work with them because we thought the terrorists might not want to draw the ire of the Chinese. China was one of the few countries in the world not in the fight against the Islamic extremists who were perpetrating atrocities in many places across the Middle East.

We had just finished our lunch and were returning to work. I had gone in the opposite direction to use one of the port-o-lets provided for us, and when I emerged, I saw them coming. I saw two large vehicles, the kind that carry soldiers in the back, a large box truck, the kind that carries supplies, and about a dozen pickup trucks with guns mounted in the beds, all racing toward us. We had little time to hide.

Moments after I screamed out the warning, I saw my brother, Touma, and I heard him yell to me, "Mekhaeil! Stay where you are! Hide! Don't let them know that you are one of us!"

I did as I was told and ran to find a place to hide, away from where he and the others were. He and my other brother, Guirguis, ran with the other men into one of the buildings and up the stairs. I hid in the bushes behind the string of port-o-lets.

Within minutes, the men in the pickup trucks began firing their guns once they were within a few hundred yards of us. I heard them yelling, "Aiaiaiaiaiaiaiaiaiaiaiaiaiaye!"

Although there were hundreds of men working on that job site, none were close to where we were, and there were no security guards or anyone else around to protect us or come to our aid. It was a huge construction site. The extremists seemed to be looking for us—and nobody else but us.

The pickup trucks began circling the building my brothers and the others were in. Once the large trucks came to a stop, dozens of men jumped from the back of the trucks and ran into the building, up to where the men were hiding. The men in the pickups kept circling, firing their weapons into the air and yelling as they did.

They all wore black masks that hid their faces and had turbans or knit hats on their heads. Most had black vests on, even though it was a warm day, and black tunics with long sleeves that covered their bodies. All had automatic weapons that fired continuously, though no resistance was offered.

I watched in horror as the men were herded like cattle from the building and into the cargo truck. They all had their hands in the air the whole time. The terrorists were right behind them, hitting them with the butts of their rifles and yelling at them. Within minutes, everyone was inside the truck. I thought I was safe.

I watched as some of the terrorists ran around to buildings nearby, looking for any others. Then I felt the barrel of a rifle hit the back of my head. I had been found.

I turned and saw a young boy not much older than I. He had come up from behind, and I hadn't seen or heard him coming. He yelled at me in Arabic, telling me to stand and put my hands in the air. I did as I was told.

"I'm not with them," I told him, just as my brother had told me to say.

He eyed me suspiciously and hit me again, this time using the butt of his rifle on my back. "Yes you are!" he said. "If not, why are you hiding?"

I repeated myself. "I am not with them!"

He gestured with his rifle that I was to go over to where the others were, yelling at me as he did. I did as I was told to do.

I kept repeating, "I am not one of them," but he didn't believe me. I was put in the truck with the others. Just as the door was being slammed behind me, I got a glimpse of Guirguis, and then we were in complete darkness.

"Oh, Mekhaeil!" he sobbed in a low whisper. "They found you! I am so sorry!" I could hear him crying.

Within a few minutes, the truck was roaring down a bumpy road. There was no talking; the noise of the engine was too loud, and no one could be heard. We could tell that we were heading up into the mountains, in the direction of where they had come from, because everyone was pushed to the back of the truck.

The engine strained while going up the steep incline. There was nothing for any of us to hold on to except each other. We were jostled about, bumping into each other, banging our heads against the walls, and bouncing up and down. It was stifling inside the truck and hard to breathe. Men were crying and gasping for air—especially those at the front of the truck, where Touma must have been.

An hour later, the truck came to an abrupt halt, and the deafening sound of the engine was replaced with the sound of men screaming, both inside and out. Then the door to the back of our truck flew open.

Dozens of men, all with guns, were standing in front of us, yelling at us to come outside. We came out one at a time, with our hands behind our heads, as ordered. As we did, a terrorist took control of each of us. I was one of the first to come out, since I'd been the last one captured.

We were marched down a dirt road a short distance and ordered to lie down. When we did, I was able to see that there were several stone buildings, maybe as many as five or six, around a large circular area where several pick-up trucks were parked.

At that point, other men came out of one of the buildings. Some were carrying orange jumpsuits, and others were carrying chains. The terrorists had us take off our clothes and put on the jumpsuits. Once we were in the jumpsuits, they put iron collars around our necks, and cuffs on our hands and feet. The collars had large circular rings on them. The cuffs on our feet were connected by chains that were about a foot long. We were handcuffed from behind. Once that was done, a long bar was hooked to the collars on each of our necks. The man who put the bar on me tugged on it to make sure it was secure.

We were then ordered to walk toward one of the buildings,

where other men stood. Someone gave a command for us to move faster, and the men started prodding us, making us go faster, yelling at us all the while. We all shuffled along as best we could, but we could only step as far as the chain between our legs allowed us to, which wasn't very far, so we couldn't go as fast as they wanted us to go.

When we arrived at the building, they unhooked the bars from the collars on our necks and shoved us inside, one by one. Once we were inside, they ordered us to sit with our backs against the walls. When we did as they told us to do, they ran a chain through the cuffs on our feet and connected the two ends to the wall nearest the door. Then the door was slammed shut.

There were no windows to the building—or if there were any, they were boarded up. We were in darkness again. The only sounds to be heard were of men groaning and weeping. No one said a word for a long time, but there was a steady hum, which I recognized as being the sound of men praying. I prayed too.

CHAPTER 2

Grim Reality Sets In

The building we were in must have been a place where animals had been kept. It felt like I was sitting on straw, and there was a faint odor of manure. My guess was that the building was a chicken coop that hadn't been used in a while.

Throughout the day, we could hear activity going on outside, and the sounds of men talking, though we weren't able to understand what was being said. We sat in silence, except for the humming. Hours later, which seemed like an eternity, the sounds coming from outside the building became less frequent. We could tell that the sun was going down because what little light there was from the cracks in the walls and the holes in the roof grew dimmer and dimmer, until it was completely black.

When we heard no sounds coming from outside our building at all, Demetrius Deeb spoke up. He was the oldest of us, and if we had a leader, which we didn't, he would have been it. He was in his midforties. His son, Ignatius, was with us too. He had just celebrated his twenty-third birthday days earlier.

Demetrius whispered, "Tomorrow we are all going to die. Tonight we must decide how we will face that death."

"But I don't want to die, Father!" Ignatius cried out. "I want to go home to see my mother, my wife, and my little boy! Isn't there something we can do to avoid that?"

"Quiet, my son!" his father told him gently but sternly. "I'm afraid not, and if they hear us, we won't be allowed to talk. We must talk softly. I say it again … in the morning, we will all be dead. Tonight we must prepare ourselves for that."

Touma, the oldest of my two brothers—who must have been sitting right next to Demetrius, because the sound of his voice came from the same direction—said, "You all know my father, Gabriel, and once he hears that three of his sons have been taken by these people, he will do everything he can to save us. He has some friends in the army who are from al-Aour. He'll go to Cairo if he has to. I think the Egyptian Army will come for us."

Guirguis added, "He will … I'm sure he will … especially because of Mekhaeil. We had to beg him to let us take him with us … it will kill him …" He started weeping, but he went on. "We should have left weeks ago, as he told us to do, and we should have left Mekhaeil behind, like he said."

Then Rushdi Bishoy spoke up. He, like Demetrius, was one of the elders of our church, and he, too, was a father. His son, Maurice, was with us as well.

"Maybe we won't die, Demetrius. Maybe they will allow us to leave. I have heard that they give Christians three options: convert to Islam, leave, or die. That's what they did with the Christians in Iraq, from what I have read in the papers."

"That was true in Iraq, Rushdi, but that was ISIS. This may be al-Qaeda. We don't know who they are. Maybe they aren't the same. And that was in Karakosh, which is where those people lived. That was their home. This is not our home. I don't think we will be given that option. Besides, they came looking for us. I think they plan to kill us because we are Copts."

"What about conversion? Do you think we will be allowed to convert?" Moghadan Ramzy asked. He was one of the younger men there, although he was still five or six years older than I.

"Maybe," Demetrius responded. "That is one of the things we must talk about. Some of you may want to do that, which is understandable. I won't. I would rather die."

"I will never convert either. I will go to my grave a follower of Christ," Cyril Bahgoury offered.

He was one of the older men in our group, but he was not as

old as Demetrius or Rushdi. He had been studying to become a priest in his younger days, but for some reason that hadn't happened yet. He was a deacon in our church and read Bible passages to us on Sundays.

"Will you, Cyril, be able to hear our confessions tonight?" Demetrius asked.

"I am not a priest, Demetrius. I'm not able to hear confessions and absolve sins. You know that."

"Yes, but you are the closest thing to a priest there is among us, and you are a deacon," Demetrius responded.

"Yes, but I'm not even a full deacon. I cannot hear confessions!" Cyril insisted.

"But you spent several years in the seminary, and you know more than any of us about our religion," Demetrius told him. "Don't you think that our church might make an exception for a situation like this?"

"I did go to seminary; that's true," Cyril stated. "But our church does not allow me to hear a confession. There is nothing to discuss. It is not an option, Demetrius. You know that. We all know that. What we can do is repent. We can all repent our sins, if you'd like."

"Then that's what we should do. This will be a long night, my brothers. I think we should bare our souls to our God before we meet Him," Demetrius responded. "And I think we should tell each other what it is we repent of."

"Maybe we should just confess to ourselves, Demetrius," Halim Nazari, another of the older men in our group, offered. "We will be talking to God, really, not to each other. I don't think it matters that we can't make confessions tonight, as long as God hears us and knows what's in our hearts."

"And I agree with you, Demetrius. I think we need to cleanse our souls before we die. I think we are dead men, too. I don't think they will allow us to leave, and I don't think any of us should convert."

"Maybe we won't die, Halim!" His younger brother, Cosmos, replied. "Maybe we can escape. Let's think of what we can do to stop them from killing us! Let's not sit here like sheep and allow them kill us without a fight!"

"Look at us, Cosmos … we are chained together like dogs. They have guns; we have nothing. What can we do? What can we do?" Halim responded solemnly. "They have offered us no food, no water … they have not even allowed us to go to the bathroom. They treat us like animals, not like human beings. Demetrius is right … we are going to die in the morning."

"Maybe not!" Moghadan said. "Maybe Rushdi is right. Maybe we can convert to being Muslims. I will do that right now if they will let me! I don't want to die. I will say whatever they want me to say. I will go back to the church once I am free from these devils."

"Not me, Moghadan! I would rather die, just as Cyril said!" Asaad Farug responded. He was a man in his late twenties, older than most but younger than Demetrius and some of the others.

"You may be right, Moghadan," Demetrius responded. "Maybe they will let you do that, but I don't think so. Let's prepare ourselves for the worst and discuss what we will do and what we will say if we are given a choice. This may be our last night on this earth, regardless of what we want to see happen."

Sarabamoon Shalhoub, who was about the same age as Asaad, in his late twenties, spoke up and said, "Demetrius is right. We can hope for the best, but tonight we should plan for the worst. We all know that we may die in the morning. We all hope that doesn't happen, but we want to be prepared for the worst. If I am to meet God tomorrow, I want to be ready." Like Asaad, and several of the others, he had a wife and children at home.

"And what say you, Raghib?" Demetrius asked. "We have not heard from you. I would like to hear what you have to say. You have been many places and done many things. You are a wise man. I value your judgment. What do you think we should do?"

Raghib Sarraf was a few months younger than Demetrius. They had known each other since childhood. They had gone to school together. After graduation, he had gone off to Cairo or Alexandria and had become a successful businessman.

Something had happened to him, and he had come back to al-Aour within the last year or two. I had heard that he lost his job and all his money and hadn't been able to find work elsewhere. He was now, like the rest of us, desperate. I didn't know much about him.

He sighed, hesitated for several moments before speaking, and then said, "Demetrius, I value your friendship—and your wisdom as well. I am so overwhelmed with grief at the moment that I don't know what to think, let alone say, but I agree with you. I think we are all dead men. To be honest, all I can think about is how they are going to cut off my head. I hope I am dead before that happens. I want to die quickly. I don't want to suffer, but I assure you all that I am prepared to die the most painful of deaths before I will convert."

At that, there was silence. Then some men began weeping.

"I think it's best not to think about that right now, Raghib, but if we are true followers of Christ, as I know we are, we should think of how He died on the cross for us," Demetrius replied.

Rushdi spoke up. "Demetrius, on second thought, maybe we should kill ourselves tonight, as the Hebrews did at Masada, and not give them the pleasure of killing us. If I could, I would do that right now. That's what I think we should do."

"I agree with Rushdi!" Abanoub Samaha said loudly.

"Shh!" Demetrius scolded. "If they hear us, we won't be allowed to talk, I'm sure. There are probably several guards right outside of these walls. We must be quiet! And Rushdi, my friend, you may feel that way, but you know that self-murder is a sin, and so do you, Abanoub, so let's not talk about such a thing."

Abanoub was the most devout man among us—except for Cyril, perhaps. He was a tall, thin man with a hawkish kind of face. He always looked stern. I don't remember ever seeing him smile.

He carried a Bible with him at all times, even at work. It was a small one, and I saw him reading it many times during the day: at lunch, when we rested, or before we began to work. He had a wife and five children at home. His oldest child was my age and was one of my best friends. I had been to his house many times. I admired him, but he scared me.

"We should not let these terrorists have their way with us!" he persisted, using a much lower voice but speaking with passion and sincerity. "We cannot let these men defile us! We must die with dignity!"

"Boctor, what do you say? We haven't heard from you yet," Demetrius asked.

Boctor Daoud was another of the young men. He was the biggest and strongest man of a group of men about his age. He was their leader. He was always laughing and telling jokes. Everyone liked him—especially the girls.

He liked to talk about what he was going to do with all the money he was making and how he was going to go to Cairo because that was where the most beautiful Egyptian girls were. He was sitting next to me, and I could hear him sobbing much of the time. He sniffled and responded, "You are older and wiser than I am, Demetrius. What you say is true, but I'm too young to die. There is so much that I want to do that I haven't been able to do yet. If there is a way to avoid it, I would like to do that, whatever that costs or whatever I have to give up. Right now, I don't care. I will say anything or do anything to avoid being killed. I just don't want to die. I agree with Moghadan."

His friend, Magdi Wassef, who was sitting on the other side of him, spoke up. "I agree with Boctor and Moghadan. I will do whatever it takes to live, if there is a way for us to do that, whatever it is."

"Nabir? Yousry? What do you say?"

Nabir Yassa and Yousry Maalouf were from Minya, not far from al-Aour, where most of the rest of us were from—except for Omar, who was from Libya. He wasn't one of us. He was dark-skinned and I wasn't sure that he was even a Christian. Those who weren't from al-Aour were from neighboring villages.

Nabir and Yousry were still teenagers, like me. They were the two men in the room who were closest in age to me. When I wasn't with my brothers, I was with them, kicking a soccer ball and playing around. They were both happy young men, excited to be on their own and making money. This was their first time away from home. They were seated next to each other not far from me.

Nabir spoke first. His voice cracked with emotion as he said, "I agree with Rushdi. I don't want to die like an animal, and I don't want to be in pain, and I agree with Boctor and Moghadan too. I don't want to die at all. If there is a way to avoid death, even if it means telling them that I renounce my faith and will convert to Islam, then I will do that."

"Shh! Be careful what you say, all of you. Think carefully before you speak. God is listening," Demetrius warned. "Remember: we are Copts!"

Yousry spoke next. "I am sorry, Demetrius, but I agree with Boctor and the others."

"Who else? Clement? What do you say?" Demetrius asked.

Clement Barakat hadn't lived in our village for very long, and I didn't know much about him. I had rarely, if ever, seen him in church on Sundays. I think the first time that I actually talked to him was when we were on the bus on our way to Sirte. He was in his midthirties, I thought. I wasn't really sure. I couldn't tell.

"As you know, I am a relative newcomer to this group," he said. "Though I am from al-Aour, I have been away for many years. I have not been back with you for too long. As some of you know, I am alone in this world. I have no wife, no children, and no family." He paused and then said, "But no one knows why that is so, and now I will tell you. All of my family was killed a few years ago, just before I moved back to our village. I was hoping to find peace there and escape all of this violence. I wanted to be alone and avoid everyone and everything, but I came here, just as all of you did, because I needed the money."

He paused again, sighed, and said, "I have lost everything. I have nothing left to lose. Please take no offense, but I don't want to confess anything to anyone aloud. I feel as if God has tested me, just as Job was tested, but I don't understand why, and I have failed the test. I am confused and, to be honest, completely depressed by what has happened to me in this lifetime. God is apparently not happy with me, and I am not happy with God right now, but I accept my fate, and I am preparing myself for the death that awaits us all."

At that, some men murmured, but no one spoke a word until Demetrius said, "We are all sorry to hear of your loss, Clement. We will pray for you. If you are to die for our faith, as I think we all will, surely you will be received in heaven as a martyr. I hope that offers you some consolation." He hesitated for a few moments and then said, "I think we have now heard from all of the men, and—"

Rushdi interrupted. "We haven't heard from Ignatius yet, Demetrius, or my son, Maurice, or from Omar."

I hadn't spoken yet either, but since I was the youngest, and so much younger than anyone else, I think they all just forgot about me. I didn't say anything.

"I'm sorry. You're right, Rushdi. Thank you. Since I can't see any of you, I just couldn't remember everyone. Let's start with Omar. What do you think we should do, Omar?"

Omar was an older man, and we all thought he was from Libya, because that is what he told someone, who repeated it to the rest of us. I didn't know him at all. None of us knew him until we arrived at work that first day. He kept to himself most of the time. He was a tall, thin, very dark skinned man, almost black in color. I had no idea how old he was. He could have been thirty, or he could have been fifty. I couldn't tell.

"These men who have captured us think I am one of you, but you know that I am not. You think I am from Libya, but I am not. You may think I am a Christian, but I am not. I am from Afghanistan, and I am a Muslim."

At that the men murmured loudly. The thought that Omar was a Muslim and that they were about to be killed by Muslims didn't sit well with them.

He continued. "But I am a Shiite Muslim, not a Sunni."

The murmuring continued, but it was lower in volume.

"Believe me when I say that if they knew I was a Shiite Muslim, they would treat me much worse than they would you. I would prefer that they continue to think of me as a Christian. I will die with you, but I will make my confession to Allah in private, if you don't mind.

"I think Demetrius is right. I think we are dead men. I don't think they will allow us to convert, even if we want to do so, and I don't think they will simply allow us to leave, either.

"I hope that Touma is right. I hope that your country will come to our assistance. I think your leaders should send some troops to rescue you and kill these people who have done this to you. It's possible that the United States or some other Western country will help us, and I hope that they will arrive before it is too late, but I don't think that's likely.

"Surely the Egyptian government knows what has happened by now. The people for whom we were working will have notified the authorities. The world probably knows by now. I think that Egypt is our best hope. Its army is close by and could be here in a matter of hours, if not less. Someone has to stop these men. We are not the first people to have this happen to them. The world will not continue to simply watch these things happen and do nothing. Maybe this will be a good thing. Maybe it will cause the good people of the world to stand up to these men who would kill us."

"I hope you are right, Omar," Raghib offered, "but no one has come to the rescue of any of those other people who have been killed by these terrorists and by the others in this world who think and act like they do, but maybe you're right … maybe that will happen this time. I think Egypt is our only hope. We can only pray that they will help."

Then Demetrius asked, "Is there anything else you would like to say, Omar?"

"Not at this time. Thank you," he responded.

"Ignatius, I apologize, my son. I know you so well that I think I know what you will say before you speak. I know how you feel. I know how your mother, my wife, feels. I know how your wife feels. I am sorry for not allowing you to speak for yourself, but let's hear from Rushdi's son first. I have offended him too, and I offer my apologies. Maurice, what do you think?"

Maurice was about the same age as Ignatius. Both men were in their midtwenties, and both men had wives and young children. I had seen both men with their families in church every Sunday for as long as I could remember. It was rare for me not to see them with their fathers and their families.

"If I am to die," Maurice said, "then I am proud to die with my father, who I love very much." At that, Rushdi began to weep profusely and rattle his chains. Maurice hesitated and then continued. "I will do as he tells me to do, whatever that is. My thoughts are for my wife and children right now, and for my mother. I don't know what they will do without us. I am praying that something will happen and we will be spared the awful deaths that await us." He began to cry and then said, "But I will die as a Copt! I will not convert! Never! That is all I have to say."

Several moments later, when the sobbing died down, Demetrius said, softly, "Ignatius? What do you have to say, my son?"

Ignatius looked exactly like his father, except for the gray in his father's hair and beard. Both men were large—not tall, but heavyset. They wore the same clothes and were always together. Ignatius rarely spoke when he was around his father, except when asked to speak. He said, "I have known Maurice and his family for as long as I have known my own family. I cannot think of anything to say more than what he has said. I love my father, my family, my wife, and my children as much as he loves his. In fact, I love his family too, just as I love many of the rest of you in this room, and just as you love your families and friends. We all love our families, and we love each other. That's how we are! That's who we are! We are Copts, and I, too, am praying for a miracle.

"However, if we are to die tomorrow, I feel exactly the same way Maurice feels … I will be proud to go to my death with my father, and with Maurice and his father, and with all of you. I, too, will never convert. That is all I have to say."

Again the room was quiet. Then Demetrius spoke. "I wish I could embrace you, my son. I love you so very much. Thank you." He was quiet for several moments. Then he breathed a deep sigh and said, "Thank you all for your thoughts. I think maybe now those of us who wish to and are ready to confess our sins to God and to each other may do so. Those of you who prefer to confess your sins privately are welcome to do so. Will you allow me to confess my sins to you all at this time?

At that, Cyril spoke up. "Again, Demetrius, I suggest that you call it a repentance, not a confession. They are similar but not the same."

"Thank you, Cyril, for that correction," Demetrius responded.

Then Rushdi spoke up. "Demetrius, I think all of the men in this room will want to communicate with God and confess their sins or repent of their sins before they die, whether openly or privately, but I suggest that we take time now, before we do that, to allow each of us to say whatever it is he chooses to say to the rest of us. Some of our younger brothers are confused about what we should do. I think that if we share our thoughts with each other before we repent, it might help these young men make a better decision.

"However, I certainly agree to listen to whatever it is you wish to say, Demetrius. You have earned that right, as far as I am concerned, without any question whatsoever, for all that you have done in this life for me and all the rest of us."

"Thank you, my friend. As usual, I agree with your suggestion. Let us do that. But first let's say a prayer. Omar, though you are not a Christian, please join us as we say the prayer Jesus taught us."

At that, all the men began to pray: "Make us worthy to pray thankfully. Our Father, who art in heaven, hallowed be thy name. Thy kingdom come, thy will be done on earth as it is in heaven. Give us this day our daily bread, and forgive us our trespasses, as we forgive those who trespass against us, and lead us not into temptation, but deliver us from the evil one, in Christ Jesus, our Lord, for thine is the kingdom, and the power, and the glory, forever. Amen."

"Now, let us sing, but very softly now," Demetrius whispered, "the song 'Be Not Afraid.'"

At that, everyone sang:

"You shall cross the barren desert,
but you shall not die of thirst.
You shall wander far in safety, though
you do not know the way.
You shall speak your words to foreign
men, and all will understand.
You shall see the face of God and live.
Be not afraid; I go before you always.
Come follow Me, and I will give you rest.
If you pass through raging waters,
in the sea you shall not drown.
If you walk amid the burning flames,
you shall not be harmed.
If you stand before the power of
hell and death is at your side,
Know that I am with you through it all.
Blessed are you poor, for the
kingdom shall be yours.
Blessed are you that weep and mourn,
for one day you will laugh.
And if wicked men insult and
hate you all because of me,
Blessed, blessed are you!"

CHAPTER 3

Dissension and Conflict

A s I sat there listening to what everyone was saying, I knew I was the only one who hadn't been asked to speak. I didn't really want to speak, and I wasn't offended because Demetrius hadn't called on me. I figured it was because I was so young. I had turned sixteen a few months earlier, just before we left al-Aour to come here.

I had never heard of Masada, and I didn't know all that much about what was going on in Syria or Iraq. Both of my parents were Coptic Christians; their parents were Copts, and their parents' parents were Copts, so I was a Coptic Christian. The idea of converting to Islam wasn't anything that I had ever thought about before. The thought had never entered my mind.

My initial reaction to all that had been said was that I would never convert, but I hadn't ever thought that anyone would cut off my head because I was a Copt before, either. I didn't think we were going to die. I believed something good was going to happen.

I felt that somehow, some way, we were going to be freed. I remained silent, but the things Boctor, Nabir, and the other young men had said caused me some concern. I was no longer as sure about the things I thought I believed in as I had been before they spoke.

Then Touma said, "If we are all going to die, including Mekhaeil, then I think we should hear from him, even though he's just a boy. As a grown man, I am responsible for my decision to be here, like everyone else in here is, but I feel responsible for Mekhaeil being here. I wish I had listened to our father and made him stay home. I begged my father to let him come with us once he turned sixteen."

"I feel the same way," added Guirguis. "I, too, feel responsible for him being here."

"Let him speak, please," Touma asked.

"I have no objection to that," Demetrius responded. "Again I apologize for overlooking him. I meant no offense. I have known Mekhaeil since the day he was born. He has a right to be heard, and I want to hear what he has to say too.

"It is so sad that any of us will die. But for you, Mekhaeil, who are so young, it is worse. So tell us, young man, what do you think of all that you have heard? What do you think we should do? What will you do?"

None of us could see any of the others, even those sitting two feet away, but I could feel the eyes of everyone upon me as I spoke. I was nervous. I wasn't used to being asked to say what I thought. My voice trembled as I spoke.

"I know my father and my mother are crying right now, worried about three of their sons, as our younger sister and brother are too. I know that the families of everyone here, and everyone else in our village, are crying as well, and I think they will do something. They love us. I think they will find a way to save us. They are probably on their way now."

"But no one knows where we are," Raghib whispered. "We don't know where we are."

"God knows where we are," I said. "He can save us, and He will. I'm sure He will. We are not going to die."

No one spoke for a few moments, and then Demetrius said, "Thank you, Mekhaeil. Hearing you speak reminds me of myself when I was your age. Your life is just beginning, and you have hopes and dreams for a better life, just as I did. You believe in our God, and you haven't experienced the evil and ugliness the world sometimes lays upon us. I hope you are right. I hope that you get to live the life you dream of. I, too, pray that He will save us."

At that, Boctor spoke out, in what almost seemed like a sneer. "Our God won't save us. We are going to die as martyrs, like we always do! He wants us to die!"

"Shh!" a dozen men hissed at the same time.

I could hear the chains rattling, and I knew the men were trying to make the sign of the cross, but they couldn't, because their hands were chained behind them.

"Boctor! Please! Not now," Cyril pleaded. "Not on the eve of the day on which you and all of us go to meet our maker! Not now! At the very least, you should have respect for those of us who believe with all our hearts, minds, and souls that Jesus Christ is our God and that He is a loving God who will hear and answer our prayers. Don't say such a thing!"

"But that is the way of our God, Cyril! This must be what He wants!" Boctor replied. "Look at us! Look at what's been happening to the Christians in Iraq and in Syria! Look at the way Christians have been treated in Egypt for two thousand years! No loving God would allow such a thing! Jesus Christ is our God, but He is turning the other cheek again, so we have no God to help us, do we? There, I've said it! We have no God who will help us!"

Again there was a loud murmur and a rattling of chains.

"Quiet! Please! Remember: there are guards right outside the door!" Demetrius pleaded. "Each of us has a right to express his opinion. If we are about to die, each of us has a right to decide how he wishes to face death. Even if we don't agree with Boctor, and I don't, please allow him to speak. Respect him. He is our brother."

"But he is wrong!" Cyril responded. "It is our duty to do our best to save his soul before he dies! It will not be good for him to meet God this way."

"Is he wrong, Cyril? Are you sure of that?" Clement asked. "You are saying what we Copts have been taught since we were children. Is that what you really believe?"

"Yes, it is, Clement," Cyril responded. "Yes, it is."

"What is it that has happened in your lifetime or in the history of our church that makes you think that God is here with us and will help us? For me, my life has been nothing but suffering and persecution because I am a Christian, and that has been the way things have been for us for centuries, since the very beginning. Do I agree with what Boctor just said? Yes, I do, and I certainly share his despair ... I know that I am so sad and so tired of all the suffering that I just don't know what to say to God, if there is a God who truly cares about us, other than to ask why. Why must we suffer so? Why have Christians continued to suffer at the hands of Muslims for over a thousand years? Why? I don't have an answer to that question, and neither do any of you. I would like to get an answer before I die, but that's not going to happen, is it?"

Again there was a murmur of the men muttering to themselves. I couldn't understand what was being said by the others, but there was still a lot of rattling of chains. Cyril then spoke up. "We have been followers of Christ for almost two thousand years, and yes, it is true, we have suffered persecutions for most of those years. Now, when our faith is being put to the ultimate test, we cannot falter! We follow in the footsteps of our ancestors. We must be proud of who and what we are. Now is the time for us to show the world that we are Christians and that we gladly go to our deaths for Him!"

"Cyril is right!" Abanoub nearly shouted. "Please, my brothers, don't turn your backs on Him now! We are being tested. Our faith is being tested. We must do as Cyril tells us and prove that we truly are followers of Christ!"

"So we are to turn the other cheek?" Yousrey asked. I was surprised to hear him speak, let alone say what he said. He was usually quiet and rarely got into any arguments. He continued. "And are we to love our enemies as ourselves, as Christ taught us?"

There was silence for several moments, and then Demetrius spoke again. "Out of the mouths of infants and babes come words of wisdom. You ask a most difficult question, Yousrey, but the answer to that question is yes. This puts my faith to the test. I know that at this moment I can't forgive those men for what they are about to do to us tomorrow. I feel nothing but enormous sadness for myself, my son, my family, and all of you, and nothing but anger at them, but I know that Jesus Christ would have us do that."

"But you have hatred for them now, don't you?" Boctor asked. "Admit it, Demetrius. You feel hate now, don't you? We all do, don't we?" he asked.

Several men murmured a positive response.

"Forgive them, O Lord, for they know not what they do! That's what Jesus commands us to do!" Cyril offered fervently.

Boctor scoffed. "Love those men? They are animals! Love these men who are not fit to be called human beings? Those men do not deserve to live on this earth! Are you serious, Cyril? I can't believe what I just heard you say. I wish that we could find a way to fight back, that we could die like men, or that I could have the opportunity to kill each and every one of them! Forgive them? Not me. I am not Jesus Christ ... I am not God. Those men hate us, and I hate them as much as they hate me."

Again there was a murmur, but this one was even louder. It seemed as if the discussion reflected a strong difference of opinion between the younger men, including my brothers, and the older men. I wasn't sure what to think. I just listened.

"Forgive us our trespasses as we forgive those who trespass upon us," someone said.

I couldn't tell who said it, but it sounded as if he was scoffing at that notion, just as Boctor had done, though I wasn't sure.

"Let's not think about that now, my brothers." Demetrius said softly. "That is a heavy cross to bear. I doubt that any of us are capable of carrying that cross at this moment."

"So what are we to think about, Demetrius?" Guirguis asked. "All I can think about is that I don't want to die and I don't want to see any of you die—especially my brother Touma, and most especially my brother Mekhaeil, for whose death I feel deeply responsible. I would gladly give my life to save his."

Demetrius responded. "You're right, Guirguis. That's exactly what we need to discuss, I think. None of us wants to die, but if there's nothing we can do about it, then we should decide how we will face death, as I said before. What do the rest of you think? Anyone else?"

Cyril spoke. "There is nothing we can do to fight these men ... nothing! We have no guns ... we are chained together, with collars around our necks and chains on our hands and our feet. So I agree with you; the only question to discuss is how we will face death, just as you said, Demetrius.

"So will we go to our deaths weeping and crying like women, saying, 'Please, please don't kill me?' Not me! I will go to my death with my head held high! Will I do anything, say anything, renounce everything, or believe anything they tell me to believe, as long as they don't kill me? Not me! I will look them in the eye and say I am a Christian! I follow the teachings of Jesus Christ! I will go to my death with a smile on my face because I know I am going to a better place, as the Christians of old did when they were thrown to the lions in the Colosseum of Rome. I will do as so many of our Coptic brothers and sisters who have gone before us have done. There are thousands of men and women who have willingly given their lives for our beliefs—probably tens of thousands, if not hundreds of thousands ... millions, even. That is our faith. That is our tradition. That is what we must do!"

Most of the men murmured support while rattling their chains.

Moments later, Raghib spoke,

"You are a true believer, Cyril; I admire you for that. And you are a wise man, Demetrius; We are fortunate to have the benefit of your wisdom at this time. The younger men in our group just want to live, and they aren't as sure as the two of you are about what should be done. I think it is a fair question: should we die as Copts, or should we lie and live to fight another day? Each of us must decide. No one will sleep tonight. There are many hours until dawn arrives. Let's talk about it."

"We should accept our fate and spend what time we have left repenting of our sins, cleansing our souls, and preparing ourselves for what lies ahead," Cyril insisted. "We will soon be standing before the throne of God, and we will be judged. We must make ready! I don't want to talk about conversion! I refuse to! I want to think only of God and where we are going."

"I agree!" Abanoub said.

Then Rushdi said, "Maybe we should repent of our sins first, as Demetrius suggests. If we do, maybe some of the things we older men say will help the younger men decide what is best to do. Those of us who are older can understand why the young men feel this way. It is harder for them, I think, than it is for those of us who have lived longer."

Then Boctor spoke up. "But what do we have to repent of? Most of us haven't lived long enough to marry and have children, as you older men have. What have we done to deserve this? What has Mekhaeil done to deserve this? And you tell us that we should willingly go to our death believing that God has a purpose for all of this?"

The chains rattled, and then Touma spoke. "Mekhaeil is a complete innocent. He has done nothing wrong, but I have, and so has most everyone else in this room, I am sure. I'm still a young man, like you, Boctor. It was only a few years ago that we were graduating from school together, but before I make my decision, and before I repent of my sins, there are some things I'd like the older men to explain to me. There are many things the elders in this room know that I don't know, and there is so much I don't know about the Muslims and why they treat us like this. Maybe one of you can explain this to me. Maybe that will help me prepare myself for what is to come tomorrow morning, whatever that may be. I want to do the right thing. I think we all do. I want to hear what you older men have to say about that and some other things."

"Mekhaeil doesn't have any idea why he is to be killed, other than that he is a Christian and these men are Muslims, and neither do I," Magdi said.

"Nor do I," Nabir chimed in.

"You all make good points. I have no problem with what you

ask, Touma," Demetrius responded. "All of us can be reminded of the things we believe in and told of things we might not know about our religion. Maybe you, Cyril, since you studied our religion for so many years, can explain to us what it is we believe and why it is we should go to our deaths as martyrs. Remind us of why we are Christians. Would you do that for us?" Demetrius asked.

"Gladly, Demetrius. I will gladly explain to you, Magdi, Touma, Nabir, Mekhaeil, Boctor, Moghadan, and the rest of you what it means to be a Christian and what we, as Coptic Christians, believe," Cyril responded.

"And what of the teachings of Muhammad?" Omar said softly. "These men, who will kill us in the morning without blinking an eye, believe that their god commands them to do this to us. They think of us, even me, as infidels. What of Muhammad's teachings?"

"Maybe you can explain that, Omar, when Cyril is finished. Would you do that for us?" Demetrius asked.

"I will," he responded. "I don't want any of you to think that all Muslims are like these men."

"All right then. We are agreed," Demetrius said. "But before we begin, may we have a prayer or a hymn."

At that Cyril began to lead us in "Be Not Afraid" again. It was a song we sang in church most every Sunday, but this time it had new meaning for me and, I'm sure, for everyone else in the room.

"Now let us be silent," Demetrius said softly. "Pray to God that His will be done, whatever that may be."

CHAPTER 4

Coptic Christians

Fifteen minutes later, Demetrius broke the silence. "Before Cyril and Omar tell us about our Coptic history and the history of Islam, I would ask that you all do your best to listen carefully to what they say and try not get too excited and say things you know might offend other people in this room. We are all in this together, and we are all brothers. Do your best to speak to each other in that way—as your brothers."

"We are not the enemy, even if we disagree with things that are said," Raghib added.

"All right then. It is now eight o'clock or so, I would guess," Demetrius said softly. "The sun comes up in less than twelve hours. Cyril, if you would ..."

Cyril heaved a deep sigh and then began. "Forgive me, my brothers, if I say things that you already know. I mean no disrespect. I will start at the beginning. Here goes.

"Let me begin by saying that we Copts are among the very first followers of Christ. St. Mark was our first pope, and he is the one who taught us about Jesus. He came to us not long after Christ was crucified. Mark was one of Jesus's disciples, though he was not among the original twelve apostles. His mother owned the house where Jesus and the apostles met on several occasions while He was in Jerusalem, and that is where the Last Supper was held. That is when and how Mark would have met Christ and seen the things he wrote about in his gospel. We know the things he told us were true because he was there.

"Mark would have been a young man—perhaps a teenager, like Mekhaeil—when he met Christ and the others. He served Christ and the apostles their food and drink at the Last Supper. Again, all of you may already know these things. All Copts are taught these things. Forgive me. I do not wish to insult your intelligence, but that is where our faith begins.

"Some of you might not know that after Christ was crucified, Mark became a follower of Simon Peter, and he traveled about with him, spreading the Word throughout the Mediterranean, ending in Rome. Many say that Mark's gospel contains much of what Simon Peter would have told us if he had written a gospel—which he didn't, to our knowledge. Mark first came to Egypt eight years after Christ was killed, and he began ministering to us at that time, but then he returned to Rome for a while.

"Ten years later, he came back to us, which would have been in the fiftieth year of our Lord, or thereabouts. He taught us about all that he had seen and heard. He had been in Antioch, Byzantium, Capernaum, Bethsaida, Rome, and all of the other places where Christianity began. He had seen it all. Our teachings and much, if not all, of what we believe came from him. He was our first bishop of Alexandria, as you all know.

"All Copts know this story too, but I will tell it for your benefit, Omar, since I think you might not have heard this before. When Mark came to Alexandria, he wanted to spread the good news about Jesus Christ, but he was careful about doing so, because Christians were being killed for their beliefs. One day he broke one of his sandals, and he found a cobbler to fix it for him. The cobbler badly injured his hand while fixing Mark's sandal, and he cried out in pain to the 'unknown God.' Mark healed the man's wound and told him about Jesus Christ. The cobbler then became a follower of Christ. Years later, he became one of our first popes after Mark. That is how our church grew … one convert at a time.

"At the time, Christians were being persecuted not only by the Romans, who worshiped many gods, but also by those in Egypt who weren't Christians, in addition to the Jews. In fact, Mark was killed in Alexandria some eighteen years later by Egyptians, not the Romans or the Jews. St. Mark was strung up with a rope around his neck and dragged through the city of Alexandria until he died. I find it comforting to think of that as I contemplate what will likely happen to me, and to all of us, tomorrow.

"To this day, our popes are called the successors of St. Mark. Our church is an Egyptian church, though we welcome people from other countries who believe as we do. The very word 'Copt' comes from the ancient Greek word '*Algyptos*,' which means 'Egyptian.'

"Because Christians were persecuted all across the Mediterranean, not just in Egypt, it was difficult for the various Christian communities to communicate with each other. As we know, Christians in Rome hid underground in the catacombs. In our country, many lived as hermits in caves, away from towns and people. There are many, many stories of Copts being killed. Most of our saints were martyrs.

"There were, however, many Christian communities in all of the countries from Jerusalem to Rome—especially in Greece, Syria, and Turkey—and all Christians, wherever they were, withstood persecutions for centuries. The largest Christian communities back then were located in Rome, Byzantium, Antioch, Jerusalem, and Alexandria.

"It wasn't until the time of Constantine in the three hundred twelfth year of our Lord that Christians were allowed to worship freely. After he won a battle at the Milvian Bridge, not far from Rome, Constantine became the undisputed emperor of the Roman Empire. One of his first actions was to institute a policy of religious tolerance toward Christians. He did this because he saw the sign of Christ in the sky prior to the battle. He had the cross painted on the shields of his soldiers along with the words '*in hoc signo vinces*,' which meant 'in this sign you will conquer.' He swore that if he won the battle, he would no longer persecute the followers of Christ. Although heavily outnumbered, he won the battle.

"He proclaimed that Christians would be allowed to worship freely throughout the Roman Empire. He himself was baptized before his death, but when he made Christianity one of the accepted religions of Rome, he asked the Christian leaders to explain to him what it was that Christians believed. He wanted to know more about Christ and His teachings so that the people of Rome could better understand Christianity.

"There was some division within all of the Christian communities, not just within the five major sites, over various issues, because most of those early Christians really hadn't been able to discuss those matters openly, or with each other, for years and years. So when no consensus was reached among the religious leaders, Constantine ordered that all Christian leaders were to meet and resolve the various issues. A conference involving hundreds of Bishops was held in Nicaea, which is in Turkey. It is now known as Iznik. Constantine himself presided over the gathering. That was in AD 325.

"Our church played a very important role at that conference. The bishop of Alexandria at the time was a man named Alexander. He brought with him an assistant, who was probably a deacon, named Athanasius. He would later become our pope. Athanasius is credited with crafting the words to what has become known as the Nicene Creed. Although it has been modified to some degree over the years, it remains a statement of our core beliefs. All of you know it, I am sure. This is what we believe. Please join me as we say this prayer to ourselves, quietly."

At that, all the men and I whispered, "We believe in one God, the Father Almighty, creator of heaven and earth, and of all things visible and invisible; and in one Lord, Jesus Christ, as the only begotten Son of God, begotten of the Father, before all worlds. Light of Light, very God of very God, begotten, not made, being of one substance with the Father, by whom all things were made, who for us, and for our salvation, came down from heaven, and was incarnate by the Holy Spirit of the Virgin Mary and was made man. He was crucified for us under Pontius Pilate, and suffered, and was buried, and the third day he rose again, according to the Scriptures, and ascended into heaven, and sitteth at the right hand of the Father. From thence he shall come again, with glory, to judge the quick and the dead, whose kingdom shall have no end, and in the Holy Spirit, the Lord and Giver of Life, who proceedeth from the Father, who with the Father and the Son together is worshiped and glorified, who spake by the prophets, in one holy catholic and apostolic church, we acknowledge one baptism for the remission of sins, and we look for the resurrection of the dead, and the life of the world to come. Amen."

Cyril resumed his history. "A hundred thirty years later, there was another large conference of Christian leaders. This one took place in Chalcedon, not far from Nicea. Again Christian leaders debated some serious theological issues. A division was created between the Christian communities as a result. This division has never been reconciled. We Copts believe that there is but one nature of Jesus Christ and that He was at all times divine, but other Christians believe that that there were times when He was on earth during which He was both human and divine.

"To this day, our faith remains unchanged. We believe that Jesus Christ is the Son of God and that He, the Father, and the Holy Spirit make up the Trinity, which we call God. That is who we are, and that is what we believe."

There was a hushed silence for several minutes. Then Boctor spoke up. "I confess to you, my brothers, that sometimes I wonder if all of that is true, especially at this moment, when I am asking myself why all of this is happening to me and to all of us."

At that, some men stirred and rattled their chains.

"Remember, my brothers: we must listen to each other and give respect to one another, even if we don't agree with what is said. Tell us, Boctor, what is it you don't believe about that prayer?" Demetrius asked.

"I am sorry. I can't help it, but sometimes I wonder if Jesus Christ wasn't just a man … a human … like Moses, David, Confucius, Buddha, or even Muhammad. Think about what you just heard. Many deeply religious people asked that very same question and came up with a different answer. Am I a heretic just to question it? Am I a heretic if I even dare to think something that is different from what the church tells me to think?"

At that, some men again rattled their chains.

"Quiet!" Demetrius reminded them. "Are you finished, Boctor?"

"No, I'm not ... and I confess I don't understand how Christ, if He was God and was not human, could allow Himself to be killed by men. I'm sorry, but those thoughts enter my head sometimes. How could God die?"

Many men gasped in disbelief.

"And what about Mary?" he continued. "Was she a woman like any other woman, or was she godlike too? Was she divine? I wonder about such things—the virgin birth and things like that."

"How can you say that, Boctor? Rushdi asked in disbelief. "We are from al-Aour! Your father and I went together, along with many others from our village, to Zeitoun over thirty years ago, and we saw the vision of Mary at the church of St. Mary! We came back and told all of the rest of our church what we had seen. After that, how can you not believe that she was truly the mother of God, given godly gifts?"

"Rushdi, I love you and your sons as I love my father and my brothers. You are like family to me. We have been together our whole lives. I remember what my father and you told us about what you and he saw. The scientists now say that it was a freak of nature and that people saw what they wanted to see."

"We went back for several years after that! It wasn't just something that happened once or twice; it happened hundreds of times. The government of Egypt accepted the reports as true. President Nasser said it was a true apparition! Even Pope Paul of the Roman Catholic Church said it was truly a miracle!"

"And our father saw it, too," Cosmos added.

"And mine as well," Moghadan said.

"And what about the Milk Grotto?" Cyril said. "Don't forget about it!"

Cyril was sitting not far from me, and I asked him, in a low voice, "What's that?" because I didn't know. I didn't want the others to hear me, but they did.

He replied, "Mekhaeil asked me what the Milk Grotto is. Maybe some of the rest of you don't know. It is a place where Mary and Joseph stopped on their way to Egypt as they were fleeing Herod's soldiers. To this day, mothers of newborns and women who wish to become pregnant now visit that place to get some of the powder that comes from the walls of the cave where Mary and Joseph stayed—perhaps only for one night.

"Baby Jesus was born in Bethlehem, far from this cave, and there are many other places along the road they traveled that are holy places: caverns, wells, and many places where miracles occurred. But as far as the Milk Grotto is concerned, Mary would have been nursing Him at the time. We are taught that a drop of Mary's milk fell on the stone and turned it white. Even now, women mix the powder from those stones with water and drink the liquid."

"If that is true—and I'm not saying that I don't believe it—I ask you, why haven't all of the women of the world come to get some of that powder? Is it something only we Copts believe?" Boctor asked.

"Boctor, your mother went there with my wife to get that powder!" Rushdi chastised. "You were fed that liquid! How can you question that?"

But before Boctor could respond, Theophilos interjected, "And don't forget about what was found in Minya not too long ago! The whole world knows about that now!"

Demetrius then said, "Maybe Mekhaeil and some of the other younger men don't know what you're talking about, Theo. Please tell them about it. That is very important ... hard to believe, really, but true. Do you mind, Cyril, if he does that now?"

"Not at all. Please ... go right ahead, Theo," Cyril replied.

"Mekhaeil, do you not know of this? I don't know how you could not know of this. It happened in el Minya, not far from our village, less than fifty years ago."

"I was born in 1999, so maybe that's why I don't know of it," I told him.

"Nor do I," Yousrey said.

"I've heard of it, but I don't really know all that much about it," Nabir added. "Some people found some ancient writings. That's all I know."

"That's right, Nabir," Theo responded. "In 1970 or thereabouts, people discovered some ancient writings that had been hidden away for centuries, on ancient Coptic papyrus paper; they came to be known as the Codex Tchacos. These writings are now part of the gnostic gospels. Scientists have dated the writings to the time Christ walked this earth.

"There is a letter from St. Peter to St. Philip and a gospel containing conversations between Jesus and Judas Iscariot, called the Gospel of Judas, and something from St. James. As I said, the age of the documents has been scientifically verified. They offer proof that the things we believe are true."

"May I speak?" Clement asked.

"Before you do, I would just like to say this to you, Mekhaeil—and to you, Boctor," Theo said. "These things we speak of are the very basis of our faith—some of the cornerstones, if you will. To be a true Copt, you must believe these things, and this is why our faith is so strong. We know these things to be true. We believe all that we have been taught."

"I'm sorry, but sometimes I wonder if people see what they want to see and believe what they want to believe. I want to know what is true and what is not true; that's all. What do I believe? That is what I ask myself. I am the one who must answer that question. I'm sorry, but none of you can answer that question for me. By saying that, I intend no offense to any of you," Boctor responded.

"May I speak now?" Clement asked again.

Some men murmured. It seemed to me as if many of the men didn't want to hear what Clement had to say, both because of what he had said earlier and because he never went to church with us, making him still somewhat of an outsider.

"Yes, you may," Demetrius answered. "Please, my brothers, let us listen to what Clement has to say."

CHAPTER 5

Clement's Heresy

"I understand what Boctor is saying and why he feels the way he does," Clement began.

As soon as he said that, chains rattled more and the men grumbled even louder. Demetrius quieted them down, and then Clement continued,

"I don't doubt that a man named Jesus Christ walked this earth, and I don't doubt that He was crucified on the cross at Golgotha. I don't doubt that Mary and Joseph were His parents, and I don't doubt many of the other things that are said about Him or them. I doubt that He was our God at the time many of those things happened."

Again the chains rattled. I think some men were again trying to make the sign of the cross. This was heresy. Even I was shocked when he said that. I had never heard a Copt say such a thing before in my life.

Cyril started to speak, but Clement stopped him and said, "I'm not finished."

"Let him finish, Cyril. We have all night to talk," Demetrius scolded. "You will be able to respond."

"But I wasn't finished, and neither was Theo. He is interrupting us!" Cyril protested.

"Let him speak, please," Demetrius insisted. "You will have a chance to talk, I promise you. What else do you wish to say, Clement?"

Clement continued. "I believe that Jesus Christ is one of the most important human beings to ever walk this earth. He has changed the world more than any other human being has ever done in the history of the world. There are others who have brought change too, such as Muhammad, Moses, Buddha, and Confucius, but none more so than Christ did. However, Cyril didn't explain everything as fully as he could have about the history of our church. Back then, some people asked the question of whether or not Jesus Christ, since He was the son of God, was a separate being from God the Father, created after God the Father came into existence. At the Council of Nicea, everyone agreed that the Holy Trinity was one God, not three. Anyone who thought differently was excommunicated.

"Later, other people asked whether Jesus Christ was part human being during the time He was on earth or whether He was God at all times He was on earth. In other words, were there two natures to Christ—one being part human and the other part God? Was Jesus Christ a human being, as Boctor just asked, or not? I say that both of those questions were, at the time, legitimate questions to ask, and that they are still legitimate questions to ask. No one knows the answers for certain.

"Before you brand me and Boctor as heretics and write us off as lunatics, please remember that the holiest and most knowledgeable people in Christianity debated this very issue in the fifth century at the Council of Chalcedon, which Cyril referred to. A major split developed between the Coptic Church and the Roman Catholic Church as a result of that conference, as he told you, so good Christian people disagreed on the answer to that question.

"Copts said Jesus Christ was, at all times, divine. The Roman Catholic Church said that Christ had a dual nature, both fully human and fully divine, and that the two were intertwined. That difference of opinion exists to this day and continues to separate the two churches.

"Forgive me, but I believe Jesus Christ was, for most of His time on earth, fully human, but I also believe He was and is the son of God, and that after His crucifixion and death He was glorified and became fully divine. But I don't condemn Boctor for asking the question.

"Was Jesus Christ a human when He was here on earth? Was He created by God, making Him, therefore, a separate God? I don't know, but I don't condemn Boctor if he comes to a different conclusion than I do or all of you do. Remember: that is what Muslims and Jews believe—that he was a human, not God—and so did some of the other Christians.

"However, I am a Christian, which means that I, like you, follow Christ's teachings as best I can, even though I don't agree with everything that the Coptic Church tells me to believe, and even though I ask God why He does some of the things He does, or fails to do some things that I think He should do. But more importantly, I ask myself, and I ask all of you, what of all the other people on earth who follow the teachings of Confucius or Buddha, or those who are Hindus or follow other religions? Are we so sure that we are right and everyone else is wrong? I ask you to just ask yourselves, who is our God? Or what is our God? And is our God different from the God of the Muslims or the Jews? The Hindus believe that there is more than one god. Buddhists believe that god is present in all of us—that we are all gods. Are they wrong too, or is there but one god, as we believe and as the Jews and Muslims believe? And is that not the same god?

"What I see happening in the world is that many religions claim to be the one and only true religion. So I ask myself, and I ask you, is it a religion we are worshiping, or are we worshiping the one and only true God?

"I do not doubt for one second, my brothers, that there is a God. The only question is who and what that is. Is He the God of the Old Testament, as the Jews believe—the God who spoke to Moses and parted the Red Sea so that the Hebrews could escape Egypt? Or is He the God who sent us His only Son, Jesus Christ, to suffer and die on a cross? Or is He the God who spoke to Muhammad through the archangel Gabriel, which resulted in a different interpretation of things? Are those different messages, or did the various messengers interpret them differently?

"And did Yahweh really tell Abraham to kill his only son, Isaac? And as Abraham was preparing to do so, did Yahweh really tell Abraham that, as a reward for his trust and obedience, his descendants would be more numerous than all the stars in the sky?

"I don't know, but I don't think so. I don't think Yahweh would have talked to Moses or Abraham, and I don't think He would have argued with Jacob or any other human being. He is God! He made the universe and all that is within it! He's not a human! He's not like us! Or we are not like Him—whichever way you want to look at it.

"I believe that the God who created the universe sent Jesus Christ to earth to die on a cross as the Lamb of God to make humans stop killing each other. Christ was the Lamb of God, sacrificed for us! People who follow Christ are told that if they have two coats, they are to give one to someone who needs it … to give away all that they own and follow Christ … to do works of charity and give alms to the poor. Who is right?

"I choose to believe that Christianity provides the best way for humans to behave toward one another. That is what two thousand years of Christianity has taught us. These men who are going to kill us don't believe that.

"The God who created the universe doesn't have to prove anything to human beings. He is so much mightier and more complex than we are capable of imagining that it is silly for us to try to think as the God who created the universe would think. Consider this, my brothers: scientists now say that the Big Bang, which is their explanation as to how the universe came into being, occurred almost fourteen billion years ago! They tell us that all that exists came from something smaller than the tip of a ballpoint pen. Scientists now say that planet earth was created four and a half billion years ago!

"The Bible tells us that Adam and Eve were created about twelve thousand years ago in the garden of Eden and that

Abraham lived two thousand years ago. I ask you, do you know what God was doing for the last fourteen billion years, minus twelve thousand years, before He created Adam and Eve? No, you don't. Nobody knows! But human beings will kill and be killed because they *believe* that they know who God is and what His plans for human beings are.

"I am as sure as I can be that the men who are going to kill us are wrong. I am sure that what they are going to do to us is not the way human beings should behave toward other human beings. But they believe they are following the teachings of their god, and nothing I say to them will stop them from killing us. Which one of us is right?

"No one knows for certain who or what God is, yet we are about to go to our graves as martyrs because we believe with all of our hearts that is what we should do. We have faith that everything we believe is true and most of what everyone else believes is false. I just don't know for certain; that is true. I believe, as all of you do, that there is but one God. That is my belief, and that is our faith. But none of us really know who God is, do we? We have beliefs that come to us from the words of other human beings, beginning with our parents, who wanted to know who God was, just as we do, and just as their parents before them did. But am I so certain of what I believe that I will die for it? Or, to put it differently, am I dying for what I truly believe, or am I dying for what I've been told to believe? That is what Boctor is asking himself at this moment.

"After what happened to my parents, my wife and my children, and now me, I am sorry to say, my brothers, that I question everything. As I said before, I know that there is a God. I believe that is true with all my heart. But I also believe that he is not just *our* God and only our God. I believe He is the God of the whole world and of all the people in the world.

"Muhammad killed people who were trying to kill him, so that he and his religion could survive, and his followers are about to kill us because we don't believe as they do. There was a time in history when Christ's followers did the same thing to them. This time the Muslims won and we lost. I don't think that God had anything to do with any of that. God is above that. Boctor is right, though he may not know why. I think that religions, including ours, and their various interpretations of who and what God is are the problem, not the answer.

"That said, I go to my grave with all of you tomorrow with Jesus Christ in my heart, and I accept my fate. In fact, I welcome it. I am tired of all the suffering. I am weary of this life. I am ready for the death that awaits me, and I will not renounce Him at this hour of darkness, though I question so many things about Him."

People were quiet, though I could hear men tossing and turning. Clement's words had made them uncomfortable. No one wanted to listen to what he was saying, but I listened. I had never thought about many of the things he was saying.

The murmurs in the room grew louder.

"Quiet! Please!" Demetrius begged. "Are you finished, Clement? I think we have been quite tolerant up to now. I think you have made your point. I would ask you to allow someone else to speak."

"I'm finished; I have nothing more to say," Clement replied.

"Cyril, is there anything else you wanted to say about our Coptic religion?"

"No, except that I will pray for the soul of our brother, Clement, despite all that he has just said. It is obvious that he has lost his faith in our God as a result of things that have happened to him during his life."

"I don't want your pity!" Clement responded. "But I thank you for your concern, Cyril."

"I hope that the rest of you will hold firm with the faith of our fathers and their fathers before them," Cyril responded.

"Thank you for listening to what Clement had to say, but I say to you younger men, please keep in mind all that Cyril has told you. That is who we are," Demetrius said. "We are Copts, and what Clement has just said is what he believes. It is not what we believe. Let us be silent for a few minutes and pray to God for wisdom and understanding at this difficult time in our lives."

CHAPTER 6

Islam

Several minutes later, Demetrius broke the silence and said, "I am certain that most of us here in this room don't agree with much of what Clement just said or with what Boctor said before him, but please remember to respect their rights to express their opinions and beliefs. They are our brothers, even if they are wrong. Now, let's listen to what Omar has to tell us. I ask him to explain to us, as best he can, what is going through the minds of these men who have locked us up like they have, treating us as they do. They haven't even offered us water, let alone food. No one has been allowed to even go to the bathroom. Why are they treating us this way, Omar? I am certain that none of us would even think about treating our worst enemies this way. Can you explain it to us?"

After a few seconds, Omar began. "First, let me repeat what I said before … I am a Shiite Muslim. I am not like these men who have captured us and treat us as they do, though we share some common beliefs. They have guns, and we do not. That is what gives them this power over us—nothing more.

"Second, please keep in mind, as I told you before, that if they knew I was a Shiite, they would treat me worse than they treat you.

"Third, please know that most Muslims in the world—and almost one in every four people in the world is a Muslim—do not think as they think and do not act as they do.

"Fourth, you should know that these men think they are doing God's will. They believe that they are fighting a holy war and that if they are killed in battle, they will go to heaven and—"

"But how can they think that their God approves of slaughtering innocent Christians who have done nothing to them! We have done nothing to them to deserve this!" Moghadan interrupted.

"Please, let him finish, and then we can ask him questions," Demetrius responded. "Omar, please continue."

"Fifth, you need to know the history between the Muslims, the Hebrews, and the Christians in order to understand what is happening now.

"Sixth, there have been many episodes of genocide over the centuries. This is no different from what happened to the Jews in Germany in the 1930s and 1940s, or to the Armenian Christians in Turkey in 1915, or the slaughter of the Tutsis at the hands of the Hutus in Rwanda in 1993, or the slaughter of Bosnian Muslims at the hands of the Serbian Christians in 1992—and those are just a few examples of similar atrocities that human beings have committed against other human beings, mostly in the name of religion. Such acts go back well before the time of Christ.

"And lastly, I think what is happening here in Libya, in Syria, and in Iraq started in Afghanistan in 1994 when the Taliban decided to rid the country of all Shiites, Christians, Jews, Buddhists, and anyone else who wasn't a Sunni Muslim.

"So although none of us has done anything to provoke this violence that has been brought upon us, we are the innocent victims of what is a jihad, or holy war, started by Sunni Muslims to ethnically cleanse their countries, and eventually the world, by eliminating anyone and everyone who doesn't agree with their interpretation of the Koran. "That said, let me tell you what I know about Islam and Muhammad, and then I will tell you what I believe.

"Muhammad was born in about AD 570, almost six hundred years after Christ, so we know much more about him than we do about Jesus Christ, Buddha, Confucius, or the prophets from the Old Testament, such as Abraham, Jacob, Moses, David, or any of the others. Despite that, there are many things we don't know about Muhammad. We know that he came from a poor family and was orphaned at an early age, so no one paid much attention to him as a young boy.

"As it is with Jesus Christ, not much is known about his early years. We know that Christ was a carpenter and little else. Most people think that He didn't begin performing miracles until He was about thirty years old, and that His first miracle was when He turned water into wine at the request of His mother at the wedding feast in Cana.

"Muhammad worked as a merchant, and we are told he traveled with caravans of merchants who went through his hometown of Mecca to the various places merchants of the day traveled. He was somewhat of an ordinary person. By all accounts, he went mostly unnoticed by those around him during the early years of his life.

"It wasn't until Muhammad was forty years old that he first began what would become his spiritual journey, which led to the founding of Islam. So he and Christ were similar in that respect; both men were in the middle years of life when their ministries began. Like Christ, Muhammad brought the world a new vision of what had come from the teachings of the Old Testament. He believed that Christ was a prophet sent by God, just as Abraham, Jacob, Moses, and the others were.

"Muhammad tells us that he went to a mountain outside of Mecca to contemplate, and while there he was visited by the archangel Gabriel, who told him that he was a prophet sent by Allah to be a messenger to his people. As commanded, Muhammad began writing down the things he was told by Gabriel. Those writings are found in the Koran, and that is when the religion we call Islam came into being. The word "Islam" comes from Arabic and means "peace purity, and submission to Allah, or God." Muhammad created the word. It didn't exist before him.

Demetrius asked, "Excuse me for interrupting, Omar, but

how is it you know so much about history and theology? We have only known you a short period of time, and that has only been while working together these last few months. You have kept to yourself, and we know little about you. Would you mind telling us more about yourself and your background?"

Omar responded, "I have found that it is best if I keep to myself. Whenever I reveal too much about myself to others, bad things seem to happen. Given our circumstances, I don't think that will be a problem now."

I heard him take a deep breath and exhale, and then he spoke.

"As I told you, I am not from Libya, though I have told people that is where I am from. I did so because I thought that it would make it easier for me to get work here, and it did. I was born in Herat, Afghanistan, in 1977, which was two years before the Russians invaded the country. They invaded on Christmas Day in 1979. It was a terrible time to be born. The Russians were merciless. They bombed the city and destroyed much of my home. Some say over half of the buildings in the city were ruined. They didn't care about religion or that we were Shiites; they only wanted to stop the protests so that the man they wanted to be president of our country could do so without resistance. His name was Babrak Karmul, but that was not his real name. He took that name after he became a communist. He founded the People's Democratic Party of Afghanistan in 1964. He was chosen by the Russians to be the leader of my country because he was a communist, and he welcomed the Russians into Afghanistan. The people of my country, whether they were Sunni or Shiite or anything else, didn't approve of what the Russians had done or what Karmul was doing to us.

"But my family survived the years of Russian occupation. It wasn't easy, and many family members and friends died during those years, but we survived. My brothers and my sisters and I were still able to go to school during those days. I had plans to attend the university in Kabul and become a teacher, but all that changed when the Taliban took over in September of 1995.

"After the Russians left in 1989, when I was twelve, there was much fighting to see who would gain control of the country. Herat was involved, but there was little fighting near us. It was mostly in Kabul, the capital. But when Mullah Muhammad Omar became the leader of the Taliban in 1994, he quickly conquered most of the country, including Herat. That was the first time that I was put in a position such as the one we are in now.

"The Taliban, who are all Sunnis, immediately instituted sharia law, which meant that women could not work, women had to wear burqas in public, no one could play music, play sports, fly kites ... many things. And they ordered that everyone must either convert to being a Sunni or leave the country immediately. Anyone who didn't leave or convert was killed.

"My family and I left. I was fifteen at the time. Herat is in the far western part of Afghanistan, not far from the border with Iran, which is a predominantly Shiite country, so we went to Massud, which is the closest big city to Herat. It is the second-largest city in Iran—much, much bigger than Herat, which had about four hundred thousand people in it before the Taliban came. Many fled at that time, as my family did.

"My family and I stayed in Massud for six years, until the United States and its allies came into Afghanistan and drove the Taliban out of power. By then I was beginning my studies at the Razavi University of Islamic Studies. That is where I learned more about Islam, and also about Christianity, Judaism, Hinduism, Buddhism, and all of the other religions of the world."

"You are an educated man, Omar. Thank you for sharing your knowledge with us," Demetrius interjected.

"You are welcome, Demetrius. As I was saying, once the Taliban was driven out of Herat, we waited to see if things would go back to what they had been before the Taliban came into power or if there would be bedlam. It took some time, but a few years later, after I completed my studies and we thought it was safe, we returned to our home. However, the Taliban didn't go away; they just began to fight the United States and its allies the same way they fought the Russians."

Omar was silent for several moments, but no one spoke.

Then he continued. "By then I was a married man. I had met my wife in Massud. She, too, was from Herat, and she had fled with her family to Massud, just as we had. We had been married for several years. We waited before having any children, because of all the fighting and the danger.

"I obtained a job at the University of Herat, which was the main reason why we moved back. It was exactly what I had dreamed of doing as a child. I was teaching theology and Islamic studies. My wife was working at the American Embassy as a translator. We were happy. Things were good. My wife was pregnant, and we were expecting our first child, a son, to be born later that year."

He paused. I heard him take a deep breath, and then he said, "That was two years ago … and then on September 13, the Taliban attacked the embassy. A truck full of explosives was driven through the gate, and men with rocket-propelled grenades and rifles assaulted the consulate. Many people were killed, including my wife and my unborn baby boy."

There was another moment of silence, and then he continued. "Not long after that, since bin Laden had been killed, the United States and all of its allies declared that they were leaving my country. They had tired of having their sons and daughters die there. That is when I decided to leave. I knew what would happen once they left Afghanistan. I knew that the Taliban would be back in power, and I wasn't going to live under Taliban rule. I was right. That is what is happening now.

"I moved to Cairo after the Sunni Brotherhood was thrown out of power, thinking that Egypt might be a safe place for me. I wish I had gone back to Massud, but there were too many memories for me of happier times with my wife there. I thought that the military was in control of things in Egypt, but I was wrong. No place is safe in the Middle East anymore.

"I was actually hoping to get to the United States. I thought that because my wife had been working at their embassy, it would help, but it hasn't. I had no idea how difficult it is to immigrate to the United States. I think it is because I am from Afghanistan and there are many Afghans trying to get into the United States. My application has been pending for two years now.

"In Egypt, because I am a Shiite, I have been discriminated against—just as all of you have been, I'm sure, because you are Christians."

"So why were you in Sirte? How could it be that an educated man such as yourself could be with us, constructing buildings?" Demetrius asked.

"I wasn't able to find employment in the academic community. Because of the problems everywhere in the Middle East, enrollment at all of the universities is way down, and fewer and fewer people are interested in studying theology. Since I am a relatively young man, and not an Egyptian, no one would hire me."

"But you couldn't find another job? One better than the one we had?" Demetrius asked incredulously.

"I had spent all my money moving from Herat to Cairo, and I had no more money left. The average wage in Egypt is a little over seven hundred pounds per week. We make five times that much here, in large part because it is so dangerous to be here. I knew that, but I was desperate, just as all of you were."

"That is true, Omar. That is why all of us are here," Demetrius responded, with sadness in his voice. "It's hard to believe that a man like you is among us. You have so much knowledge to share with the world, and it will soon be lost."

"I lost my apartment. I had no car. I was desperate," Omar continued. "I didn't even have any good prospects for finding a position. My great hope, for which I prayed every day, was that the United States would let me in, but it seems that no longer matters anymore, doesn't it?" he asked ruefully.

"Unless there is a miracle," Demetrius responded, "none of that matters anymore. All of your hopes and dreams—and all of ours, as well—will soon be gone. But before I interrupted you, you were telling us about what happened after Muhammad created the Islamic religion. Please continue."

"After several years, Muhammad began to preach to others the message he was receiving from Gabriel and from God, and he began to attract some followers. However, as with Christ, his message was not well received by the community in which he lived. He was not put to death, as Christ was, though. Muhammad fled Mecca and went to a place called Abyssinia, which is now called Medina, where his message was received better, but there were many there who did not accept him or his teachings.

"Unlike Christ, the Buddha, or Confucius, but much like David and some of the other Hebrew leaders of the Old Testament, Muhammad was a man who fought to gain power, and then he had to fight to keep what he had won. He and his followers fought with those who didn't agree with him and what he was saying. After ten years of fighting the tribes in and around Abyssinia, or Medina, he made a peace with those people. Not long after, he and an army of ten thousand soldiers, we are told, returned to his hometown of Mecca and militarily captured it.

"Ever since, as you know, large throngs of people have been making the pilgrimage to Mecca to honor him. It is estimated that over two million people make that journey every year."

"Do both Sunnis and Shiites make the pilgrimage?" Demetrius asked.

"Yes," Omar responded.

"Side by side?" Boctor asked.

"We all go as a group. Remember: you cannot tell us apart. We are the same people," Omar told him

"I don't understand the difference, really," Demetrius responded. "It makes little sense to me. I hope you will explain that to us. I am sorry to interrupt. Please continue."

"Not long after he established Mecca as the headquarters of the religion he founded, and after his message was firmly established and codified as a new and different religion, he died. That was in AD 632, so he lived to be sixty-two years old, but his message, as found in the Koran, ultimately unified most of the people who lived in Arabia, most of whom were either Hebrews or Christians at the time. There were also, as now, pagans and followers of other religions in the area.

"He taught his followers that there was but one God—not three, as Christians believe … Father, Son, and Holy Spirit."

"We don't believe that there are three Gods, Omar," Cyril interjected. "We believe that there is but one God, which we call the Holy Trinity."

"I'm sorry if I misstate your beliefs, but that is what many Muslims, if not most, believe. But as I was saying, Muhammad required complete submission to God. He commanded daily prostrations and prayers to God. He commanded a strict social order in families and religious communities. He demanded that people dramatically change the way they lived, and people did as he commanded.

"Muslims, and that includes me, believe that the Koran is the word of God as told to Muhammad, just as you Christians believe that the Bible is the word of God. What many non-Muslims don't realize is that the Koran incorporates many of the stories from the Old Testament, and much of the New Testament is in it too. However, the stories are, in some cases, slightly different in places.

"Muslims believe there is truth in the Torah and the Bible. As I said, if you read the Koran, you will see that much of what is found in the Torah and the Bible is in the Koran too; yet these three religions, with the same or similar historical foundations and backgrounds, have been at war with one another for centuries. The question of why and how that can be is not for me to answer. I can only explain to you what I know and what I have learned in my life."

Everyone was quiet as Omar spoke. Many in the room likely had never heard a Muslim explain his faith the way Omar was doing. I hadn't.

Omar continued. "What many people don't understand, as Demetrius just mentioned, is why the Sunni Muslims hate the Shiite Muslims so much … and here's why. When Muhammad died, he didn't name a successor. Because of that, his followers weren't sure what to do. Who was to be their leader? Many wanted a blood relative to be the leader of Islam, much as with monarchies throughout history. Many thought Muhammad's cousin, whose name was Ali, was the chosen one.

"There were others in the Islamic community who felt that the leader should be the best person in the religion. They didn't want to create a monarchy—or royalty, if you will. They favored a man named Abu Bakr, who was a close confidant and adviser to Muhammad during many of his later years. They wanted him to be the caliph, or successor, to Muhammad.

"They were unable to reconcile their differences, and the two camps basically broke off from one another and went their separate ways. Now, as history has shown us, Abu Bakr was a military genius. He spread the faith over the land at the point of a sword.

"It wasn't long after Muhammad died before this entire part of the world was dominated by Muslims, and that included the Shiites, who were busy spreading the faith too. They, too, conquered parts of Arabia. Both groups survived and prospered, though they quarreled and fought during all of those years, just as they do now. They never reconciled their differences.

"To this day, the difference between the two groups remains the same. Shiites say that only a blood relative of Muhammad should be the caliph, and the Sunnis say it should be the person chosen by the Islamic community. Shiites still believe that Ali and his successors should be the caliphs. We have holy days to honor Ali.

"At this time, most Muslims are Sunnis. Four out of every five Muslims in the world are Sunnis, if not more. So we are greatly outnumbered."

"But why do they hate you so?" Demetrius asked.

"It has been that way for over a thousand years, since AD 632, when Muhammad died. I cannot explain it any better than I have. This is a fundamental difference of opinion—or, I should say, belief—and hundreds of thousands, if not millions, of people have died because of that difference."

"Are there any other differences? Different prayers? Different customs?" Demetrius continued.

"All Muslims say the basic prayer. We believe that there is no God but God and that Muhammad is his prophet, and all Muslims say that in prayer every day. Sunnis pray five times per day, and Shiites pray three times per day. In our prayers, we say that Ali was the one chosen to follow Muhammad, and we believe that to be the truth. Obviously, Sunnis don't say that.

"Some holy days are different, and as I said, we have a day on which we honor Ali, who is our founder. But the main difference these days—other than how we select our leader, which remains the most significant issue—is the interpretation of the Koran and sharia law.

"The extremists read the same words all other Muslims read, but they interpret them differently. They say that Muslims should go back to the Koran and behave as men and women behaved almost fourteen hundred years ago, without regard for all that has been learned and all that has changed in those many years.

"We can only imagine what life would have been like during the days Muhammad walked the earth, or what it was like when Christ walked the earth, but times have changed. Attitudes have changed. People have changed. Extremists wish to go back to the social order that existed back then."

"But why must they now kill Christians and others who don't agree with them, Omar? Why now? What has happened to change things?" Demetrius asked.

"I can only tell you what I think … I don't know," Omar responded. "I believe it started in Afghanistan with Mullah Omar, and it may have begun when Osama bin Laden formed al-Qaeda, or it could be a result of what happened in Iraq when Saddam Hussein was overthrown by the United States and its allies, or it could be because of the Arab Spring, which began in 2011. I cannot say with certainty."

"But what is your opinion?" Demetrius persisted.

"ISIS didn't come into existence until the United States invaded Iraq and Saddam Hussein was killed. There are many who think that ISIS would not have come into existence if Saddam Hussein had not been killed, and I am one of them.

Hussein was a brutal dictator, and he was in complete control of the country. There was little dissent because he didn't tolerate any dissent. If he were still alive, he would probably still be in absolute control of Iraq, and many would say that would be a bad thing, but maybe we wouldn't have ISIS. Who knows? But that's what I think.

"Shiites and Kurds, as well as Jews and Christians, were discriminated against under his regime, and many of them were killed, despite his insistence that his was a secular government—even though he was a Sunni. All ISIS soldiers are Sunnis. Most of their leaders are former generals and officers in Hussein's army. That is a matter of fact, I believe, but that doesn't answer your question.

"In my opinion, ISIS is not, truly, a political group, although it seeks to take over Syria and Iraq. They are religious fanatics. They do what they do in the name of Allah. As their very name implies, they want a pure Islamic state in Iraq and Syria, just as Mullah Omar did in Afghanistan. They are seeking to regain control of the Middle East—much as Abu Bakr did in the days after Muhammad died, I believe."

"But are we sure that these men who captured us are part of ISIS and not al-Qaeda or some other group?" Demetrius interjected.

"That is a good question. I don't know, and that is why I said a few minutes ago that the followers of Osama bin Laden are involved in this too. He is the one who created al-Qaeda in 1989, after Russia withdrew from Afghanistan. It's surprising, really, that bin Laden would have created this group when he did, after the United States had provided so much help to those who fought against the Russians, including bin Laden himself, but that's what he did. And al-Qaeda's main goal is now to drive the United States and all other Western influences out of Arabia.

"Al-Qaeda is, for the most part, a political group, or it has a political mission, but it is based entirely upon a religious belief—a Sunni religious belief. Osama bin Laden was from Saudi Arabia, and he was a Sunni. Still, al-Qaeda, ISIS, and the Taliban are three separate and distinct organizations, and all three are composed of Sunni Muslims.

"Please keep in mind that I am a Shiite, not a Sunni, and I am not saying that there are no Shiites who are behaving badly in the world today. Iran is a Shiite-dominated country, and they have been as repressive as the Sunnis since the shah of Iran was deposed. There is blame to be shared for what is taking place these days. Sunnis are fighting Shiites in many parts of the world as I speak.

"So although al-Qaeda is an entirely Sunni Islamic group, it includes people from all over the earth. Many are just terrorists who want to kill other people, I believe, and they are being paid money to do so. They reap the plunders of war, but they say that they do so for the purpose of purifying the region of outside influences, meaning the United States and all Western powers.

"Initially al-Qaeda went into the Sudan after Russia withdrew all of its military forces from Afghanistan, but it wasn't a very large group at the time, and it wasn't active for a few years. However, in 1993, it organized and carried out the bombing of the World Trade Center. It also claimed responsibility for the downing of two Black Hawk helicopters that year.

"Once the Taliban came into power in Afghanistan in 1994, Osama bin Laden was welcomed into the country by Mullah Omar, with whom he had fought against the Russians. He was allowed to set up terrorist training camps there. Afghanistan became bin Laden's headquarters. As I recall, he was banned from returning to Saudi Arabia at that time.

"From their bases in Afghanistan, al-Qaeda began to conduct more terrorist attacks, and it began to recruit more followers, too. Osama bin Laden had an enormous amount of personal wealth, and he used that money to buy the weapons and the people he needed to carry out those attacks. In 1998, the US embassies in Kenya and Tanzania were attacked by his followers. In 2000, the USS Cole was damaged by bombs placed on the ship by his followers. That attack killed seventeen American soldiers and injured many more.

"Of course it was on September 11, 2001, that al-Qaeda accomplished its most notorious attack, and that is when the entire world began to take them even more seriously than before. That is when Mullah Omar protected bin Laden and refused to turn him over to the United States. That is what caused the United States to enter Afghanistan and drive the Taliban from power."

"But Christians and Jews weren't killed in Afghanistan, were they?" Raghib asked.

"There weren't many Christians or Jews there at that time. Even before the Taliban took over, 99 percent of the people in Afghanistan were Muslim. Almost 85 to 90 percent of those were Sunnis. Once the Taliban conquered the country, it imposed sharia law everywhere, and it made Shiites either convert to being Sunnis, leave the country, or die.

"So yes, the Taliban did persecute any and all who were not Sunni Muslims, and that included the few Christians or Jews who were there. And don't forget what it did to the two ancient statues of Buddha several years ago. Mullah Omar called them 'un-Islamic.' So Buddhists, Christians, Shiites, and all others have been targeted for elimination by the Taliban."

"But they didn't behead people, did they?" Moghaddan asked.

"Oh, yes they did. There were beheadings, but the practice wasn't as common and as widely known then as it is now. Now they take videos and put them out over the Internet. They seem to be proud of what they do. We didn't hear as much of beheadings then, and the beheadings weren't reported in the news or on television. But the change in that may be because they have beheaded American, British, French, and Japanese journalists, among others, recently. Now they seek ransom money and say that if the ransoms aren't paid, the beheadings will occur. Actually, I think the main reason we hear and see so much these days is because of the Internet and the ease with which anyone can post things for the world to see.

"But though the two groups are similar, they are different. In Afghanistan, the Taliban wants a country that is entirely free from anyone other than Sunni Muslims. The goal of al-Qaeda is to rid all of Arabia of all foreign influences. We thought ISIS would be confined to Syria and Iraq, but now they are in many other countries. The Taliban was only in Afghanistan at first, but after the United States drove them from power, they fled to Pakistan, and now the Taliban is in Pakistan too, but nowhere else.

"The Taliban was and is made up only of Afghans and Pakistanis, whereas al-Qaeda includes Chechens, Uzbeks, Filipinos, Syrians, Koreans—people from many different countries. ISIS was originally only Iraqis, but now Syrians have joined them—or they have joined the Syrians; I'm not sure which. Again, the groups are divided along religious lines, and there are many more Sunnis than Shiites, as I mentioned before.

"I have heard that the Taliban doesn't approve of the tactics of ISIS and al-Qaeda and that it is trying to disassociate itself from those two groups. So while both groups are doing horrible things, they are doing them for somewhat different reasons; one is more religious, whereas the other is more political. In fact, I've heard that ISIS is fighting the Taliban in Afghanistan, but I don't know if that's true or not."

"And you blame the Taliban for being the cause of all that is going on here in the Middle East?" Cyril asked. "Why is that?"

"I do blame them—Mullah Omar, in particular. If it weren't for the Taliban, I don't think al-Qaeda would have become what it has become. I think the radical Islamic philosophy of having a country completely free of any religious diversity comes from the Taliban too. So yes, I blame the Taliban as being the main group responsible for what is going on in the world these days."

"And that is all because of how it interprets the Koran," Demetrius asked.

"Yes, with its extreme position on sharia law, whereby women are not allowed to work outside of home and are required to wear burqas. Girls can't go to school, men must wear beards, no one can play music, no one can play games, there is no kite-flying—all sorts of things. But the main thing is that all who live in Afghanistan must be Muslims—and Sunni Muslims at that."

"However, I do want to say one thing about that—and by 'that' I mean the way women are treated under sharia law. The United States and many Western powers deplore that particular policy, but let me suggest that they are being hypocritical. It is true that women have risen and now have status nearly equal with that of men in those countries, but it wasn't long ago that women were not allowed to vote or own property in the United States. Also, many nuns in the Catholic Church wear habits and clothing that is not much different from the burqas Muslim women wear. The Middle East is not as modern as the United States and Europe, and that is part of the problem; there is a dramatic difference in culture.

"However, since Demetrius asked me to try to explain what is going on, I would say to you that much of what is going on in the world today has happened before. History is repeating itself, I believe, and what is happening to us has happened to many men before us, for exactly the same reasons.

There was quiet in the room when Omar stopped talking. Then Rushdi asked, "Omar, I have heard that Muhammad himself ordered the beheading of many people, including Jews, when he was alive. Is that true?"

"That is not true. Some people say that an incident occurred when Muhammad supposedly ordered that nearly a thousand Jewish men and boys be killed in the town of Medina. It was during that period of time when Muhammad had an army of followers and was fighting against any and all who opposed him in Medina before he went on to conquer Mecca.

"The Jews who were killed had betrayed Muhammad, and that is why they were killed, but Muhammad didn't order them killed. Someone else did. Muhammad put someone else in charge and told that person to decide what to do with those who had betrayed him."

"And they were beheaded?" Rushdi asked.

"That is true," Omar replied.

"Christ never did anything like the things Muhammad did. Do you think that has anything to do with the differences in the two religions, Omar?" Cyril asked.

"Christ lived at a time when Rome ruled the world. Maybe if he had lived when Muhammad lived, things would have been different. For Christ, a military solution was not possible, but—"

"If God wanted it to happen, God could have made it happen, I believe," Abanoub interjected.

"In the Old Testament, Yahweh helped the Jews defeat their enemies," he responded. "Their God was very much involved in what happened to them back then. Again, in Christ's day, a military victory over the Romans was impossible, in my opinion, but I cannot deny that God is capable of doing anything. Maybe God chose not to do anything to teach humans a lesson."

"Which is what we believe Jesus Christ did," Cyril affirmed. "He died on the cross to give us a new covenant—a new way of behaving. We believe that, Omar."

"Muslims believe that Jesus Christ was a great prophet, but we believe that Muhammad is the last and greatest prophet," Omar responded. "That is the biggest difference between our two religions. And while fundamental and orthodox Muslims are very strict, there are some Jewish and Christian communities that are just as strict in their interpretation of the Torah and the Bible, and violations of the law are not tolerated. Orthodox Jews and Charismatic Christians can be equally as fervent and equally as strict, I believe, as orthodox Muslims. We are as ardent in our beliefs as you are."

"But we aren't running around beheading people, Omar," Demetrius interjected.

"No, Christians and Jews aren't, and these men are not orthodox Muslims; they are radicalized Muslims—radicalized Sunni Muslims," Omar responded.

"And they are crazed ideological terrorists," Raghib added, "who apparently see nothing wrong with what they are doing. These are dangerous people."

Omar continued. "In the Old Testament, Yahweh was stern with those who disobeyed him. He was prepared to destroy Sodom and Gomorrah, as you know. Many say the god of the Old Testament was full of fire and brimstone. These men who have us chained up like this think they are doing nothing wrong by killing us; they think that it is God's punishment. To them they are doing Allah's work by ridding the world of heathens and infidels. Men have acted this way for centuries. Until we find a way to prevent this kind of action, I believe it will continue. I don't see a peaceful resolution to the problem at this time, I'm sorry to say.

"That is as much as I have to say about Islam and my beliefs. I hope it has been helpful."

Again the room was silent. Then Demetrius spoke.

"Thank you, Omar, for sharing your knowledge of Islam and Muslims with us. Let us be quiet for several minutes, my brothers, and think about what Omar has told us. Please consider all of what you have just heard, and we will talk about these things in a few minutes."

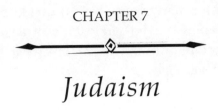

CHAPTER 7

Judaism

"My brothers, I have been giving much thought to what we have heard tonight, and I want to share one thought with you. These terrorists who have captured us recognize the Bible as a holy book, and accept that Jesus Christ was a prophet, just as Abraham, Moses, David, and others were prophets. They are descendants of Abraham, just as we are. They call us 'People of the Book.' I still don't understand why they hate us so just because we believe in Christ. I thank Cyril and Omar for trying to help me understand it better than I do, but I am still confused. I don't hate them. I truly don't," Demetrius told us.

"And don't forget the Hebrews," Omar whispered. "They are part of this. We should include them in this conversation too."

"Omar makes a good point. We must know and remember the history of the Jews to understand the tortured history of this land of ours, even though they have little to do with what is happening to us now," Rushdi said.

"Maybe you will tell us what you know about that, Rushdi. Will you?" Demetrius asked.

"I would rather someone else do that, Demetrius, if you don't mind," he responded. "I don't feel much like talking."

"But none of us went to school in Cairo, as you did, Rushdi," Yousrey said. "None of us knows what you know. We only know what our fathers, the priests, and the elders have taught us. We would like to hear from you."

I knew that Rushdi had gone on to college in Cairo after finishing school in al-Aour. I knew that he became a professor and taught there for many years, but I didn't know what subjects he taught. I also knew that he had lost his job a year or two earlier and had been back in our village ever since. He had a big family and many mouths to feed.

"Yes, please do," Yousrey asked. "Most of us just finished our schooling. None of us went to college, as you did. We don't know what you know."

Demetrius replied, "Yousrey makes a good point. Most of the men in this room are young enough to be our children. They don't know what we know. Please, Rushdi, share with us some of your knowledge of these things. Would you do that for us?"

"We are about to die. My brothers, are you sure you want to spend our last hours on earth listening to a professor lecture you on Jewish history? Cyril has told you about our Coptic faith, and Omar has told you about Islam. Do you really want to hear from me about the Jews?" Rushdi asked.

Rushdi was a tall, thin man with piercing black eyes. Whenever I saw him in church or in his home, or anywhere, he always had a serious look on his face. I knew he had been a professor and was very smart. I was intimidated by him.

Like all the other men, he had a full beard with much gray in it, and he wore a black cap over the top of his head at all times, except when in church. No one wears a hat in church. Most Copts are clean-shaven, but in Sirte, all of the men allowed their beards to grow.

"I do," Moghadan responded. "We may not have many hours left to live, but I'd like to hear what you have to tell us. So please, Rushdi, tell us what you know about the Jews."

Other men muttered their agreement with that request.

"I will do as you ask, my brothers," he responded.

"Thank you, Rushdi," Demetrius said.

"And please explain to me why these terrorists aren't killing any Jews. Why is it only us Christians?" Moghadan interjected.

"Before you answer that question, I want to know why we

have to talk about this at all. If we're going to die in the morning, less than eight hours from now, why waste our time talking about these things? I, for one, don't really want to hear it," Clement said.

"Clement," Demetrius responded, "We all listened to you, so now, please, listen to what others have to say … unless most of the rest of you agree with him. Do the rest of you think this is a waste of what time we have left on earth?"

"I agree with Clement," Boctor said. "This is a waste of time. It's only going to confuse me more."

There were grumbling sounds, but I couldn't make out what they were saying. Then Moghadan spoke up. "I am much younger than you, Clement, and younger than most of the rest of you, but I'm not the youngest man here; Mekhaeil is, and Magdi, Nabir, Yousrey, and Boctor are about the same age as I am, but I am hearing things I didn't know.

"If I am to die tomorrow, I would like to have a better understanding of why I am to die. I want to know if the Jews have anything to do with this. I, too, want to know why it is that only Christians are being killed. I would like to hear what you have to tell us, Rushdi."

"If that is what the majority of men in this room wish for me to do, then I will do so," Rushdi responded.

Demetrius then asked, "How many agree?"

Most of the men mumbled an affirmative response.

"How many disagree?" he asked.

A few men mumbled a negative response.

"All right then," Rushdi said, "here goes. First of all, I think it's important for you, Moghadan, and all of the young people here to understand that the Old Testament is all about the Hebrews—or, as we call them, the Jews. The Torah is their holy book, just as the Koran is the holy book for Muslims and the Bible is the holy book for Christians, and it was written by many people over a long period of time, right up until the time before Christ.

"The Jews believe that Moses wrote the first five books of the Old Testament about fourteen hundred years before Christ was born, and the other books were written by other people, many of whom are unknown, but all of the people who wrote the Old Testament were Jews."

"Is it Hebrews or Jews?" Magdi asked. "I never understood why they're called both names."

"In the Bible, Abraham is called a Hebrew because his father's name was Eber; the word 'Hebrew' refers to the fact that Abraham was the son of Eber. After that, descendants of Abraham were called Ebers, and that name became the word 'Hebrews.'"

"But what about the word 'Jews'? Where did that come from?" Yousry asked.

"That was different. The word 'Jew' comes from the fact that two of the twelve ancient tribes of Israel lived in Judea, and those two tribes were called 'Jews' because they were from Judea. I don't know about the other ten tribes. So all children of Abraham were called Hebrews, and it seems to me Jewish people should really be called Hebrews, not Jews."

"And what of the word 'Israel'?" Nabir asked. "Where did that come from?"

"That comes from the Torah. It is written that God, who they called Yahweh, among other names, changed Jacob's name from Jacob to Israel. Jacob was the grandson of Abraham, and in the Bible, he argued with God.

"The word 'Israel' comes from two words—'argue' and 'God.' That is where the name supposedly comes from. The book of Genesis says that God told Jacob he was to be called Israel from then on. So from that moment onward, the descendants of Abraham, through his grandson, Jacob, were called Israelites, and that's where the country gets its name, as I understand it. But not all Israelis are Jews, remember."

"So Muslims and Christians who live in Israel are Israelis too?" Moghadan asked.

"That's true, Moghadan," Rushdi answered. "And almost thirty percent of the people who live in Israel are Muslim or Christian— mostly Muslim. The Muslims who live there call themselves Palestinians. I don't know what Christians who live in Israel call themselves. I think they're called Israelis. If not, they should be."

"So how are the Muslims and Jews different from us if Muhammad recognized Jesus Christ as a prophet and Jesus Christ was a Jew?" Moghaddan asked.

"Jesus Christ wanted the Jews of his day to follow the customs and traditions of Judaism better than they were," Rushdi responded. "What makes them different from us is that neither Jews nor Muslims believe that Jesus was the Messiah. and we Christians don't recognize Muhammad as a prophet, and neither do the Jews."

"But Muslims, Jews and Christians all believe what is in the Old Testament, and everyone traces their roots back to Abraham, correct?" Yousrey asked.

"Yes, they do," Rushdi responded.

"And why don't Christians and Jews recognize Muhammad as a prophet of God?" Yousrey continued. "He obviously convinced the world that he was a messenger from God. If Christ was the most important person ever to walk the face of the earth, it seems pretty obvious that Muhammad has to be not far behind him, right up there with the Buddha, Confucius, and Moses, yes? We can't deny that, can we?"

"We recognize that he started a new religion—Islam, which has been around for over fourteen hundred years—and no one can deny that one in every four people in the world follows his teachings now," Rushdi responded. "But I don't think Christians, Jews, Buddhists, Hindus, or any others besides Muslims recognize Muhammad as a prophet at all. I'm unaware of anything that Christians and Jews accept as truth from Islam, other than those beliefs they have in common. We believe what we believe, and they believe what they believe."

"But all three agree on a number of things, including the Bible and many of the stories in it, right?" Yousrey continued.

"That's true, Yousrey," Rushdi said.

"That makes no sense," Boctor said. "So these people who have us chained up like this believe, as we do, that most of everything in the Bible is true. Is that what you're telling us?"

"For the most part, yes, that's right," Rushdi replied.

"So what don't they believe about us? Why do they hate us so?" Boctor asked.

"For one thing, they don't believe that Jesus was God and that He died on the cross," Rushdi answered. "That's the biggest thing."

"They don't? So what do they think happened to Him?" Magdi asked.

"They think that God took Him up into heaven. They don't believe that God could die," Rushdi responded.

"That's what we believe too!" Abanoub stated.

"Yes, that's true, but we believe He died on the cross first, and that on the third day He was resurrected, and then He ascended into heaven. There's an important difference there," Rushdi answered.

"So they hate us and are going to kill us because of that?" Boctor asked incredulously.

"We believe that He died for our sins," Rushdi replied, "and that He allowed himself to be killed for us in order to teach all of humanity a lesson, and—"

"And that is what we should do tomorrow!" Cyril interjected. "We should go to our death as Jesus went to His death, and we should do that to show the world that we are followers of Christ—that we will gladly lay down our lives and join Christ in heaven!"

"And," Rushdi continued, "to make a new covenant with the world and show men, by his example, that men shouldn't kill each other—that might doesn't make right, as had been the way of the world for thousands of years before Him, just as Omar explained a while ago."

"But that's the way things still are, isn't it? Might still makes right, and the group with the most guns wins, right?" Clement added.

"You may be right, Clement, unfortunately. Before Christ, the nation with the strongest army would kill anyone else they wanted to, take their land and their property, and keep them as slaves until a more powerful country came along and conquered that nation."

"And after Christ, the same things continued to happen," Abanoub interjected. "The Romans still ruled the world, and then came Genghis Khan, Attila the Hun, the Muslims, the Ottoman Empire, the British Empire, the Germans, and the list goes on and on. And now it's the United States of America. That is human nature. Our God, Jesus Christ, is unique. He gave us a new covenant to follow—one that was completely different from anything that went before Him. We must remember that always."

"So Muslims believe that there is a God, but they don't think Jesus is God?" Boctor asked.

"That's right. They believe Jesus was a prophet, just as Muhammad was a prophet," Rushdi replied. "Muslims believe that Muhammad is the last and greatest prophet—greater than Christ, Moses, or anyone else."

"And the Jews? You were telling us about the Jews, and then we started talking about the Muslims again. What about the Jews? What do they think of Muhammad or Christ?" Moghadan asked.

"As I said before, they don't believe that Christ was the Messiah or that Muhammad is the last and greatest prophet," Rushdi responded.

"How can they not believe that Christ was the Messiah?" Abanoub asked. "Look at all that He did! There has been no one in the history of the world who changed the world more than Christ did … ever!"

"As Yousrey pointed out a few minutes ago," Rushdi responded, "Muhammad changed the world too, Abanoub; and all reasonable people would have to agree, I think, that he changed this part of the world as much as, if not more than, Christ did. Christianity flourished in Europe, not here in the Middle East."

"And remember, after Muhammad died, people in this entire area of the world were Muslims for over a thousand years," Omar added, softly. "And that is the case to this day, as you know."

"But Copts and other Christians persevered through all those persecutions, and we are still here," Abanoub responded. "Don't forget that. We are strong, and we are prepared, once again, to be martyrs, if that is God's will for us."

"That is true," Omar responded. "And I am very much impressed by the strength of your faith. I am learning things about you that I didn't know."

"And in the days when Jesus Christ walked the earth," said Rushdi, "the Jews wanted the Messiah to come and do as Moses had done, or as David had done, or as others had done before in their history, and rid them of their oppressors, who were the Romans at the time. The Romans had conquered them and basically made slaves of them, much as the pharaohs of ancient Egypt had done to them over a thousand years before."

"But after all the years that have passed since Christ was crucified, and as the followers of Christ continue to multiply all over the world, can't the Jews see that what Christ did was save humanity, and that He really was the Messiah?" Abanoub asked.

"No," Rushdi answered. "They say there are still wars to this day and that there is still disease, pestilence, and many other bad things in the world. They say that the Messiah, who they think is still coming, will not allow those things to happen."

"So they don't think that anything we believe in is true?" Guirguis asked.

"Like I said before, there are some things we believe in that they also believe in, Guirguis," Rushdi replied. "They don't believe that Jesus was God. They don't believe that He performed miracles. Jesus was a Jew, and they think of Him as a heretic rabbi. Most of the early Christians were actually Jews who believed that He was the Messiah, but there are still many things we have in common with Jews, such as the Old Testament and our common ancestry."

"So when did the Jews who followed Christ become Christians and not Jews?" Touma asked.

"At some point—and I don't know exactly when that was—they stopped calling themselves Jews and began calling themselves Christians. Remember: St. Paul, who was then called Saul, was a Philistine who was hunting down Jews who weren't following

Jewish laws and traditions when Jesus appeared to him on the road to Damascus. After being blinded and chastised, Saul became Paul, and he became a believer at that moment."

"So Jews were killing Christians, too?" Boctor asked.

"You mean back at the time of Christ?" Rushdi responded.

"Yes," Boctor answered.

"They were persecuting them. Yes, they were. The religious leaders in Jerusalem wanted to stop all Jews from believing in anything Christ said. They punished any Jews who became followers of Christ. To my knowledge, they excommunicated them and ostracized them. The Romans killed Christians, as we know, and so did the Egyptians in the years after His death, as we also know, and so did others. The Jews were part of that too. It wasn't easy being a follower of Christ back then."

"Or now," Demetrius added.

"Or now," Rushdi affirmed.

"And they killed Christ, right?" Magdi asked. "The Jews, I mean, because they considered Him to be a heretic, right?"

"They convinced the Romans to kill Christ because He was inciting riots or disturbances or some such thing. The Jews didn't actually kill Him. The Romans did," Rushdi replied.

"Same thing," Boctor said.

"Maybe yes, maybe no," Rushdi responded. "Some people blame the Jews; some don't."

"I do," Boctor stated.

"So why do the Muslims hate the Jews so much?" Moghadan asked.

"They have hated them for centuries," Rushdi responded.

"But why?" he persisted. "For the same reason they hate us, or for a different reason?"

"Mostly because the Hebrews lived in what is now Israel, and its capital, Jerusalem, is seen as holy land by Muslims, Christians, and Jews. When the Muslims captured Jerusalem not long after Muhammad died, they controlled it for hundreds of years before the Crusades, during which the Christians sought to recapture and reclaim Jerusalem from them. Jews were still there during all of those years, living as second-class citizens, just as we Christians did under Muslim rule."

"Why is Jerusalem a holy place for Muslims?" Sarabamoon asked.

"You have all seen pictures of Jerusalem, yes?" Rushdi asked.

When several men, but not all, responded affirmatively, he continued,

"Well, the most recognizable landmark is what is called the Dome of the Rock. It is a mosque with a huge golden dome on top that stands high above most everything around it. If you have seen a picture of Jerusalem, you have seen it. The mosque was built by Muslims not long after Muhammad died, and it was built because of a vision Muhammad had. It was built on top of an ancient Jewish temple. Both Jews and Muslims revere Jerusalem," Rushdi responded, "as we Christians do, too."

"This makes no sense!" Boctor said again. "Muslims recognize Jesus as a prophet, though they refuse to recognize Him as God, as we do; and they recognize Jerusalem to be the Holy Land, as we do; we are all sons of Abraham, and yet they are going to kill us because we believe He died on the cross and they don't. That's it? That makes no sense!"

"Keep your voices down," Demetrius reminded everyone.

"But we were talking about Jews, not the Muslims," said Moghadan. "We got sidetracked. I want to know why they aren't killing Jews too. Why only Christians?"

"They would be killing Jews too, Moghadan, if any were here!" Rushdi responded. "There just aren't that many Jews left here in Libya, or in Syria, Iraq, or Afghanistan. They were run out years ago or killed long ago. The Iranians, the Palestinians, and many Arab countries want to see them run out of Israel and out of the Middle East to this day."

"And remember 1967, when a million Muslim soldiers were ready to attack Israel and kill all the Jews?" said Raghib. "They were badly defeated in what was called the Six-Day War, but don't think for a minute that there aren't some Muslims who still want to kill all Jews. Many still do, but they can't, because Israel is too strong."

"They want the land returned to the Palestinians, who are Muslims," Omar added. "Many did not accept what happened in the years after World War II, and they still don't."

I asked, "What happened after World War II?"

"Mekhaeil," Rushdi responded gently, as if I were an idiot for not knowing all of this, "you should have paid better attention during history class. After World War II ended, the Jews who had survived the Holocaust had nowhere to go. They didn't want to return to or remain in Germany, and no one else wanted to take them in—at least not in large numbers—so those people were looking for a place to go. Jerusalem was their most desired destination.

"The British had been the rulers of Palestine, Egypt, and other places around this part of the world since 1917. In 1946, after the war ended, and before Israel officially became a sovereign nation, Jews began returning to Jerusalem in small numbers as a result of an agreement reached between many countries after much debate. Ultimately it was the British who agreed to allow Jews to go back to Jerusalem in larger numbers, and it was the British who gave Israel its sovereignty.

"At first the British were allowing about fifteen hundred people a month, or something like that, but the Arabs who lived there were furious, and they refused to allow the Jews to settle there and wanted all of that to stop. All of their Arabian neighbors agreed with the Palestinians. Pressure was put on the British by the United States and others to allow even more Jews to settle there, despite the opposition from what was a predominantly Muslim community.

"That went on for about two years. Then, in May of 1948, the British just up and left, leaving the Jews and the Arabs who lived in Palestine to fight it out. More and more Jews arrived from all over the world, as they could see this was an opportunity for them to regain what they considered to be their rightful homeland, and the Jews won. The Arabs never accepted that. The fighting continues to this day, and a peaceful resolution doesn't seem possible."

"But these terrorists aren't killing Jews; they're killing us! Why?" Yousrey asked.

"As I said before, it's because there aren't many Jews here, and they know that Israel would not allow it. Israel would kill them if they tried," Rushdi responded. "Israel isn't involved in what is going on in Syria, Iraq, Libya, Afghanistan, or anywhere else, really—at least not publicly. You never hear them mentioned except when it comes to the issue of Iran obtaining nuclear weapons, and then they are quite vocal."

"But why is that?" Boctor asked. "Why isn't Israel involved in all of this? I still don't know the answer."

"Actually it's quite busy defending itself," Omar interjected. "You can bet your life on that. I assure you that Israel is involved in everything that's going on in the region. We just don't know what it is doing. You can be sure that if we were Jews, Israel would be here already. They would come save us. I have no doubt about that."

At that, Asaad spoke up. He had been quiet for some time.

"So why doesn't our country come to our defense?" he asked.

"I have no answer for that," Rushdi responded, "except to say that the last time Egypt fought with Libya, it didn't go well, and Egypt is having enough troubles of its own right now. Other than that, I don't know. But I hope it will come save us. Though I doubt that it will."

There was silence in the room for a long while after he spoke.

"So I still don't understand," Touma said. "Why does everyone hate the Jews so?"

"Who would like to answer that question?" Demetrius asked.

"I have talked enough," Rushdi said. "Let someone else try to explain that, please."

When no one else offered, Demetrius said, "Omar? You are a professor of theology; would you help us with this?"

CHAPTER 8

Misunderstanding and Dislike

"I will do my best," Omar responded. "That is a difficult question to answer, Touma. Much of what I will say is just my opinion. I will try to be as factual as possible, however, and let's use the term 'dislike' instead of 'hatred.' The use of the word "hatred" is not helpful to this discussion.

"First, let me say that it is important for you to know it is a fact that there are not many Jews in the world, yet they have been the object of much scorn and ridicule for centuries, for some reason.

"Second, you should know that there are many religious groups in the world, but five are generally recognized as being the greatest, largest, or most significant religions in the world; these are Christianity, Islam, Buddhism, Hinduism, and Judaism.

"Third, as I said before, one in every four people on this earth is a Muslim, one in every three people on earth is a Christian, one in every seven people is a Hindu, and one in every sixteen people is a Buddhist, yet only two people in every one thousand people on earth are Jews."

"No! That can't be true," Guirguis exclaimed. "Really?"

"Shh!" Demetrius hushed.

"Is that true?" Guirguis asked again, incredulously.

"It is true," Omar responded. "Trust me on this. I found that hard to believe as well, but it is true. And remember: there are few Jews in China, India, and Pakistan, where over half of the people on earth live; and there aren't many Jews in Africa or

South America either. It's only in this part of the world, including Europe, and in the United States that Jews can be found in relatively large numbers."

"I find that hard to believe," Cosmos said. "Is that true, Rushdi?"

"It's true, Cosmos," Rushdi responded. "In fact, something else surprised me: there are as many Jews in the United States as there are in Israel."

"I am not the expert on this, Cosmos, but if Omar and Rushdi say it's true, then I believe it," Demetrius added.

"Jews have fled many countries over the years or have been forced to leave as a result of discrimination, hatred, dislike ... whatever you want to call it," Omar said. "And those relatively small numbers undoubtedly have something to do with that."

"Everyone remembers what happened in Germany during World War II," Rushdi added, "but I don't think the world will allow anything like that to happen again—not to the Jews or anyone else."

"As I was saying," Omar continued, "it's important to keep the issue in perspective. This is a problem for the Middle East and no place else on earth. What happened to the Jews in Germany under Hitler, when as many as six million Jews were killed, can't be forgotten, but there are so many extremely wealthy and powerful people in the world who are Jewish—especially in the United States, Europe, and other places—that I don't think we're likely to see anything like that happen again either.

"So when you ask why so many people dislike the Jews, the question is really more about what happened over the last several thousand years, throughout the history of the Jews, than it is about what is going on in the world now, and the only place it is happening is in Israel—because of the Palestinian issue, I think."

"So what you are saying, as I hear it, is that our problem exists because Muslims hate Christians, and it has nothing to do with what Muslims think about the Jews. Is that it?" Moghadan asked.

"I think that's true," Omar responded. "Those are two separate issues. Jews aren't involved in what is going on here in Libya, at least not openly, and there aren't as many Jews in Syria, Iran, Iraq, Afghanistan, Saudi Arabia, or Egypt as there are Christians."

"But as you have told us, there seem to be more things in common with the three religions than there are differences!" Touma interjected. "All believe themselves to be descendants of Abraham! All believe in the Bible as a holy book. So I don't understand why the Muslims hated, or disliked, the Jews so much back then. Why did they, Omar?"

"I'm getting to that, Touma," Omar responded. "I'll give you my opinion later. Here are some more facts. Since all of you are Egyptians, it's important to keep in mind that Egypt was conquered by Rome just thirty or forty years or so before Christ was born. Egypt had been the dominant civilization in the area for three thousand years before that, ruled by pharaohs, who were considered semigods for most of those years, until Alexander the Great and the Greeks conquered it a few hundred years before Christ.

"Now, after that, Rome controlled Egypt for the next six hundred years and then some. Remember the story about Cleopatra, the queen of Egypt and the last heir in the Ptolemy dynasty, and a Roman general, Marcus Anthony. They fell in love with each other, and together they fought the Romans, but they lost."

"I remember that," Yousry said.

"Me too," Nabir added.

"Good. That's the history of your country. You should know that. My point is that it wasn't long before Christ appeared on earth that the great and powerful Egyptian civilization ended. First it was the Greeks, and then it was the Roman Empire for over six hundred years. When the Western Roman Empire fell, there was a period of about a hundred and fifty years when Christians were in charge, for the most part, but in the middle of the seventh century, the Muslims conquered this entire area.

"As I also told you earlier, Muslims have ruled this part of the world for the last fourteen hundred years, and during all that time, all the way back to the days of ancient Rome and before,

Jews were suppressed or, in some cases, made slaves, as we know. There was a period of about a thousand years when they were the ruling class in Israel and in Judea; this was after the exodus from Egypt and before the coming of Alexander the Great.

"So when you think of it from that perspective, when an entire group of people are considered to be slaves—or a defeated enemy or second-class citizens, if you will—for about two thousand years, maybe that explains the historical bias against them. Does that make sense?" Omar asked.

"Yeah, that makes sense," Moghadan responded. "In a way, it's hard to believe they were treated that badly for so long and survived."

"But the most surprising thing, to me, is that they prospered— even during many of those days," Omar said. "They were successful in business and other things. They found a way to thrive, not just survive. I admire them for that," Omar said.

"How much worse for them was it back then than it is now?" Boctor asked.

"There was a period of time when all Jews had to wear black badges identifying them as Jews. Jews weren't allowed to ride horses or camels, only donkeys and mules. There were many times throughout the years when large numbers of Jews were killed, with no recourse. It was condoned, if not permitted, by the rulers.

"There were also many times throughout the history of this region when Jews were simply told to leave and were put out of a country. Many times when they were put out of a country, they had to leave all of their accumulated wealth behind. They left, literally, with only the clothes on their backs. That happened in Jerusalem and this part of the world in the first century, not long after Christ died, when the Jews revolted against Rome. They were easily defeated, and then they were exiled.

"There were other times, as now, when Jews and other non-Muslims were told that they had to convert to Islam or leave. And there were times when the option of death or conversion was given, too. This isn't the first time such a thing as this has happened."

"But it's not happening to the Jews now. It's happening to us," Abanoub said.

"That's true, Abanoub, and we'll talk about that later, but to further answer your question, Touma, Jews were considered to be impure by Muslims. For centuries, Jews had to bow down to Muslims on the street; they could not touch the food of Muslims, and Jews weren't allowed to build houses that were higher than Muslims' houses.

"Muslims were allowed to insult and berate Jews, with no one to stop them. It wasn't against the law for a Muslim to do so. Jews were taxed higher than Muslims. In many places, Jews were not allowed to live anywhere but in a specifically designated part of a city.

"There were some times when things weren't as bad as that, if the leader of the country was sympathetic or kind. For the most part, however, that's the way things were for the Jews for centuries."

"Think about that," Rushdi interjected. "To have that kind of attitude toward another group of people just because of their religious beliefs—it's deeply rooted in Muslim society, isn't it?"

"It is," Omar acknowledged.

"Did you ever feel that way, Omar?" Boctor asked.

"No, I didn't. I truly never did, and that is, I'm sure, because there were no Jews in Afghanistan, where I was born and raised."

"But you would have seen it in Iran, wouldn't you?" Cyril asked.

"You would think so, but I didn't," he responded. "Remember: I was going to school, and people are more understanding in that environment."

"That's true," Cyril acknowledged.

"So what makes you think things are so different now, Omar? Just seventy-five years ago, Hitler was killing every Jew he could find; and fifty years ago, a million Muslims wanted to kill every Jew in Israel. A hundred years ago, hundreds of thousands of Jews were killed in Russia. I'm not so sure you're right about things being entirely different now," Raghib said.

"The difference between what it was like hundreds of years ago, or even fifty years ago, and what it is like now is mainly that Jews now have someplace to go where they are safe—where they won't be persecuted. They can either go to Israel—which is still a dangerous place to be, as we all know, but it is the only predominantly Jewish large-scale community on earth—or they can go to the United States.

"I think it's because the United States will protect them. Since you mention Russia, millions of Jews immigrated to the United States around the turn of the century, and because the United States has become so powerful—the most powerful country on earth—I think they are safe there. I don't think anyone would challenge them even in Israel, because of the support it has from the United States."

"I don't know about that," Boctor replied. "Look at what happened to the Americans in Afghanistan."

"Or Iraq," Moghadan added.

"Or Syria," Yousrey added.

"The Americans demolished the Iraqis in Kuwait, and they did the same thing to Saddam Hussein in 2003," Saraboum said. "And they did it in Afghanistan, too. Nobody can stand up to them. The Taliban and the others use suicide bombs, car bombs, bombs in the roads, and sniper attacks; that's the only way they can fight them. And the United States doesn't like to see its soldiers die no matter how they die, but especially in those ways."

"And they hid in the mountains of Afghanistan. Here they have nowhere to hide," Theo added. "The Jews will be protected by the Americans. I think that's true."

"So, to conclude, what I would tell you is that those days of discrimination and prejudice against the Jews are gone, really, except for these current Islamic extremists. They are returning to the mentality of hundreds of years ago. I don't think Jews are hated or disliked as they once were. Those days are over."

"What these men want, Omar, is to have a country where only people who think like they do can live; that's discrimination," Cyril said. "And they are still discriminating against us for that very reason. You are wrong, my Muslim friend. Muslims discriminate against Jews and Christians to this very day."

"My point was that the discrimination had nothing to do with Judaism," Omar responded. "That was the question I was asked to answer."

"You said that Jews aren't disliked as they once were, Omar," Theo continued, "and I think you're wrong. Nothing has changed in over a thousand years. I agree with Cyril."

"It is just my opinion. I gave you facts, and then I gave you my opinion," Omar responded.

"Omar, I think you're mistaken too," Raghib told him. "Maybe you never had that attitude in Afghanistan before the Taliban came along, but the government of Iran—who are Shiites, as you know—still wants to completely remove the Jews from this area of the world, and we know they're not the only ones," Raghib told him. "The leader of Iran said something like that not long ago, didn't he?"

"That was Ahmadinejad. He was the president for five years, and he said some stupid things," Omar responded. "He's gone now."

"So did many others in Iran, Omar," Rushdi responded. "He wasn't the only one, and Iran is being sanctioned by the United States and its allies for its policies. Israel is scared to death that Iran will get a nuclear weapon and wipe it off the face of the earth. I think you're wrong about this, Omar."

"They have a new leader now, and he is much more moderate," Omar replied.

"So you think that the centuries of hatred and discrimination against the Jews are over, Omar?" Demetrius asked.

"Yes, I do, for the most part. I think that most Muslims in the world don't feel that way anymore. I think it's only the extremists who think that way," he responded. "Except for the Palestinians who live in Israel, that is."

"Omar," Demetrius offered, "with all due respect, we Copts have lived under persecution and discrimination at the hands of Muslims for centuries. I think we have been persecuted just as much as, if not more than, the Jews. I don't think you realize the extent of our suffering. We are here because of that discrimination."

"That is a different situation, I think," Omar responded. "Muslims' discrimination against Christians is an entirely different matter, both from a historical point of view and to this very day. It's not the same thing at all."

As I sat there listening to what Omar was telling us, I detected a powerful odor, as if someone had gone to the bathroom not far from me. None of us had been allowed to relieve himself in over eight hours. I tried to clear the smell from my nostrils, but I couldn't. It smelled really bad in our room. I had urinated in my jumpsuit hours prior. I couldn't help it. I was sure others had done so, too.

I was hungry and thirsty, too. I had never been deprived of water for so long in my life. My shoulders, back, and other parts of my body ached. I was miserable, but I was listening to every word that was being said.

Then Clement spoke up. "We're going to die in the morning! Can we stop talking about the Jews? They've got their problems, and we've got ours; and right now our problems are a whole lot worse than theirs. Can we stop this? Now?"

"I think you're right, Clement. On this I agree with you. Touma, did Omar answer your question?" Demetrius asked.

"Yeah, I think so," Touma replied, "but I don't think he's right. I think there is still much hatred in the world for Jews, and it's coming from Muslims. I still don't understand why they hate them, or us, so much, but I don't want to talk about it anymore. Thank you for answering my question."

"Let's be quiet for now. Say some prayers to yourselves ... please," Demetrius asked.

CHAPTER 9

Christianity in the Middle East

After several minutes, Demetrius said, "I have been thinking about what we have heard from Omar, Cyril, and Rushdi, as well as from Boctor and Clement, and I have some questions. I'd like to hear more about the history of Christianity in the Middle East after the coming of Muhammad. From what Omar says, Christians were the oppressors during many of those years. I wasn't aware that was the case, at least not in Egypt and this part of the world, and I would like to hear more about that.

"Who would be willing to tell us about that? Rushdi? You are the most learned man among us. You know as much about the history of our people and our country as anyone. Would you tell us what you know about that, please?" Demetrius urged him.

"All right, my friend, although you may not like to hear some of the things I have to say about this aspect of Christianity. But as we prepare ourselves for what is to come tomorrow, now is not the time to speak anything less than the truth. Please keep in mind, as I speak, that much of what I am about to say is not the history of the Coptic Church. It is mostly about the history of the Roman Catholic Church.

"What Cyril told you earlier was, for the most part, completely true, and I will try not to repeat things he has already told you, but for most of the almost three hundred years after Christ's death, Rome persecuted all Christians, though there were periods of limited tolerance during some of those years. Christians and

Jews were treated at best as lower-class citizens during all of those years, but Jews weren't persecuted as we were, though they were driven out of Jerusalem and this area in the first century, as Omar told you.

"What Cyril didn't mention was that while that was taking place in Rome and in the countries controlled by the Roman Empire, Christianity was spreading throughout areas outside of the boundaries of the Roman Empire too, in places like Afghanistan and as far away as India. So Christianity was growing during those years, despite what Rome and Jews were doing to suppress that growth.

Also, during Constantine's lifetime, Jerusalem became Christianity's holiest of cities—even as much as, if not more so than, Rome. Much was done to improve and beautify Jerusalem during those years, although Constantine's mother, Helena, deserves most of the credit for that. Many churches were built during his era, but that was all because of her influence over him. Constantine's mother turned Jerusalem into a jewel of a city, as only an emperor's mother could have done; and for that, we recognize her as a saint.

"Because of the rise of Christianity and the continued presence of the Romans in Jerusalem, the influence of Jews was greatly diminished during those years. In fact, there was a period of time when it was a criminal offense not to be a Christian. What happened back then is much like what is taking place now, only the reverse. Non-Christians were ordered to convert to Christianity or leave. Many Jews left Jerusalem and Judea and went to Turkey and other places to the north and east.

"So for the next three hundred years or so, after Constantine died, Christianity flourished in this part of the world, up until the time of Muhammad, and during most of those years, there was not much tolerance of other religions. There were some emperors who came after Constantine who reverted back to worshiping the Roman gods and did things to renew the persecution of Christians, but by that time Christianity had developed to such a point that there were too many of us, and the various Christian communities easily withstood those difficult periods.

"Also, there were other groups, such as the Zoroastrians, the Gnostics, and many pagan cultures back then, but Christianity, in various forms, was by far the most dominant religion in Europe, North Africa, and here in the Middle East—including Afghanistan, and as far away as India, as I said before.

"Europe was a different story. When the Western Roman Empire came to an end, which occurred at the end of the fifth century after Christ, there was much lawlessness because there was no one to prevent it from happening. People looted the churches and the pagan temples, both of which were full of silver and gold. Religious statues and artifacts were destroyed by the invading barbarians, much as ISIS and other terrorists are doing now in Tikrit, Ramadan, and other Christian places. It was a bad time in the history of the Roman Church, as well as for Italy and all of Europe. It was called Europe's Dark Ages.

"Fortunately for the Roman Empire, and for civilization as we know it, one of Constantine's most significant acts, and perhaps his greatest accomplishment, was to create an empire in the East. He could see that there was more commerce taking place in the eastern part of the Roman Empire, and he wanted to take advantage of that. To do so, he created a new city, and he named it after himself.

"He chose a spot through which merchants would most likely travel from east to west, and north to south, which was also a location on the water by which sea traffic would have to pass, going from the Mediterranean to the Black Sea. That city is now called Istanbul, but back then it was called Constantinople. We are told that nothing was there before, but after the Romans were finished, it was the most magnificent city in the world. That became the capital of what was called the Eastern Roman Empire.

"It took the Romans twenty years to build it, and the Romans used all of their ingenuity and knowledge to build it as well as anything in the world could be built at the time. That city, and the Eastern Roman Empire, lasted for almost another thousand years after the Western Roman Empire fell to one of the Germanic hordes in AD 476. It was not until AD 1423, when the Ottoman Turks captured the city, that the last remnants of what had been the Roman Empire officially disappeared off of the face of the earth. Artifacts remain, but the empire was destroyed.

"When the Western Roman Empire fell, there began a period of time in the history of Europe known as the Middle Ages— though the first few hundred years are called the Dark Ages, as I said, but that didn't affect the people who lived in China, Africa, Arabia or other parts of the world. That is because there was no central government in Europe, as there had been under Roman rule. None of the great countries, such as Germany, France, Spain, England, or any of the others we now know, were in existence then. Those places were called Flanders, Burgundy, Aquitaine, and some other names you probably never heard of.

"The Middle Ages lasted for almost a thousand years, from the end of the Western Roman Empire in AD 476 until the late 1400s, just before Gutenberg invented the printing press, and right before Columbus discovered the new world. During all those years, Christianity dominated most of Europe."

"Please, Demetrius! How much more do we have to listen to?" Boctor interrupted. "We have one night more to live on this planet; I don't want to spend it studying history! With no disrespect, Mr. Bishoy, I never liked history!"

Before Demetrius could respond, Magdi spoke up. "I'm sorry, Boctor, but I would like for Professor Bishoy to continue to explain these things."

"Me too," Yousry said.

"Me as well," Cosmos chimed in.

I was happy they said what they did. I also knew very little of what Rushdi was talking about.

"Demetrius?" Rushdi asked. "Do you want me to continue?"

"Please do, my friend, but maybe you can summarize some things to make it go faster," he responded.

"I will do my best," he said. "I am getting to the heart of what I have to say, so let me say this … much happened during those thousand years—too much to discuss with all of you tonight, as our time here on earth is dwindling by the minute, as Boctor so delicately points out.

"As far as Christianity is concerned, however, those thousand years were a time when the Roman Catholic Church, which was centered at what is called Vatican City, in Rome, grew more and more powerful. There were times when kings took orders from the popes in Rome. There were other times when there were two popes, and countries waged wars over who should be recognized as the true leader of the Roman Catholic Church. There were yet other times when the church was actually the head of several countries and governed as a king or emperor might do. Those countries were called papal states.

"It was during those years that there were many violent clashes between Muslims and Christians. There were wars, called the Crusades, during which Christians sought to wrest Jerusalem and the Holy Lands from the Muslims. There were at least six major Crusades, which were holy wars, and they took place over a period of several hundred years.

"From the time the Muslims captured Jerusalem, which was shortly after Muhammad died, up until the end of the eleventh century, Muslims ruled this entire part of the world, which included Egypt, without any significant challenges whatsoever.

"But as Omar told you, Jews and Christians were allowed to practice their religions, for the most part, although there were periods of time when new rulers persecuted the Jews harshly."

"And the Christians were persecuted just as much, if not more, during those times," Cyril chimed in. "Omar didn't mention any of that."

"I was asked to talk only of the Jews, Cyril," Omar replied.

"That's true, Cyril," Rushdi acknowledged. "And at all times, both Jews and Christians were seen as inferior people. They were both required to wear armbands or badges that identified them as something other than a Muslim at times. Christians had to ride donkeys and mules, but never horses or camels, just as the Jews did.

"And did that include us, Mr. Bishoy?" Moghadan asked.

"Yes, Moghadan. We Copts were treated just like the Jews and other Christians during those years," Rushdi responded.

"So at the very end of the eleventh century—in AD 1095, as I recall—a pope by the name of Urban II called for all Catholics from all across Europe to join together in what would best be described in today's world as a holy war against the Muslims who held the holiest city on earth, Jerusalem, captive."

"That is like what the Muslims are calling a jihad today, yes?" Magdi asked.

"That's right, Magdi. It is very much like what the Muslims are doing today in many respects, I am sad to say.

"Hundreds of thousands of Catholics answered the pope's call, noblemen and peasants alike, and began a march through what is now Turkey, Syria, and Lebanon on their way to Jerusalem, and they had the support of the Christian leaders in Constantinople, even though the two religious communities did not see eye to eye on some things. At that time, there was the Roman Catholic Church in Rome and the Greek Orthodox Church in Constantinople."

"And our church, the Coptic Church in Egypt, was completely separate and apart from both of them—right, Professor Bishoy?" Moghadan asked.

"That's right, Moghadan," Rushdi responded. We have always had our own popes, even though we agreed with the teachings and doctrines of either or both, at times. We kept our independence and never yielded to the popes in Rome or the leaders of the Eastern Orthodox Church on matters of theology."

"In the Eastern Orthodox churches, are they called popes, as with us and the Roman Catholics?" Maurice asked.

"No, they are not. They are called bishops, and there is a group called a synod of bishops who make decisions affecting the entire congregation."

"What about the Russian Orthodox Christians? Were they part of the Crusades?" Maurice continued.

Rushdi sighed and said, "No. Let's not get into that. There

were battles against the people in what is now Russia and other countries that were part of the Soviet Union about the same time, so the Russian Orthodox Church wasn't involved in the Crusades, but let's not talk about them now, please. I've been asked to hurry things up, as you know."

"Were Copts part of the Crusades?" Touma asked.

"Please, Touma, you are getting ahead of things. There was a Crusade—it was the fifth one, I believe—with the purpose of freeing the Christians in Egypt, meaning us, from the Muslims, but that Crusade never got close to Egypt and was a complete failure. So the answer to your question is no, Coptic Christians were not part of any of the Crusades, to my knowledge, though some Copts may have joined the fight. I don't know.

"So as I was saying, Pope Urban II is the one who united all Christians in the entire Roman Catholic Church, as well as many of the Christians who were part of the both the Eastern Catholic Church and the Greek Orthodox Church, and convinced them all to go to Jerusalem and recapture it from the Muslims. And he promised every single man who went to fight the Muslims that he would be forgiven for all his sins and would go to heaven; that was called a plenary indulgence, and it was a very powerful incentive for many of the Christians of that day."

"So this huge army of Christians, all of whom had to eat along the way, basically plundered and pillaged any and all who stood in their way on that mission. They created churches and fortifications along the way. It took them years to get to Jerusalem, but in 1099, three years after the soldiers began the long march, the city of Jerusalem was captured by Christians.

"For the next ninety years or so, Christians ruled Jerusalem and all of the surrounding areas, but not Egypt. It was from Egypt that the Muslims gathered enough strength to take Jerusalem back from the crusaders in 1189."

"That must have been a bad time to be a Coptic Christian," Asaad said.

"We don't think of it that way, Asaad," Rushdi responded. "We are known for our ability to withstand persecutions. It was that way then, and we survived that crisis, just as we will survive this crisis. And there were more Crusades. The Roman Catholic Church didn't accept defeat. It organized several more Crusades and kept up the fight for the next hundred years or so.

"A few years later, in 1192, crusaders went to win back what had been lost a few years earlier, and after several battles, a truce was declared whereby the Muslim leaders were allowed to keep what land they had recaptured, but they agreed to allow Christian pilgrims to visit Jerusalem, and all the holy lands, and not be harmed.

"However, not too many years later, at the beginning of the thirteenth century, another Crusade was organized, but this one went very badly for the entire Christian community. There were still differences between the popes in Rome and the leaders of the Eastern Catholic Church and the Greek Orthodox Church, and—"

"Wait a minute!" Moghadan interrupted. "What's the difference between the Eastern Catholic Church and the Greek Orthodox Church?"

"Basically the difference between them was all about the pope in Rome. Some Christians accepted the pope as the leader of the church. Other Christians, like those who were members of the Greek Orthodox churches, didn't accept the pope in Rome as their leader, so they were separate in that way. Most of their beliefs were the same, but they didn't accept the pope as their spiritual leader.

"They didn't like the fact that popes were always Italian. The Greeks and the Italians have always fought with each other, it seems. Historians tell us that when the Fourth Crusade began, the two religious communities were actually trying to find a way to mend the fences and unite, as they had been united centuries earlier, but that didn't happen. Things got worse—much worse.

"What happened is that the crusaders from Europe, under the banner of the Roman Catholic Church, at the urging of the pope in Rome, engaged in a bloody battle against the Christians in Byzantium, and the Roman Catholics won. The battle began over money, we are told, because the soldiers demanded to be paid their wages but weren't. The crusaders—who were given plenary indulgences—slaughtered the Christians who lived in Constantinople and plundered massive amounts of gold and silver.

"They destroyed many historic religious buildings—and artifacts, too—for the gold and silver in them. It was a terrible time for Christianity. To this day, the wounds from that time have not healed, and that was almost eight hundred years ago."

"It sounds much like what ISIS and these terrorists who have captured us are doing—destroying Christian churches and artifacts and killing people. Doesn't it?" Clement asked.

"Please! Clement! I have heard enough from you tonight! What's your point? That it's okay for them to do this to us?" Cyril interjected. "Stop!"

Demetrius then tried to pacify both men while chains rattled.

When quiet was restored, Rushdi continued. "You are right, Clement; it was a terrible time in history, and it is much like what the Muslims of ISIS have done in Tikrit and Ramadi. They have destroyed ancient churches, shrines, statues, and religious treasures, just as those crusaders did in Constantinople years ago."

"But that was Christian versus Christian, Rushdi. The Muslims were the common enemy. So what did the crusaders do then, after sacking Constantinople? Did they go after the Muslims?" Theophilos asked.

"Yes, Theo, they did, but it was a complete failure," Rushdi responded, "and there has never been any serious attempt to reconcile the differences between the two Christian groups ever since. Some historians—and I am, as all of you know, one of them—say that the sack of Constantinople, the queen city on earth at the time, was the greatest crime ever committed against humanity, and it was committed by Christians against other Christians. That was in 1204.

"In fact, less than fifteen years ago, Pope John Paul II wrote a letter to the leaders of the Greek Orthodox Church and apologized for what the crusaders did eight hundred and some years earlier.

"But getting back to the battle between the Christians and

the Muslims that was the Fourth Crusade, as I said, it failed miserably. Only one tenth of all crusaders actually reached the holy lands, and they were easily beaten back. The Fifth Crusade was the one that was supposed to free Egypt, but it failed.

"There was a sixth Crusade in 1228, and that succeeded, but only for a short period of time—maybe fifteen years, as I recall. All of the other Crusades failed, and there were several others. The last was in 1290 or thereabouts.

"Muslims remained in control of the area during all of those years except when the crusaders were victorious on those two occasions I mentioned. The Muslims continued to have control over all of Arabia and Northern Africa up until the late nineteenth century, really, although there is, as you would expect, much that happened during those years that we don't have time to talk about. But I do want to tell you about one more period in the history of the Muslim–Christian battles."

"What about the Jews? Weren't they part of them, too?" Moghadan asked.

"Not really," Rushdi responded. "The Jews were never powerful enough to fight either the Christians or the Muslims, so they were the victims of whatever group was in control. The most they could hope for was to be left alone, but that didn't happen too often over the centuries. The Jews are more powerful now than they were back in those days. Israel may now be the most powerful country in the Middle East."

"Because they have the support of the United States!" Sarabamoun whispered loudly.

"Maybe that's why … or maybe it's because it now has the military strength it never had before."

"That's because of the United States too!" Saraboum persisted.

"Maybe, but for whatever reason, Israel is now more powerful than it has been for almost two thousand years, but that's not what I wanted to tell you about, and this will be the end of what I have to say on this topic. I will now talk about the period of time not too long after the Crusades ended, because I think it's important to discuss the Spanish Inquisition."

"Thank you, Rushdi, for all that you have told us," Demetrius said, "but before we hear from you about the Spanish Inquisition, let's sing one of our songs and say some prayers."

At that, he led us all in the surrender song, again. We sang, "We surrender our lives to you ..." and we all thought that we were about to do just that in a few short hours.

CHAPTER 10

The Spanish Inquisition

"Rushdi, do you think we need to hear it?" Demetrius asked. "Is it that important?"

"Yes, I think it is if anyone here wants to understand the history of the differences between Muslims, Christians, and Jews and why things are the way they are now ... Yes, I do," Rushdi responded.

"Okay ... please, tell us about the Inquisition," Demetrius said, "but make it as brief as you can, please."

"We've been talking about how the Muslims have discriminated against us for years and years, and they have. Now I'm going to tell you about a time when Christians persecuted Muslims and Jews."

"Why do we have to listen to this?" Boctor asked. "So we can hear how they have a right to do what they're going to do to us?"

"Boctor, please ... we're all going to die tomorrow ... I didn't ask to do this ... I thought you young men wanted to hear this," Rushdi replied.

"I do," Touma said.

"So do I," Moghadan added.

"Me too," Nabir chimed in.

"Do the rest of you men want me to go on?" Rushdi asked.

Most of the men mumbled positive responses.

"Okay, then. I will," Rushdi said. "I know it won't make any difference, but I think it's important for you all to know so you can better understand how things got this way."

"It wasn't like this until ISIS and al-Qaeda came along," Guirguis said.

"No, that's true," Rushdi responded, "but it's been this way in the past, and that's why I'm telling you about it. Sometimes people don't remember the past, but you have to know the past and try to learn from past mistakes," Rushdi replied.

"So you think this Spanish Inquisition you're going to tell us about was a mistake?" Boctor asked.

"Yes, I do," Rushdi replied, "just as it was a mistake for Hitler to do what he did, or for the Ottomans to do what they did to Christians in Armenia a hundred years ago, as well as the other atrocities men have committed against other men in the name of religion. Yes, I do think those were mistakes that should not have been committed and should not be repeated, Boctor."

"Then I want to hear about it too," he said.

"Good. Here goes," Rushdi replied. "History has laid blame at the feet of the Spanish for what was truly a Catholic policy established by various popes in Rome, beginning in the late twelfth century. I think the Spanish deserve blame for what took place in Spain over a period of about four hundred years, but they were doing what several popes had told them to do. It was the Roman Catholic Church's response, I believe, to what Muslims had done to Christians in Egypt, Arabia, and the Middle East for hundreds of years before that, as we have discussed already."

"As Omar told you, when the Muslims conquered Jerusalem, Egypt, and this entire area after Muhammad died, they persecuted Christians and Jews and made them both second-class citizens, and there were times when Christians and Jews were forced to either convert to Islam, leave the country, or die, as is happening now, and that practice continued for centuries—though there were a few brief periods of religious tolerance, depending upon who the leader of Islam was at the time.

"So when Muslims swept across Arabia and the Middle East, they also conquered much of North Africa. As you know, Spain and Portugal are but a few miles from North Africa, and the Muslims crossed the water and then conquered the people who lived there. They then controlled Spain and Portugal for several hundred years. The Christians in both countries fought for years to win back that land.

"That was before the Crusades, which didn't take place for another three hundred years, or more. Apparently the Roman Catholic Church wasn't as interested in Muslims occupying Spain and Portugal as much as it was in Muslims occupying Jerusalem. Why the popes didn't have a Crusade to rid the Muslims from Spain and Portugal before coming here, I don't know, but they didn't.

"Actually, the Portuguese regained their independence from the Muslims, who were called Moors, or Berbers, two hundred fifty years before Spain did. The Spanish recaptured parts of their country a little at a time. By the end of the fifteenth century, the Moors controlled only the very southern part of Spain.

"But what the Roman Catholic Church did in the latter part of the twelfth century was issue a decree—or what was called a papal bull, or edict—to all Roman Catholics that said all Muslims and all Jews and anyone else who did not believe in the teachings of the Catholic Church would either have to convert to Catholicism or leave whatever country they were living in."

"Just as the Muslims are doing today," Omar said softly.

"That's right," Clement chimed in.

"And there were many instances where Muslims and Jews were forced to leave whatever country they were in. Many people who refused to leave and refused to convert died, but many people claimed to convert to Christianity, and they did so only to avoid being persecuted, killed, or to avoid being forced to leave their homes and all of their belongings behind. So the problems truly began long before Spain initiated what history now refers to as the Spanish Inquisition.

"And the Spanish didn't really do much about those issues until King Ferdinand and Queen Isabella began their reign, which was over two hundred years later.

"You see, what they did—Ferdinand and Isabella, that is—after they defeated the Muslims and recaptured Grenada and reunited all of Spain, was say to the Muslims who were there, 'Convert, leave, or die,' just as the popes in Rome had commanded them to do. Many Muslims converted, or said they did; but in reality, those people didn't convert. They kept their religion and continued to live in Spain, pretending to be Christians.

"And to be honest, from what I have learned, the problem was mostly with the Jews in Spain—more so than the Muslims. I think most of the Muslims just left and went back to Morocco, or wherever, in North Africa. They were defeated by the sword. The Jews weren't involved in those military battles, but Ferdinand and Isabel wanted Jews to convert or leave too.

"Later on, Martin Luther began what became a revolution, or reformation, against the leaders of the Roman Catholic Church. Over a hundred years later, the Inquisition included ferreting out Protestants, too, but I am getting ahead of myself. That was in the middle of the sixteenth century. Martin Luther was born in the late 1400s. He was one of the first of those who protested against the popes in Rome, though I am sure there were many others we never heard of who questioned some of the things going on in Rome during those years.

"So what the Inquisition was all about, really, was questioning whether or not those Muslims and Jews who said they had converted to Christianity in order to remain in Spain were truly converts or were just saying that to stay in the country, keep their wealth, and not get killed. But, you see, it all started two or three hundred years earlier, as I told you."

"You should say it began when Muslims said that Christians had to convert to Islam or die, Cyril! They're the ones who started it, not the Christians!" Abanoub said heatedly.

"Shh!" Demetrius warned. "Not too loud!"

At that, the door flew open and several men rushed in, screaming at us in Arabic. We all understood what they were saying, although the dialect was a little different.

"Shut up, you filthy pigs! It smells like shit in here! We should kill you right now! You are not human beings; you are swine! Do you hear me? You are swine! But even swine must be fed, so we will give you water. If you move, you will die! Don't move!"

At that, two of the men, each of whom was carrying a bucket of water in one hand and a ladle in the other, went from man to man, holding the ladle below the chin of each of us.

The moon must have been large that night, because when the door opened, we were able to see each other—though not too well. We were all up against the walls, and the shadows made it difficult to see, but I was able to make out several of the men. I especially sought out the eyes of my brothers, Touma and Guirguis, but I wasn't able to make eye contact.

When one of the men held the ladle to me, I stuck my face in it as best I could and gulped down as much water as possible. I wasn't able to get much, because he took it away before I was finished drinking and dumped what was left on my head before moving on to the next man. I held the water in my mouth and swished it around as long as I could before swallowing the last of it.

After our captors had been gone for what seemed like an hour, though it was probably nowhere near that long, Demetrius whispered, "As you were saying, Rushdi, this practice of ordering people to either convert, leave the country, or die began centuries ago and is not a new thing."

"No. No it isn't," Rushdi responded. "That's right. That's my point, and the Inquisition is a perfect example of it."

"You know, I have listened to all that has been said here tonight, and I have learned a great deal about our history that I didn't know, but I'm still not sure who actually started this horrible practice," said Theophilos. "I think I heard Omar say—or maybe it was Cyril, or you, Rushdi ... I don't know—that it started back in the days after Constantine. Is that right? Is that when it started?"

Theophilos and his brother, Halim, were inseparable. They were much older than me, maybe ten or twelve years older, but I had known them since I was a child. I hadn't been able to tell them apart for years. Both men were tall and thin, and both men had thin beards that were exactly alike, and they both wore the exact same cap on their heads. They usually wore the same clothes, too. After working with them for a couple of months, I finally figured out how to tell them apart. Theophilos's voice was deeper, and he had a small mole above his right eye. They were very nice men, and I liked them both very much.

"Did they do things like that back in the days of ancient Egypt," his brother, Halim, asked.

"No, Halim, they didn't," Rushdi answered. "Back in those days, before the coming of Christ, countries conquered other countries and then enslaved the peoples they conquered. They didn't try to convert them to their religion, or at least I don't believe they did. What do you think, Cyril?"

"I think you're correct," Cyril answered. "In those days, things were decided by the sword. Conquering armies weren't so much interested in making the people they conquered think like they thought; they were more interested in the land, jewels, riches, camels, or whatever they could steal. Mostly, they made slaves of those they conquered."

"The Greeks imposed rules and regulations, and created better-organized societies, but they didn't make those they conquered worship their gods. They made them follow their rules, though," Cyril offered.

"So it began with the Romans then?" Theophilos continued. "Were they the first ones to make people convert to their religion?"

"Not the early Romans, such as those in the days of Christ. They allowed the Jews to worship as they pleased. I guess the earliest I can put it is in the days after Constantine, when some of the emperors who followed him made people convert and killed those who didn't," Rushdi said.

"Actually, that's ironic, because, as I think of it, that may have been one of the things that made the Roman Empire so great … they allowed the people they conquered to live in a civilized society by constructing much better roads, buildings and other things, and they created rules and regulations that provided a legal structure for all to follow and obey, much like the early

Greeks. More than anything else, they were plumbers ... great with moving water and disposing of filth and waste. They ruled with an iron hand, though, and theirs was the greatest civilization the world has ever known.

"So what the Romans did after Constantine was just like the things these extremists are doing to us," Clement added.

"As I have said, that's right, except they did those things to the Jews and pagans—not the Muslims, because they weren't in existence yet," Rushdi replied. "History is repeating itself, as you can see."

Everyone was quiet for a while, and then Abanoub spoke up.

"Demetrius, I think I've heard enough. I don't think this is helping us any longer. It makes me feel as if, somehow, we Christians are responsible for this! I don't want to hear any more of this!"

"I agree with him," Boctor added. "I am tired of this too. I don't want to hear any more of it."

Demetrius then asked, "How many of you feel the way Abanoub and Boctor do? Should we stop this and move on to something else now?"

There were some groans and some muted replies, but most people seemed to want to hear more—especially the younger people, like me. I was learning things I never knew.

"Abanoub and Boctor, I think you are outnumbered. Rushdi, please continue."

Boctor cursed, and Abanoub said something I couldn't understand, but it was clear that most people were interested in what Rushdi was saying.

"So this was the policy of the Roman Catholic Church for centuries, but the Spanish Inquisition, as most people know it, didn't really start until the very end of the fifteenth century," Rushdi told us." However, as I have said, it was around for centuries before that—just not as effective. But it was in Spain for centuries after that too."

"And I'm sorry, but did I hear you say that this Inquisition applied to the Jews who were in Spain more so than it applied to the Muslims?" Halim asked. "Didn't you say that?"

"That's right, Halim," Rushdi responded. "Jews actually became the bigger problem—a much bigger problem for Spain, as I am about to tell you.

"What I find to be the most ironic part of the Spanish Inquisition is that the two people who are generally regarded as being most responsible for it are highly regarded by historians for some things that they accomplished during their reigns. Those two people were King Ferdinand and Queen Isabella. What they accomplished far overshadows all of the wrongs they may have committed as a result of the Inquisition, in my opinion. History has basically forgiven for them for the sins they perpetrated in the name of religion."

"Why do you call them sins?" Abanoub asked. "Christians were only doing what had been done to them. Those weren't sins. The Church ordered it. Why shouldn't they make certain that people who called themselves Christians were truly Christians? Why couldn't they make Spain a purely Christian country, especially after the Muslims had oppressed them for almost eight hundred years!"

A few men rattled their chains in agreement with that. Then Omar said, "Is it wrong when they do it to you but right when you do it to them?" Omar asked.

"You mean to *you*, don't you, Omar? You are a Muslim, not a Christian," Maurice hissed.

His father, Rushdi, immediately spoke up. "Maurice! Please … don't speak that way to Omar. He is a good man. Not all Muslims are like these men who have captured us."

Maurice immediately apologized. "I'm sorry, Father. Forgive me for insulting you, Omar."

Then Omar responded, "It is true. I am a Muslim, as I have told you, and I am not proud of what Muslims extremists are doing now or what the Taliban did to me in Afghanistan, and I must make peace with you, my brothers, with whom I am about to die, as well as with myself and my god. I am trying to make sense of what I have witnessed in this lifetime. We are all children of God. I regret what is happening to you, and to me, because of a difference in our religious beliefs."

"Thank you, Omar, for being so understanding. Please, all of you … please respect Omar and his beliefs. He has done nothing to harm us. We have no quarrel with him … especially tonight," Demetrius said.

"But that is the point of what we are doing, Demetrius!" Boctor said excitedly. "That is why we are doing this! That is what we are doing here tonight—trying to make some sense out of what is happening to all of us, including Omar. And we are about to be killed by Muslims … and he is a Muslim. I can certainly understand why Maurice said what he said. I don't blame him for it. I feel that way too. I'm sure his brand of Muslims, the Shiites, did many horrible things to Christians over the years too."

Demetrius jumped in and said, "Please, forgive them, Omar. They are young men, and this is an extremely difficult situation, as you know. No more, Boctor! Rushdi, how much more of this?"

"Not much," Rushdi answered. "I'm almost finished."

"Then continue, please," Demetrius asked.

"So let me ask you all this question: when you hear the names King Ferdinand and Queen Isabella, what do you think of?"

"The discovery of the Americas," Nabir answered immediately.

"That is correct, Nabir. Yes, it was in 1492 that King Ferdinand and Queen Isabella commissioned Christopher Columbus, a Portuguese sailing captain, to lead the *Niña*, the *Pinta*, and the *Santa Maria* and find a passageway by sea to the Orient. They had no idea that there were two continents in between Europe and Asia.

"History has glorified them for their willingness to fund the expedition. Needless to say, the monetary rewards of gold and silver Spain realized over the next two or three hundred years as a result of Columbus's discovery undoubtedly had something to do with their prestige, but there was something else that happened in 1492 that gave an enormous amount of glory and praise to King Ferdinand and Queen Isabella. Does anyone know what that was?"

"I do," Raghib replied.

"Other than Raghib," Rushdi continued.

When no one responded, he said, "That is the year when they finally defeated the Muslims in battle and won back the only remaining vestige of Muslim rule. That battle was fought in Granada, in southern Spain. To Spaniards, at the time, that may have been even more important than discovering the new world. Ferdinand and Isabella were revered by their people. They had won back the country of Spain from the infidels. They could do no wrong in the eyes of their countrymen.

"But think about it … Look at all that was happening in Spain at that time: the discovery of the Americas, reclaiming Spain from the Moors after almost eight hundred years of captivity, and, while that was going on, the Inquisition. It was a most remarkable period of time. It didn't involve Egypt or the Middle East at all— at least not directly—though it was, as I say, a most remarkable period in the history of the world for everyone, I'm sure. It was much like when men landed on the moon, perhaps.

"So Ferdinand, who was the son of the king of a region in Spain called Aragon, and Isabelle, who was the queen of an adjacent region called Castille, married in 1469. By doing so, they united all of Spain except for that part of Spain that was held by the Moors.

"Together, their two armies succeeded in bringing about the defeat of the Muslims twenty-three years later, and it just so happened to occur in the very same year as Columbus discovered the Americas. Isabella died twelve years later, but Ferdinand remained the king for another twelve years after that. They ruled Spain for over forty-five years, and some call that the Spanish Golden Age because of all that was accomplished during their reign.

"The Inquisition—which they began as part of their rule, even before the conquest in 1492—lasted long after they were gone, though. It is said to have lasted for another three hundred fifty years, up until 1834, when the purge finally ended.

"They sought to cleanse the Church and make certain that all Catholics were true believers. The Jews who were driven from Spain were allowed to take nothing with them except for what they could carry. Many injustices were perpetrated in the name of Christianity. Many people were killed, and there was much discrimination."

"Just as what is happening now in the name of Islam," Clement said.

"And just like what had been done to Christians in Egypt, Arabia, North Africa, Afghanistan, and all over the Middle East for centuries!" Abanoub said again.

"Please!" Demetrius urged. "Now is not the time to say who was right and who was wrong or what is right and what is wrong. We are discussing these things so that we may all understand a little better what is happening to us. Remember: tomorrow, we will all likely be dead. Are you finished now, Rushdi?"

"Yes, I am," he replied.

"Thank you for that explanation. I learned some things I didn't know, and I hope that our younger brothers have learned some things too, but I think it's time to move on. Are we ready to repent of our sins?" he asked.

"Wait! Before we do, would someone explain to me what happened between those days and now? When did England, the United States, France, and all the other European countries, who now have so much influence over our country and the world, become so powerful? Was it after the world wars or before?" Magdi asked.

"Magdi," Rushdi said kindly, "you should have paid more attention in your history class too! You should know this."

Some of the men snorted. Nothing would make them laugh this night.

"Let me ask the group: Do you want to hear about that period in history or not? What say you all?" Demetrius asked.

Again there were murmurs and grunts, but most of the people, who were young men and hadn't been educated the way that some of the older men had been, wanted to learn more about how things had happened and why we were in such a predicament.

"Rushdi has talked for a while. Let's let him have a rest." Demetrius said. "Who will explain that to our younger brothers?"

When no one volunteered, Demetrius asked, "Rushdi, no one knows this subject better than you do. Would you mind?"

"Okay, I will do as you ask if that's what the men want to hear. I will tell you what I know. I have given many, many lectures on such topics over the course of my life, and this may be my last one."

CHAPTER 11

The Age of Colonization

"You have all now heard things about the history of our church and the history of Christianity, Islam, and Judaism, and now I will tell you about that period of time when European countries basically conquered the world. It is important because it explains, to some extent, how religion was spread across the world. It involves us, too, but that is only more recently—as in the last hundred years or so.

"History calls it the Age of Colonization, but it was truly a time when European countries pillaged the weaker countries in the world. Mostly it was Spain, England, and France, but Portugal, Denmark, and the Dutch were involved too. Those countries, because they were on the Atlantic Ocean and had a well-established shipping industry, had a great advantage. They also had strong armies and navies.

"After the fall of Rome, and throughout the Middle Ages, no European nation ever came close to gaining the power the Western Roman Empire had, and no civilization has come close ever since, but with the discovery of the Americas, the world changed. For the most part, this part of the world, where we live, remained relatively unchanged. Muslims remained in command. No Europeans came here during those days, except during the Crusades.

"Not long after Columbus discovered the Americas, trade routes to China, India, Indonesia, and the Far East were established. Europeans immediately began to trade heavily in those areas. Prior to that time, the goods were transported to and from those countries mostly by caravans of camels, which was time-consuming, perilous, inefficient, and expensive.

"In many cases, if not most, the Europeans took over the countries by military force and actually established governments there. In some cases, the control of countries went back and forth as the Europeans fought each other over them. In other cases, such as India, one country took control of one part of it and other countries took control over other parts.

"In North, South, and Central America, all of the European powers were involved in what was basically a landgrab. In some parts of what was called the New World, they found enormous amounts of gold and silver, such as in Mexico, Peru, Ecuador, and other countries in South and Central America. In doing so, they acquired great wealth.

"Surprisingly—to them, that is—little gold or silver was found in North America, but there were many natural resources there, which were eventually harvested from that part of the new world. As you all know, I expect, England and Spain took the largest chunks of land, but France, Portugal, and the Dutch got their share too. It was a time when the stronger countries in the world took advantage of the weaker and less-developed countries in the rest of the world.

"European nations grew even more powerful as a result of the massive amounts of gold and silver they stole from the Incas of Peru and the Aztecs of Mexico, among others. Not surprisingly, after the discovery of the Americas, European nations fought with each other even more often than before to see which countries could profit the most from their ill-gotten gains. Again, the three most powerful countries were Spain, England, and France, and they profited the most.

"England, which called itself Great Britain by then, claimed control of a large portion of North America, as did France and Spain, and they, together with the Netherlands and Portugal, laid claim to Central and South America. The consequences of those conquests remain visible today.

"The people in the country we now know as Brazil speak Portuguese to this day. Most people in Mexico, Central America, and South America speak Spanish. French is spoken in parts of Canada, but English is the language of the United States and most of Canada. In India, English remains the second-most commonly spoken language. All of that is a result of that period in history called the Age of Exploration or, as I said before, the Age of Colonization.

"Importantly, as I just mentioned, because Great Britain ruled most of what is now India, the people learned to speak English. Great Britain also cast their influence, therefore, on what is now Pakistan, Afghanistan, and Bangladesh, and that control existed until the early to middle part of the 1900s. Their influence remains to this day.

"Great Britain controlled parts of the Middle East and Africa, too, including Egypt, until 1948. They also took over Australia and New Zealand. There was a time in the middle of the nineteenth century when Great Britain claimed to rule the world.

"Through all of that, here in Egypt, our Coptic Church remained independent and strong, and—"

"But when that was going on, what was happening to the people of all of those other countries, as far as their religions were concerned?" Magdi asked.

"All of the European countries were Catholic at that time. Muslims were not a part of it at all, and neither were the Jews. It wasn't until the seventeenth century that the Protestant movement began in earnest and the strength and influence of the Catholic Church was reduced in several countries—especially in England and the Netherlands, but not in Spain or France. So Catholicism was being spread across the world in those days— Roman Catholicism."

"Italy, Greece, and Turkey weren't involved?" Moghadan asked.

"Or Germany or Russia?" Cosmos added.

"Not in the colonization period; that's right. As I said before, because they were on the water, England, France, and Spain—and the other three, Denmark, the Netherlands, and Portugal—dominated the seas. When they conquered a country, they sent priests along with their soldiers and did their best to convert the inhabitants to Catholicism. In some cases, they did so with brute force, and that's what happened to the Native American Indians of North America and to all of the indigenous people in Mexico, Central America, and South America, as well as in India, the south of Africa, Indonesia, and China, too … all over the world, really."

"What about China?" Nabir asked. "Why weren't they involved in colonizing other countries? They were on the water; weren't they interested in acquiring new land?"

"Maybe the Americas were too far away from China. Is that the reason?" Guirguis asked.

"That's a good question, Guirguis, and I don't know the answer," Rushdi responded, but my guess would be that China—even though it was so big, and probably so strong, as it had so many inhabitants even back then—didn't take to the seas to conquer neighboring lands because it had enough land where it was. It had already conquered most of the countries that were around it, over time. It didn't start out as the huge country it is now. I don't have a good answer for that. Do you, Omar?"

"There is another reason, I think," Omar responded. "I don't think China was as advanced, militarily speaking, as the Europeans were at the time. The Europeans were constantly fighting with each other, and in the process, they were developing new means of warfare: bigger ships, bigger guns, and better methods of fighting.

"Great Britain, which thought it was so powerful that it could conquer anyone in the world, tried to conquer China. It wasn't able to do that, but it took control of Hong Kong and kept it for quite a long time. It only recently gave it back to China, but no one has ever actually conquered China, though Japan tried to, but was unsuccessful, during the Second World War. So to answer your question, I don't believe that the Chinese had any interest in the new lands at the time, except for reasons of commerce, though many Chinese traveled to the new country and settled there later on. That's the best answer I can give you."

"But was China ever either a Christian or a Muslim country?" Theophilos continued.

"No," Omar responded, "and because it was never conquered by a European power is the reason for that, though there are Muslims and Christians and other religions there, in small proportions. Most are Taoists, or they follow the teachings of Confucius. Nowadays, under Communist rule, religion is discouraged."

"And Russia?" Halim asked.

"Russia was a Christian country until the Communist revolution led by Lenin in 1917, and then Stalin took over and banned religion. It was not a Roman Catholic religion or a Greek Orthodox religion. It had its own brand of Christianity, called Russian Orthodox, but there are many Muslims there too, and other, smaller, religions.

"Russia, like China, is a very big country; this was especially so during the years when it was the Union of Soviet Socialist Republics," Omar responded. "There are many smaller religions, as I just said, but the five largest religions in the world are Christianity, Islam, Judaism, Hinduism, and Buddhism, and all five are there, but mostly it is a Christian country."

"So Christians dominated the whole world then, except for China and here in the Middle East?" Touma asked.

"For the most part, that is true. Now one third of the people in the world are said to be followers of Christ, but that number is declining. There were times when the number was much higher, but there have always been many, many other religious communities that did not follow the teachings of Christ, Muhammad, or the Jews, just as there are now.

"Buddha lived about five hundred years before Christ, and so did Confucius, and Hindus have been following the teachings of various holy men since at least fifteen hundred years before Christ. Those religions haven't changed much over the centuries, but those religions never spread too far from its base of followers, either. They never tried to force others to become what they are. Most Buddhists and Hindus live in India, China, and the Far East."

"So where we live and throughout all of Arabia, the predominant religion has been Islam, both Sunni and Shiite, since the days of Muhammad, and Europe, together with North and South America, has been predominantly Christian during all those years. Other than that, the rest of the world was either Buddhist or Hindu—is that about it?" Moghadan asked.

"I think that's a fair statement, Moghadan," Rushdi responded.

"But in Africa, the only other major continent, there are many Christians," Omar added, "as a result of hundreds of years of work by missionaries from Europe and the United States. There are many Muslims throughout Africa, too, and there are many places there where the people continue to practice their ancient religions, which are not Christian, Muslim, Buddhist, Hindu, or Jewish."

"So after the European countries conquered most of the rest of the world, including us, when did they lose all of their power and influence?" Magdi asked.

"At the beginning of the twentieth century. So it hasn't been that long ago," Rushdi answered.

"All of Africa, most of the Middle East, and much of India, Indonesia, and other parts of the world remained under the colonial rule of one European country or another at the beginning of the twentieth century. Things started to change about the time the First World War ended, and that's when people in the various countries began to rebel against their rulers and regain control of their countries.

"Things changed even more after the second World War, as we know. Mahatma Gandhi is given credit for convincing the British to up and leave India in 1947, which was an enormous amount of land, and that's when they left the Middle East, too. So by the end of the Second World War, most of the world was free of colonial rule ... but not the Middle East ... not us."

"Is that true?" Cosmos asked.

"Yes, it's true. Here in Egypt, we gained our independence in 1922, and Saudi Arabia did so in 1932; but Syria wasn't independent until 1946. Iran wasn't independent until 1979, Libya gained its independence in 1951 and Algeria became independent in 1952. Morocco, Tunisia, and Sudan became independent in 1946, and Yemen wasn't an independent country until 1967. So you see, it wasn't that long ago that things were very different around here from the way they are now," Rushdi responded. "Some of that occurred while I have been alive. Much of that was told to me by my father."

"But none of that was about religion, right? It was all about money and power, correct?" Moghadan asked.

"That's true. As I said, there were, and there still are, Christian missionaries all over the world seeking to convert people who they viewed as being pagans into becoming believers in Christ, but now they do so in a peaceful way, by persuasion, not by force ... not like it was back through the centuries, as Cyril explained to us," Rushdi answered.

"But these Muslims who have captured us are going back to the way things were fifteen hundred years ago, and they want to convert people to their brand of religion at the point of a gun ..." Omar interjected.

"Or a sword," Clement added.

"So why aren't the Christians of the world coming to rescue us?" Boctor asked.

"I can't answer that, Boctor," Rushdi said. "I don't know."

"Most countries, especially democratic countries like the United States and Great Britain, try to separate church from state. Back in those days, the church played a much larger role in politics than it does now. That's what I think," Omar responded.

"And there is no money in it for them," Clement added. "We have no oil, Boctor! They don't care about us. It is all about money."

"Is this all about money?" Touma asked.

"No, Touma, what is happening to us is not about money. It's about religion," Rushdi responded. "An extremist brand of religion."

"But they are capturing people and saying that unless they are paid a huge ransom by the government of wherever those people came from, the people they capture will be beheaded. Several countries have paid huge ransoms to these terrorists," Sarabamoon said. "Why not us?"

"That's true," Rushdi responded, "But no one will pay a dime to ransom any of us, I'm afraid. Egypt has no money, and we are Copts."

"That's not right!" Guirguis said. "Someone should come to rescue us: our country, our religion, other Christians … somebody."

"We can only pray," Demetrius responded.

"No one cares, Guirguis. No one cares about us" Clement said. "Not our country, not even our fellow Copts … no one."

"That's not true!" Demetrius responded. "You can believe that our Coptic brothers and sisters are praying for us now. It's just that we have no military and no ability to fight these men."

When he said that, I'm sure everyone felt the sadness and hopelessness of our situation. We were all silent for a few minutes, and then Demetrius spoke again,

"I think we have spoken enough of history and what has brought us all to where we are now. I think it is time for us to think about where we will be going tomorrow. Let us be still for a while and think to ourselves about what is likely going to happen to us then. Each of us is about to face our maker; we must be prepared for that. I think it's time to confess our sins—or repent them, as Cyril says.

CHAPTER 12

History Repeating Itself

"Demetrius, before we move on to that, I would like to know what others feel about all that we have just heard," Theophilos said.

"As I understand it, what is about to happen to us has been happening ever since a few hundred years after Christ walked the earth. It started, I guess, when some of the Roman Emperors after Constantine made Jews and others convert to being Christians, and then, after Muhammad, there were times when the Muslims made Christians and Jews convert to Islam. But what about the beheadings? When did that start?"

"The earliest beheadings that I'm aware of were when the Jews were beheaded in Medina after they betrayed Muhammad," Cyril responded.

"Why beheadings?" Boctor asked incredulously. "I can't stop thinking about them cutting my head off. That was over fourteen hundred years ago! Haven't they outlawed that yet?"

"No, I'm afraid they haven't," Cyril said. "And it's been going on forever, and it's still going on, I'm sorry to say."

"I don't want to have my head cut off," Boctor said.

"France, which considers itself to be one of the most civilized nations on earth, used the guillotine as punishment up until the late 1970s, not all that long before you were born, Boctor."

"No! Really?" Boctor asked. "That's hard to believe. France? No way!"

"I'm afraid so, Boctor, and many people thought that it was the most humane way to kill someone," Raghib added.

"I can't believe that," Boctor continued.

"It was only stopped in France when then president Mitterand banned capital punishment altogether. If it weren't for him, they'd still be using it. They thought it was the most humane way to kill someone," Omar added.

"The most humane way?" Boctor asked. "Really?"

"Yes," Omar responded. "Think about it … with the weight of that large blade coming down at a high rate of speed, death would occur immediately. The other most favored method was poisoning, and that would take quite a while—or it could, I assume. And it was, and is, supposedly, quite painful. And then there were the firing squads."

"But that's not how we are going to die, Boctor said. "These men will use swords. The best we can hope for is that the swords will be sharp and they will swing hard and fast so it will be over quickly. I would much prefer the guillotine, now that I think of it."

No one spoke for several minutes after that comment. Then Omar said, "In Saudi Arabia, that is how the government still executes some of its people, with the public allowed to watch."

"Even now?" Boctor asked.

"Even now," Omar responded, "but people aren't allowed to take pictures."

"And those aren't the only two countries in the world in which the governments authorize the practice of beheading people," Raghib added. "Beheadings are legal in Iran, Qatar, and Yemen, too. Those are the ones I know of; there may be more."

"But there haven't been nearly as many public beheadings in quite a few years," Rushdi said, "because the whole world condemns it … until ISIS started doing it again here lately in such a brutal and public way."

"The whole *civilized* world, that is," Demetrius added.

"People say that ISIS is doing it now to scare people and to intimidate them," Raghib added.

"'To horrify people' would be more accurate," Boctor said.

"Or to attract people," Omar said.

"To attract people? You think people become jihadists because they want to be a part of beheading other people?" Abanoub asked.

"That's what I've heard," Omar responded.

"Really? Why? Why would people want to do that to other people?" Touma asked.

"I have no idea. I can't understand it, but that's what journalists who interview these people are saying—that the brutality of some of the things ISIS is doing is one of the reasons why people come from all over the world join ISIS and al-Qaeda," Omar replied. "And some of those people come from the United States, Germany, and France."

"England, too," Raghib chimed in,

"Especially France," Rushdi offered. "There are many Muslims in France these days, and some of them have been there for years. They're causing quite a few problems there now."

"And in the Netherlands, too, right?" Cyril asked. "Weren't there some arrests made there, too, not long ago?"

"That was for something else, I think," Omar said. "I think that was for someone saying bad things about Muhammad, but I could be wrong."

"There are Muslims all over the world," Omar stated, "and more and more of them are becoming jihadists, so everyone should be worried about a global jihad. That's what I fear is taking place."

"With all due respect, Omar, you seem to be saying that it's the Sunnis, not your Shiites, who are doing all this; but the Shiites are just as much to blame, aren't they? They have a repressive regime, and they're in Iraq fighting the Sunnis now," Theophilos said.

"And the Iranian Army is winning!" Rushdi added. "The United States and others don't want them to win because they're afraid the Shiites will become too powerful and gain control of Iraq."

"That's true. The Iranian Army is in Iraq, and they are winning," Omar told him. "No one else had been able to stop ISIS, but they have, and the United States isn't happy about that. You are correct. They want the Iranians to stay out of Iraq."

"Why?" Boctor asked. "Somebody has to stop them, and no one else is able to, so let them slaughter each other. Sorry, Omar, but that's how I feel. I hate Muslims, though I don't hate you."

"Please, Boctor, we are taught not to hate," Demetrius said softly.

"I hate them, Demetrius," Boctor responded. "Sorry."

"Many people around the world, especially in the United States, don't want the Iranian Shiites to get control in Iraq, because they're afraid of what the Shiites will do to the Sunnis if they do. They think the Shiites will slaughter them. They weren't treated well by Saddam Hussein for many years, and after he was overthrown, the Shiites, who are in the minority in Iraq, were given the opportunity to run the government, but that didn't work out too well."

"That makes no sense to me!" Touma stated in a loud whisper.

I was surprised how emotional Touma was about this. He wasn't one to get easily agitated. But he'd never been chained up like this before, either, about to die.

"If the Iranian Army, which is composed of mostly Shiites, is the only group in the world who is willing or able to defeat ISIS, then they should be welcomed with open arms by everybody in the world to fight ISIS! Otherwise the people of the world should go in and fight ISIS themselves. It's wrong to sit back and let ISIS murder people, behead them, destroy historical and religious places, and do nothing about it because of politics! That's wrong!" he said.

"I wish the Iranian Army would come kill these people who have captured us," Boctor chimed in.

I heard Guirguis say, "I agree!"

"Me too," Magdi said.

Others voiced their agreement with that sentiment.

"We all wish they'd come here now," Omar said, sadly, "but they won't.

"This is ISIS or al-Qaeda, we don't know which, and the Iranians are a thousand miles from here. They don't care about us. Nobody cares about us. Nobody's coming to save us," Clement stated.

"Our only hope is Egypt," Raghib said.

"We have no hope," Clement responded. "We are dead men, like Demetrius said hours ago."

There was silence in the room, and then Sarabamoon said, "So, from everything I've heard, and everything I know, it seems as if religion has been the main thing people have fought over, and killed each other over, for the last two thousand years, since the days of Christ ... is that about it?"

He was one of the middle-aged men. I didn't know him well, but I had seen him in church for years. He was one of the few men who didn't have black hair. He had brown hair. His father and the rest of his family were from our village, but I had never met his mother. He had a beard and was a short, stocky man.

"Gold and silver, too," Clement responded.

"Or oil," Raghib offered, "which is the same thing."

"Or better," Clement responded.

"But from what I'm hearing, more wars have been fought over religion than gold, silver or oil. Am I wrong?" Sarabamoon persisted.

"One could certainly make a good case that you are right about that, Sarabamoon," Rushdi responded.

"So Jesus Christ comes to earth and tells mankind to love each other, not to hate each other, and his legacy turns out to be the exact opposite; people kill each other in his name. Is that about it?" Sarabamoon continued.

"No, no, no ... don't say that," Cyril responded. "It is a battle, but we—you, me, and all of us here—are fighting that battle right now. We are Christians, and we will be martyrs in Christ's name. We will win the war. God is on our side."

Clement started to say something, but Demetrius shut him up.

"So we're going to die only because we are Christians? There's no money in this, so why do they want to kill us? What does killing us prove? What does it accomplish?" Boctor asked. "No one gets gold, no one gets silver, no one gets oil, no one gets any money … so why are we being killed?"

"It's a good question, Boctor," Omar replied. "I don't have an answer for you, except to say that the terrorists are killing Christians and sending a warning to the world that they will do it again and again, until they are stopped."

"Or until they win," Boctor replied. "Someone has to stop them."

"It's almost as if they want someone to try to save us," Cyril said. "Like they want to make the whole world so mad at them that the whole world says that it can't go on … and then they can die as martyrs. That's the only way it makes any sense to me."

"I think that's right," Theophilus said. "To them it makes sense. When they die, they will die as martyrs, and that is their reward. They want to die as martyrs. They do suicide bombings all the time—all over the world, it seems. They don't care. Life on earth is meaningless to them."

"So there's nothing we can say or do to change their minds?" Boctor asked.

"I'm afraid not," Omar responded. "This isn't a theological debate; it's mass murder. I don't think there is any reasoning with them, and by that I mean that no one in the world can reason with them. They will stop at nothing until they get what they want, which is a completely pure Islamic world—and a Sunni world at that."

"Are you getting the picture here, Boctor?" Clement asked. "You are going to die in the morning … understand?"

"He refuses to believe it," Moghadan offered.

"I think he's just trying the best he can to figure out some way that we all aren't going to die in the morning," Magdi, who was his best friend, said. "I don't blame him. I hope he figures something out for all of us before it's too late."

"I hope he's not thinking that maybe we'll be allowed to convert," Yousrey stated. "I hope not."

Then he asked, "If they do allow you to convert, you won't, will you, Boctor? You'd never convert, would you?"

"I am thinking about it, but I know that if I were to do that, my mother would kill me if they didn't," Boctor responded. "Of that I'm sure."

"I have decided. I won't." Yousrey said.

"I don't think we'll be offered that opportunity," Clement said. "We're dead men."

"So what have we learned from what we have heard over the past several hours?" Rushdi asked. "How are things any different for us, Demetrius? How has this helped us? It may have made us become further apart."

"I was hoping that it would help the younger men understand why all of this is happening to us," Demetrius answered. "And as I said at the very beginning, I think we are preparing ourselves to meet our maker in the morning."

"It helped me to see that history is repeating itself—that what is happening to us is what has happened in this part of the world for most of the past two thousand years, all in the name of religion," Moghadan said. I thank you, Demetrius, for having us do this."

"All in the name of religion … even though we both believe there is only one true God," Clement scoffed.

"Their god is not my God," Abanoub stated.

"Nor mine!" Cyril joined in. "I will gladly die for my God."

"Remember that we are Copts," Demetrius said softly, "and that we should all gladly go to our deaths as martyrs. In the end, good will win out over evil."

All of the other men grunted their approval, and then a silence fell over the room.

CHAPTER 13

Demetrius Repents

Several minutes later, Demetrius said, "So, my brothers, can we repent of our sins now? As you know, I think we should all hear what each of us wishes to say, but I understand that many don't agree with that. What should we do? And how should we do it?"

"I think we should confess our sins to ourselves," Cyril said. "We will be communicating directly with God."

"I agree," Raghib said. "and, please, take no offense, but I don't want all of you knowing about the things I've done in my life that I'm not proud of. That's why people go to confession with only a priest, who is sworn to silence."

"We can't have true confessions, because we don't have a priest. There is no way around that, I acknowledge," Demetrius responded. "But St. Paul told the early Christians to confess their sins to each other and pray for each other so that they may be healed. I think we should do as St. Paul told us to do, though ours are repentances, not true confessions, as Cyril has told us repeatedly."

Many of the men didn't seem to be too receptive to that idea. There were murmurs, but I couldn't understand all that was being said. then Demetrius said, "Let's do this: let the men among us who want to make a repentance openly do so, and those of you who don't want to do that don't have to. This is supposed to be a time for each of us to prepare himself to meet our Father in heaven. This is a time each of for us to cleanse himself, to truly repent of the sins he has committed, and to ask God for His forgiveness. We don't have to agree on this. With your permission, I will go first."

Everyone indicated that they would allow Demetrius to make his repentance, and so he began. "My brothers, and my son, I ask that you hear me as I repent the sins of my life ..."

Although I couldn't see him, because we sat in complete darkness, I closed my eyes, and I could see him in my mind as clearly as if he were standing right in front of me, dressed in his finest clothes, as I had seen him on so many occasions in my life.

I had attended the same church as he did since I was an infant, just as most everyone else in the room had done for years. Demetrius was one of the most respected elders in our church. I don't remember being there a single Sunday when he wasn't.

He would always be standing at the front of the church before Mass when people entered, and again at the end of the Mass, as people were walking out of the church. He always had a smile on his face as he shook my hand when I came and when I left. He did that with everyone, not just me.

To me, he was an old man, but he worked as hard as anyone did, and what we did was hard work, so he wasn't feeble or infirm by any means. He had a full beard, just as everyone else did, except for me. Magdi and Moghadan, who were just a few years ahead of me in school, both had scraggly beards that really weren't beards at all, and many of the men took pleasure in teasing them about their beards. With me, they just laughed.

Demetrius had a beard that was mostly white, even though the hair on top of his head was black with streaks of gray running through it. On Sundays he would wear an ornate black knit cap over his head, which he would take off when he entered the church. On all other days, he would have a cap on his head, but it would be a different one every day, and the caps were various colors, too. He was always smiling.

He was a large man—not too tall, but large around his midsection. Whenever he had to climb stairs or carry heavy objects, he would tire easily. He climbed a ladder only when it was absolutely necessary. One of the younger men would usually do those things for him. However, he was probably the best carpenter in our group. I thought he was.

As I sat there, I pictured a bright, sunny day, a Sunday, and we were standing in front of the church. I was with my family. All those around me were dressed in their finest clothes, as had been the case so many times before. Demetrius was smiling, greeting me warmly.

What I remembered most about him, though, was his eyes ... they were kind eyes, and they were blue. Few people in our town had blue eyes, but he did, and I remembered his laugh. He had what people call a belly laugh. It started in the area of his stomach and erupted from his lips. It made me laugh to hear him laugh. It was more of a rumble than a laugh.

I couldn't recall a single time when I heard him raise his voice in anger, and I know for certain that I never heard him curse or use vulgar language, though most of the other men did while working—especially the younger men. Here was a man whom I respected as much as my own father. I had no idea what this man could have done wrong that he needed to confess to us. I wanted to hear what he had to say.

I closed my eyes, leaned back against the wall, and listened ...

"My brothers, this is not a time for me to brag about myself or to tell you stories of any of the good things I may have done in my life. This is a time for me to confess to you, and to our God, the bad things I have done in my life—the things I am not proud of. This is not easy for me.

"My son, Ignatius, is here with me, and I feel his presence as clearly as I feel my heartbeat. He is my oldest child, and I have loved him dearly from the day I felt him kicking in his mother's womb. I love him—just as I love my other children, my wife, my brothers, my parents, and the rest of my family—now more than ever, because I know I am about to lose him and the others. I am sorry for things I have done and failed to do in my life.

"When we go to confession at our church, we begin by telling our priest how long it has been since we have been to confession. We state that we are sorry for the sins we have committed since our last confession and for all of the sins in our life. We have been in Sirte for over three months now, and I have not been to confession since I left home.

"Tomorrow is my final day on earth, just as it is for each of you. I make this confession to you as if I am speaking to God himself. This is not the time for false pretense. He knows what I have done. I know what I have done. This is a time for honesty. This is a time for me to admit to Him what I have done … or failed to do."

Some men squirmed as Demetrius spoke, and the chains rattled when they did. It was hot inside this hellhole we were in. It smelled like a urinal, or like one of the uncleaned port-o-lets at the job site. Everyone was hungry and thirsty. My mouth was parched again.

The water we had been given was long gone. I could barely muster enough saliva to wet my lips. I had gone to the bathroom in my pants twice now, and so had probably everyone else, I was sure. The stench in the room was unbearable, but there was nothing we could do. Despite our pain and our discomfort, no one made a sound as Demetrius spoke.

"Some of you know me only through church and from working together—especially you younger men. Raghib and Rushdi have known me since we were little boys, but even they don't know all of the secrets I have kept inside me. We all have secrets. There are things we all have thought, said, and done that we want to keep to ourselves.

"There are things I am about to tell you that no one knows … things I feel … things I am not proud of … things I would say only to God, or to a priest. But these are things I must say to you, because of what is to happen to us tomorrow."

"You don't have to do that, Demetrius. You don't know for certain that we are to die tomorrow. Something might happen. Somehow, we might be saved," Cyril interjected.

"I am as certain that we are going to die tomorrow as I have ever been certain about anything in this life, Cyril. You are welcome to believe what you wish about what will happen tomorrow. I am preparing myself for death. If I wait until the morning to see what is to happen, it will be too late to repent. We may not have the time to do so. Now is the time. The hour is near.

"As I think back to my childhood days, and my earliest recollections of life, I see myself as a young boy running around our village with Raghib and Rushdi and the others. I see my house—the same house where my father still lives to this day—and all of the other houses in our village. In some ways, little has changed since those days. I have seen my entire life flash before me many times this night.

"Our village has grown. There are more houses now than before—many more. There are more people in our village now than there were back in those days, but our church is the same. Father Ignatius, for whom my son is named, is still there, and Father Maurice, who came before him, and for whom Rushdi named his first born son, is long gone.

"Five priests have been our shepherds over the years. I think of them, and of the many confessions I have made to them and the others, and I ask myself, 'What have you done with your life, Demetrius? What is it you are most proud of, and what is it you are most ashamed of? What is it that you need to confess?

"Yes, this is not like any other confession. It is not about what I have done since my last confession. It is about what I have done, or failed to do, in my entire life. I ask myself what I will say when the Lord asks me that question tomorrow, as I'm sure He will: 'What have you done with your life, Demetrius?' What will I say to Him? What I say to you now is going to help me be prepared for what I will say to Him tomorrow.

"As little boys, we ran around, played games, laughed, and had fun. We were sheltered by our parents, our church, and our village. Though we were in the minority in Egypt, we felt secure in our village and in our homes. Our parents would scold us and tell us what to do, and we would do whatever we were told to do, but we pushed them as far as we could before we would be punished, as children will do.

"I think we tried to think of ways to upset our parents or our teachers. That's what little boys do, but I don't think any of us did anything in those early years that would be of concern to God. All children are good, I think. It is when they get older that they are changed by the world around them. That's when the evil one tries to enter our lives.

"As we got older, we became more mischievous—and I was certainly no exception, as Raghib and Rushdi can testify. There were pranks we would pull, the three of us, and things we would do to get ourselves in trouble just to show off to our friends and prove how different we were from all of the others, and to impress the girls. Again, I don't think any of us did anything during those years to bring the wrath of God upon ourselves. Those, too, were normal things young boys do when going from children to adolescents.

"During our teenage years, however, we became defiant and even more emboldened. I was no exception. We were trying to become men, and we wanted to be strong, fearless, bold … and different from the others. I stole things from the market. I threw rocks at people and ran away. I made fun of boys not as big or as strong as I was. I rebelled against my parents.

"At times, I resented being made to go to church on Sundays. I questioned the very existence of God, as some of you may be doing here tonight. I think those things are normal too.

"And there were the girls. That's all we could think about, even though our parents would warn us and the priests told us of what sins we would be committing if we didn't follow the teachings of the church. But I, like every other boy, thought of nothing else. I pestered those girls more than I should have, but those things, too, are normal.

"I don't think God expected us to be able to avoid sin and temptation. Like Adam and Eve, we were unable to avoid the temptation of the apple—which some might call physical love and others might call knowledge or something else. Few can avoid that temptation.

"Actually I think that is a good thing. When men are no

longer attracted to women, the most basic fabric of civilization is destroyed. Some say that physical attraction to a woman is the most powerful force in a man's life, followed closely by the need for money.

"In fact, I think He allowed us to be tempted and He knew that we would sin. We are all sinners. There is no one who is pure. We are human. He wanted us to exercise our free will and, after doing so, decide to be good. He did not want us to be good just because we were told to be good or because He made us good.

"I think He did that so we would understand what is good and what is evil, and then we could choose to be good. He put us here to be tested. He wants us to pass this test and be with Him in heaven if we do. We are facing a major test now, my brothers, and we want to pass this test.

"As I look back on those days when I was still a child, I wonder what my parents wanted for me and what God wanted for me. I didn't think of that back then. I did what Demetrius wanted to do. But as I think back, even now, wondering what I could have done differently with my life, I'm not sure what God or my parents would have had me do differently.

"Actually, that is what I regret most about my life. What I mean by that is this: just like all of you, I have heard many of the parables that Jesus used as a way to show His followers how to live as God wants us to live, and one of the parables among all of them that haunts me to this day is the one about the black sheep. That may surprise you, but it's true.

"Think about it. In that parable Jesus tells us how the good shepherd will do all that he can within his power to find one of the sheep from his flock that is lost and bring that lost sheep back into the flock. All of us understand that to mean that the lost sheep are the members of our church who have strayed away, just as a sheep that strays away from the flock becomes lost.

"I was not that lost sheep. I have never strayed far from the flock, and I have never even wandered to the edge. So why does that parable haunt me so? As I look back at my life and ask myself, 'Demetri, what have you done with your life?' I say that I have done little with it, and I ask myself why that is. Why have I done so little with my life? I think the answer is, in part, that there was so little expected of me. We come from a small village. Most of our families have been there for generations. Our families will probably be there for many generations to come. In many ways, I did exactly what was expected of me.

"Granted, I could have done what Rushdi did, which was to do well in school and go on to university; or maybe become a priest, as Cyril tried to do; or become a teacher, as Rushdi did; or become a successful businessman, as Raghib did. I tried, but that wasn't me. I didn't succeed at those things. I was a carpenter. Maybe I wasn't as smart as the others were, or maybe I didn't try as hard as they did. I don't know. For whatever reason, after finishing school, I went to work with my father, building things.

"Although he told me that he didn't want me to follow in his footsteps, I really think that's what my father wanted me to do. I think he wanted me to work with him and to be like him. That is what he did with his life, and that is what his father had done with his life before that, and that is what my son, Ignatius, has done with his life too. Please don't misunderstand; there is nothing wrong with that. Christ was a carpenter too. That's not my point.

"Not long after we graduated from school, Demiani and I were married. Demetri and Demiani—it was a match made in heaven, people said. Her father was a builder too, and the two families built us a house not far from where I grew up. It's about halfway between my father's house and her father's house.

"We had little money, but that didn't stop us from having children. First came Ignatius, then Sofia, then Youssef, and then Hannah. We would have had more, but God did not will it. I have been blessed. I praise God every day for all that I have been given in this life.

"We were happy. We loved each other, and we loved our children and our families. We all went to the same church we had gone to since we were children. Ignatius has followed in my footsteps.

"He married soon after he finished school, as I did, and now he works with me. I expect Youssef might someday do the same thing, as will my grandson, probably. Again I say to you that there is nothing wrong with that.

"As I prepare to go to my grave, I find myself ashamed of myself for what I have not done. I believe my life has been a failure—that I have done nothing to glorify my God and to make the most of the gifts He has given me. That is my greatest sin. That is what I am most ashamed of—that I have not done more."

At that, chains began to rattle, and when they did, he began to cry. I could hear him softly sobbing. It brought a tear to my eye to hear it. He cried for several minutes, and when the sobs subsided, he took a deep breath and said, "I am sorry, my brothers. Forgive me. I thank you for listening to my confession."

The room remained silent for several more minutes, and then Raghib spoke. "That's it? Demetrius? Are you finished? Have you nothing else to confess? No affairs with any of the women in the church? No taking money from the poor box? Nothing?" he asked incredulously.

"I have looked at other women, and I have had impure thoughts, Raghib, as you know, because we have talked of such things, but most of that was before I was married. I have never acted on those impulses, and no, I never stole money or anything from the church or anyone else."

"I don't understand," Cyril asked. "What are you confessing to us? If you have nothing else to confess, you are a saint. I doubt that any of us can say that we have led a life so pure as the one you have led."

"And you are a leader of our church," Abanoub added. "You are respected by all. You, of all people, should be welcomed into heaven, Demetrius. We all love you. How can you think that of yourself? I don't understand."

"Did you not listen to me? I have done nothing with my life! I have done nothing to make myself worthy of heaven. I am like the man to whom much was given by the master and nothing of value was returned," Demetrius answered.

"What are you talking about, Demetrius? You have led the life of a Christian! You have been a good son, a good father, a good husband, and a good parishioner. What else could you have done? What else should you have done?" Raghib asked.

"Do you remember the parable of the master who gave three servants bags of silver and told them to take good care of his money? It is found in the gospel of Matthew. This is the parable that troubles me the most, above all others."

"Of course I remember it! I remember it well. We all do," Raghib responded.

Demetrius continued. "When the master returned, the servant who had been given five bags of silver gave the master back those five bags and five more. The servant who had been given two bags of silver gave the master the two bags back plus two more. The servant who had been given only one bag of silver had put the bag in the ground so as not to lose it, and he gave the master back the one bag of silver but nothing more.

"The master was furious at the servant who had done nothing with the bag of silver, and he cast the man out of his house. He told the man that he could cry and gnash his teeth, but he was banished forever from the master's house. I think I am like that servant."

"Demetrius, please … don't think those thoughts. You are a good man. God will greet you with open arms. I am sure of it," Raghib told him.

"No! That is not true, and there is nothing any of you can say to make me feel any differently. I ask for your forgiveness, and I ask for God's forgiveness. That is my confession. I repent of my sins. Thank you all for allowing me to say it to you."

"I think we all would disagree with you, Demetrius," Raghib said.

"And if I had been a better man, a better carpenter, a better husband, a better father, a better provider to my family, I wouldn't be here with my son, about to die," he cried. "I have failed them all. I am a failure in this life. I am not worthy of heaven."

No one spoke for several moments, and then Cyril said,

"Demetrius, as you know, and as all Copts know, no one is worthy of heaven. We are chosen by grace, not by our merit. But if you are not worthy of heaven, none of us are. You are a righteous man. You should be proud of yourself."

Then Raghib said, "Demetrius, my friend, my life has been nothing like that. You are no sinner, but I am. I was not going to speak, but after hearing what you have just told us, I will give my confession too."

CHAPTER 14

Raghib's Repentance

"I have been a sinful man," Raghib began. "I am not proud of it. I know that I will not be going to heaven by repenting of my sins, which is why I wasn't going to bother doing so, my brothers, but after hearing what Demetrius has said, I have decided to do so, in order that you can hear from a true sinner about what he has done—not from one who thinks following the good shepherd is a sin. We are all going to die tomorrow, so I have nothing to lose. Here is what I have to say.

"My life has been like that of the first servant in the parable of the talents, which Demetrius shared with us moments ago. I grew up with Demetrius and Rushdi. I remember Cyril and Theophilus, who were a few years younger than we were, and I remember a few of you here who are much younger than we are from when you were just boys, but I left our little village as soon as I could, once our school days were over.

"I went to Alexandria to seek fame and fortune. I had no idea what I would do, but I knew that I didn't want to stay in our village all of my life. Like all of you, I was raised well by my parents, and I was a good Coptic boy, just as Demetrius, Rushdi, Cyril, and the rest of you were. When I got to Alexandria, the first thing I did was go to St. Mark's Cathedral. I knew no one there, of course, but I was sure that the priests there would help me, and they did.

"They fed me, gave me a place to stay, and found me a job

with one of the parishioners. As fate would have it, that was an extremely fortunate occurrence for me. I thank God and our church for what happened to me back then, although there were times, as now, when I wished I had stayed in our village and worked alongside Demetrius. But, as most of you know, my father was the town's butcher. I had no desire to follow him in that line of work.

"I went to work for a man named Haroun Ibrahim, who owned a carpet business. I began as a laborer. That was hard work. I was still just a boy, not much bigger than Mekhaeil, and those carpets were heavy. They are twelve feet wide and could be a hundred feet long. We had machines to help us move the carpets around, but there was much heavy lifting to be done too.

"I was one of several young men who had few skills and little else other than a strong back. I was able to do what was required of me, but it wasn't easy. For many the work was too demanding and too hard. Many young men came and went, but I was not going to be denied. I worked hard, and Mr. Ibrahim noticed me. I arrived at work early, and I was always the last to leave. I never complained, no matter how difficult things got. Every now and then he'd offer a word of encouragement to me. It didn't hurt that he saw me in church every week either. I'm sure that helped me too.

"After a couple of years, Mr. Ibrahim came to me one day and asked if I would be interested in learning how to make the rugs. You may not know this, but Egyptian rugs are quite precious—and quite expensive as well. They are different from Persian rugs, which are made in Iran and Turkey, although they are sometimes confused with them. They are unique, and he was quite proud of his product.

"Egyptian rugs are handwoven in an extremely time-consuming process, but the quality of the rugs was superior to those made by machines. I knew nothing of how carpets and rugs were made, especially at the beginning, but I wanted to learn. I wanted to advance in order to make more money. I jumped at the opportunity I was given.

"I worked for several years doing that. I learned about the fabrics used in the making of the rugs, which were mostly different kinds and qualities of wool, and I learned about the dyes and the various patterns. I learned all that I could about how Egyptian rugs were made.

"I was proud to be working on a product that came from our country. I learned quickly, and I became a competent rug maker. There were people working beside me who had spent their entire lives making rugs, so I was by no means the best, but I had a likable personality, I guess, and Mr. Ibrahim continued to notice me in the factory and in church. Again I say it—I thank God and our church for the opportunities I was given in this life.

"I was very fortunate to be working for a man who was a Copt. There were many Muslims who worked for Mr. Ibrahim, but there were mostly Christians, Coptic Christians, at his business. I did not experience the discrimination other Copts did in Alexandria at that time and continue to experience now, for that reason.

"By then I was in my early twenties, and I was a man with a purpose. I was going to make something of myself. I was going to make as much money as I could. I had ambition, and Mr. Ibrahim saw that in me.

"I saved every pound I could. I had found an apartment not far from my work or from the church that was a modest, but decent, place to live. I bought a motorbike and drove around the city whenever I wasn't working. I was working hard and doing well for myself.

"After a few years in the rug-making department, Mr. Ibrahim came to me one day and said, 'Raghib, I have been watching you. I notice how hard you work. I see that you are one of the first to arrive every day and that you are one of the last to leave. I see you in church every Sunday, and I see how you act and how you behave. I am thinking that you could be a good salesman. Would you like to give that a try?'

"Again I jumped at the opportunity. I had to go from being a worker who brought lunch with him in a box and buried his head in his work each and every day, to becoming a man who could present himself to the public and sell rugs to people. I had to create a new image of myself. That is what a salesman does; he interacts with people and convinces them to buy whatever it is he is selling, and I was determined to be good at it. It was a huge change for me—perhaps the biggest change in my life.

"I had to buy new clothes, new shoes … new everything. I bought nice suits and nice ties, not like the clothes that I had worn as a child or as a laborer in the factory, or at any other time in my life, and certainly not like what we are wearing now. I became a new man.

"All the while, I was earning more and more money. I began to eat at nice restaurants. I rarely brought lunch with me to work, and I began to meet women—all kinds of women, not just the women in church on Sundays or the women at work. It was a big change for me, and I liked it. I had grown a beard to make me look older, but I shaved it off because I thought it would help me be a better salesman.

"I quickly became one of Mr. Ibrahim's better salesmen. I knew much more about the rugs than almost any of the other salesmen because I had spent years making those rugs. Through hard work and long hours, I soon became one of the best salesmen in all of Alexandria, and again, Mr. Ibrahim noticed.

"After another few years, Mr. Ibrahim asked me if I would be willing to go to other countries, such as Europe and the United States, to sell his products. I told him that I would. He told me that I would need to learn how to speak proper English for that. I told him that I would gladly do whatever it took and do whatever he recommended. I enrolled in a program that same day.

"By that time, I owned a car. It was a fancy car, and women were attracted to men my age who owned such a car, and there were many women who were attracted to me during those days. I won't tell you much more of those days other than to say that I was a sinful man. I am not proud of it now.

"Within a year, I was speaking the language well enough that Mr. Ibrahim sent me to England, the United States, and other English-speaking countries, just as he said he would, to sell

Egyptian rugs to the big department stores throughout the world. I was making more money than I ever dreamed of making.

"As I said before, I'm not proud of some of the things that I did back in those days, but I am proud of myself for having been successful at what I set out to do. I drank heavily, I cavorted with many women, and I stopped going to church. I often couldn't find a Coptic church in places I traveled to, so that was an excuse for me not to go.

"After a while, I didn't go to church even when I was in Alexandria or Cairo. I rarely came home to our village—not even to see my parents, my brothers and sisters, or my friends. I was too busy.

"For almost fifteen years, I traveled the world and saw many sights, all the while making more and more money. I had become a wealthy man, a very wealthy man."

He hesitated for a few moments as if thinking of what life was like for him during those days, and then he continued.

"But two years ago, Mr. Ibrahim took ill, and things changed for me. By then he was in his late sixties and was not well. He had worked his whole life at his business, and he had become an enormously successful businessman, but in the process, he had not taken good care of himself.

"One day he summoned me back to Alexandria and asked me to become a vice president of the company. I really didn't want to do that, as I was quite happy with the life I was leading. Going back to Alexandria and being in the office each and every day was nowhere near as glamorous a life as the one I had been leading.

"However, I could not refuse him, and I did what he asked of me. I was by his side most days, helping him to make all of the major decisions regarding his business. He trusted me. He confided in me. He knew that I had learned the business from the ground up, much as he had. He had trained me well.

"Business was good. Egyptian rugs had become even more desirable to wealthy Westerners over the years, and our profits continued to rise. Mr. Ibrahim treated me as his son, and I treated him as if he were my father. I devoted my life to his business, just as he had done.

"I never found time for a wife, though I was with many women who wanted to marry, and I never had any children, but I had become what I set out to become. I had become a successful man. I was in my early forties at that time, and I thought my life couldn't get any better. I was on top of the world."

He paused as he said those words, took another deep breath, and then went on.

"All that changed when the Muslim Brotherhood rose to power. When Mohammed Morsi was elected as the president of our country, things got much worse for Copts, as we all know, but that was not so much the case for my company or for me. I know for a fact that after the Muslim Brotherhood took over, Copts were fired and Muslims were hired in their place in government and in many businesses. Discrimination was rampant throughout the city and the country—but not at our company.

"There were many other companies who made Egyptian rugs in Alexandria, Cairo, and other parts of Egypt, but none had been as successful as we had been in developing international clients. Most of those other companies were run by Muslims, and there were many of our competitors who envied our success. There were warning signs, and things were done to us that we felt were discriminatory, but we were able to overcome them and carry on.

"However, after the military overthrew Morsi and put him out of office, the Muslims became enraged and turned their anger against the non-Muslim community. They were convinced that Copts had something to do with the military taking over the government, but they couldn't fight the military regime, so they took it out on us. Incidents began occurring all over Egypt.

"As you may know, our pope was said to have approved the ouster of Morsi. Even though that may not have been the truth, the Muslims didn't need proof. Many churches were destroyed. Most were damaged. Many innocent Copts were killed.

"In late July of 2013, within a few weeks after Morsi was ousted and the violence began, Muslims attacked our business. It happened at night, after most of the workers had gone home. I was in the office, by myself, when alarms began going off, informing me of what was going on. Armed men with torches had broken through the gates and were setting fire to our buildings. These were thugs out to destroy us.

"I grabbed a gun from my desk and ran out to see what was happening. By then the building I was in was engulfed in flames. Most of the materials we used were extremely flammable. Men were running through the buildings with torches in their hands, screaming and setting everything on fire that wasn't already burning.

"As they ran toward me, I shot at them. I killed several men, but there were too many of them, and they began running toward me. Once I had no bullets left in my gun, I turned and ran.

"I knew the building well, and I was able to escape. I tore off my coat and tie, and ran through the crowd back to my home, leaving my car behind in the company garage. I packed my bags, rented a car, and left that night. I stayed in a hotel in Cairo.

"The next morning, the headlines in the *Daily News* were about the fire and how four Muslims had been shot and killed. I wasn't named as a suspect, but I knew that it wouldn't be long before the trail would lead to me.

"I couldn't go back to Alexandria, and I had nowhere else to go. The factory and our offices were completely destroyed. I knew what would happen to me if I were captured by the authorities— or worse, what would happen if the Muslims found me—so I took a bus and came home the next day. I have never gone back.

"I have been in hiding ever since. I lost everything I had. I am a wanted man. I don't use my real name anymore. I am on the payroll here as somebody else. I have gone through all of the money and things I was able to take with me that night. I took this job as a last resort. I have nowhere else to go. So here I am … chained like a dog, awaiting execution, with nothing left of all that I amassed and nothing to show for what I have done with my life."

He paused for several moments and then added, "And I am

a murderer, an adulterer—a lost sheep who has wandered far, far from the flock, who is as poor a Copt as one can imagine, I think." Again he hesitated. "So, my brothers, do you think God will forgive me for my sins now that I have repented them?"

No one spoke. There was complete silence.

"No, I don't think so either. I don't think God will forgive me for my sins. I am doomed, I fear."

Again there was silence. Moments later, Abanoub asked, "Do you think that God won't forgive you because you killed those Muslims who destroyed our churches, killed our fellow Copts, and ruined your business?"

"Or that if we fight back, we are committing a sin?" Boctor asked.

"It's not that so much—although killing other human beings is, as we all know, a mortal sin—as it is the life I led. I don't regret killing those men at all. I regret not being able to kill more of them, to tell you the truth. It's that I did not lead a Christian life.

"If I could live longer, I would try to repent and make up for the things I have done or I have failed to do. I think that there are many reasons why I am not worthy. I can think of few reasons why I could be considered as being worthy of heaven, to be honest."

"But that is what a confession is for, Raghib. We don't know how He thinks or how we will be judged," Demetrius said softly.

"Thank you, Demetrius. You have always been a kind man. I don't think a repentance, since this is not a confession, made hours before my death can make up for a lifetime of greed and debauchery, do you? As I said, I believe I am doomed."

"Jesus Christ preached forgiveness. If you are truly sorry for the sins of your past, and if you have made a full and complete repentance, then maybe there is hope," Demetrius offered.

"Demetrius, there is more, but I don't wish to share any more of the sins of my life with you. I am resigned to the fact that I am a sinner and that I am to die in a few hours. I thank you for your concern, but please leave me to my thoughts. I accept my fate. I pray only that God will show mercy on me. I will confess other sins to Him privately."

"As you wish, Raghib. Thank you for sharing your thoughts with us. Before the next person speaks, let us sing our confession song ..."

At that, all the men joined him in singing.

> I love you, my gracious Lord, my most holy one.
> You've washed my heart as white as
> snow with the blood of your Son.
> You forgave all my sins, O Lord,
> and held reconciliation.
> On me You put a bright new
> robe—the robe of salvation.
> You freed me from captivity, Lord—
> the captivity of Satan.
> Away You cast my transgressions,
> into forgetfulness.
> Far as the east is from the west,
> Lord, You put away my sins.
> You've omitted my iniquities as
> though nothing was done.
> You have dispersed my sins, O Lord,
> as a cloud would disperse.
> Through the grace of Your only
> Son, I got the perfect peace.
> With every breath I bless You,
> soul and body in accord.
> All praise and worship are due
> to my beloved Lord.

CHAPTER 15

More Men Repent of Their Sins

After several minutes, Demetrius asked, "Who would like to go next?"

"I will," Moghadan said.

"Please, go ahead," Demetrius told him.

"I am a sinner," he began. "Ever since I was a little boy, I have been disobedient and defiant. I have disobeyed my parents. I have disobeyed the laws of God. I have disobeyed the rules of our church. I have done nothing with my life to bring joy or happiness to my family or my church. I am ashamed of myself, and now I'm going to die before I can do anything to atone for my sins," he said, and then he began to sob.

Chains began to rattle as many sought to offer some comfort to him.

Demetrius hushed the men and asked, "How old are you now, Moghadan? Are you twenty yet?"

Moghadan sniffled, and said, "No. Not yet. I'll be—or I should say I would have been—twenty next month."

Demetrius sighed and said, "Not even twenty years old ... this is so sad."

He was quiet for several moments, and before he could speak, Yousrey said, "I feel the same way."

And then Magdi said, "Me too."

The three of them had been best friends since they were children. They had completed their schooling a few years ahead of me but hadn't been able to find much work since. They had gone to Cairo together for a short while and tried to find work there, without success; and they'd been to Alexandria a couple of times with no luck, which was why there were here with the rest of us.

Then Demetrius continued. "I say this to all of you young men … and I mean it from the bottom of my heart. What is to happen to us tomorrow is wrong for a number of reasons, but the most important reason is that it is a sin against all that is good. You should not die now. We all know that you want to live so you can become men and decide for yourself if you will be a good man or not a good man, as I said before. Those are choices all of us make.

"But you are, in all likelihood, going to be deprived of that opportunity because of nothing that you have said or done. None of you have done anything to deserve what is going to happen tomorrow. These are evil, misguided men who think they are doing the work of their god by killing us just because we believe in Jesus Christ and not in the teachings of Muhammad, as they do.

"Take my son, Ignatius; he is several years older than you are, and he has become a fine young man, a good husband, a good father, a good Copt, and a good man in every way. But he wasn't always this way. He was just like the three of you—rebellious, disobedient, and defiant, just as I was when I was your age. I think that is the way it is for most young men. In fact, I would go so far as to say that is the nature of human beings, so please don't think you are bad.

"Let me explain. You have all heard of the concept of free will, which means that you have the freedom to decide for yourself what you will do with your life. Some people say that your fate is predetermined—that God knows before you are born what your life will be like. And we believe that is true. We don't doubt it, because we believe God knows everything. But for many people, that doesn't make sense.

"If you have free will, they reason, how could it be that God knows what you are going to do? To many it sounds as if God is just creating these beings, such as the three of you, knowing exactly what they will do with their lives and yet is still saying that you have the freedom to decide what you will do with your lives.

"To me, and to all Copts, that makes perfect sense. If you believe that God is all-knowing, all-seeing, and all-powerful, as I do, and that He created all that is, all that has been, and all that is to be, as I do, then you accept the fact that God is in charge and has a plan for you.

"God wants you to succeed. God wants you to be happy. All that God asks of you is that you accept Him as your Lord and Savior and obey His commandments. The three of you do accept Him as your Lord and Savior; you have told us that you do. You have shown us that you do.

"The three of you are good boys—or, I should say, good young men. Look at you. You go to church regularly, although not every Sunday, and you are here doing your best to make some money so that you can meet a girl, get married, buy a house, and have children someday. You are good workers, all three of you, and every man in this room will swear to that. You have done nothing wrong. You should not be afraid to meet our God tomorrow. You three are innocents. If you are to die, this is in accordance with God's plan for you, and you will be rewarded for your obedience to Him—I am sure of it."

"So if that is true, Demetrius, why is this happening to them?" Clement asked. "Are they being punished for something they did or something they failed to do?"

"There is evil in the world. We all know that. The evildoers are powerful. We cannot know what God's plan is for what is to happen. I have no explanation other than to say we accept it," Demetrius responded.

"And what about earthquakes, plagues, sickness, death, and things like that?" Boctor asked. "Are those part of God's plan for us too?"

"Be careful, Boctor," Abanoub warned. "God hears what you say, and He knows what you are thinking."

"If there were no challenges, no obstacles, life would be easy, wouldn't it? Demetrius added. "I can't explain it any better than that. I cannot think as God thinks. None of us can."

"So God put those things here to challenge us?" Clement asked.

"I didn't say that, Clement. Remember: I am not a priest. I am just like you, my brothers, just older. I don't know everything. To be honest, I know very little, but I know that there is a God and that God is good."

"That's what these terrorists say all the time—'Allahu Akbar! God is great!' I would say that their god is not so great. If their god would have them kill us for no reason other than that we are followers of Christ, then their god is evil, too," Abanoub said.

"Maybe we have the same God," Cyril offered, "and they just don't realize it."

"But we are the ones who will die in the morning, Abanoub. How can our God allow that to happen? Is our God stronger than their god or not?" Clement replied.

"Shut up, Clement! You have already told us you don't believe in the same things we believe in! Just shut up and die with the rest of us! I don't want to hear you talk any more tonight!" Abanoub told him.

"Shh! Please! Let's try to stay as calm as we can be under these circumstances," Demetrius cautioned. "And please try not to say anything to offend anyone here with us. It will only make it worse for all of us."

Abanoub persisted. "But he has been saying these things all night, and—"

"I know … I know. Everyone, please stay calm—or as calm as you can," Demetrius urged us, and then he went on to say, "We must trust that there is a reason for what is going to happen to us—that some good will come out of it. Who knows, maybe because we die the world will take notice and do something about it. Maybe things will change because of what happens to us."

"I would much prefer that something happen to them and

that they die and we don't," Boctor said. "Then we would know for sure that something good came of this."

"I can't argue with that," Demetrius responded, "but getting back to you, Moghadan, and what you said, I would say this to you, and to Yousrey and Magdi as well: you three have done no terrible things; you have killed no one—"

"As I have," Raghib interjected.

"And you have committed no crimes—or none that you have told us about. From what you have just said to me and to all of us, you are sorry for whatever you have done that was not pleasing to God or to your family. That is good. That is a good repentance. You are repenting of your sins, and you are asking for forgiveness. You have seen the errors of your ways, and you are saying that you are sorry for what you have done and what you have failed to do. I believe that you will be forgiven and that you will be with God tomorrow.

"Let me ask all of you, everyone in the room. We have just heard what Moghadan, Yousrey, and Magdi have said. They are sorry for their sins. Though we are not priests, and this is not a confession, I ask you, do you believe that the sins of these three will be absolved?"

All of the men rattled their chains and voiced agreement.

"There. You have heard all of us tell you that we believe you will be absolved of your sins," Demetrius said.

I don't think Moghadan and the other two really believed what Demetrius told them. I didn't. We couldn't absolve anybody's sins. We weren't priests. I think everyone realized that Demetrius was just trying to make them feel better.

"Really? Do you think God will forgive us?" Moghadan asked.

"Yes, I do!" Demetrius assured him. "Your life, and the lives of Yousry and Magdi, is being cut short through no fault of yours. I have had a full life. I wish it could be much longer, but I have found a woman to be my wife whom I love very much. I have had children whom I love very much. I have been blessed with a young grandson whom I love very much. I am a fortunate man in that respect, and I thank God for those blessings. I have had plenty of time to make decisions and to do things that are pleasing to God.

"You have not lived long enough to experience those things. It makes me cry just to think of how your life is going to be ended before it really begins … the same for all the rest of you, young and old, too. It is so sad, but you should not think that you are unworthy. And remember what St. Mark taught us: 'He who covers or hides his sins will not prosper, but he who confesses his sins and forsakes them will have mercy.' And God will have mercy on your souls. I'm sure of it."

"And if we confess our sins, He who is faithful and just will forgive us our sins and cleanse us and make us righteous. That comes right from the Bible," Abanoub added.

"And Jesus told his apostles that if they forgave sins, then sins were forgiven," Demetrius added.

"But only a priest can forgive sins," Cyril reminded everyone, "and there are no priests in this room."

"What Cyril says is true, but remember: before there were priests, followers of Christ confessed their sins to each other, and that is what we are doing. It is the best we can do. So please, have faith. Do you remember the act of contrition?"

"I do," Moghadan responded.

"Then say it … all three of you," Demetrius said.

The three of them spoke together: "Father, I have sinned against heaven and before you. I am no longer worthy to be called your son. I am sorry for all my sins with all my heart. I detest my sins because they offend thee, my God. I firmly resolve, with Your help, to sin no more. I ask You to forgive me for my sins. Amen."

The other two mumbled along with him, but I could clearly hear Moghadan's words because he was sitting closest to me.

"If you were honest about what you have told us, and you are truly sorry for your sins, I am sure that the three of you are forgiven and that you will meet God with clean hearts," Demetrius told them.

"I agree," Theophilos added.

"You really think so?" Moghadan asked.

"I have no doubt about it," Demetrius replied.

"I hope you're right," he replied.

I knew Moghadan pretty well. I talked to him more than any of the others, except for my brothers. I could tell that he was really scared of what was going to happen to us in the morning, but I think he was more afraid of going to hell than he was about having his head cut off.

I still expected a miracle to happen. I didn't believe I was going to die; I just knew that somehow, some way, we were going to be saved.

"And the same goes for the rest of you young men, who are not much older than these three. Make a good confession and trust in your God to be with you at this time of need."

"Demetrius," Moghadan said, "if God forgives us for our sins, as you say He will, then I'm sure He will forgive your sins, too."

"Thank you, my son," Demetrius responded. "I hope you are right. Anyone else? Touma? Guirguis?"

At that, Touma said, "I'll go next."

CHAPTER 16

Touma Repents

Touma was five years older than me. After he finished school, when he couldn't find a decent job in al-Aour, he went to Cairo with a couple of his other friends, who weren't with us, and he was gone for several years. He'd come home several times each year, but he'd been out of the house for a while.

In fact, Guirguis took his room when he left, and he didn't want to share it when Touma came back. He wanted Touma to sleep on the couch in the living room area. I was in the smaller room with my younger brother, and I was looking forward to the time when both of them would be gone, so I could get a room to myself.

I wasn't sure what he was going to say, but I thought it would probably be a lot like what Moghadan and the others had said. I was wrong.

"I am a sinner, and I wish to confess my sins, or repent of them, as Cyril says I must do. This isn't easy for me, because I am about to say some things that my brothers, Guirguis and Mekhaeil, don't know about me, and neither does anyone else … things that I'm not proud of.

"As most of you know, I went to Cairo not long after I finished school, but not to go to university. I went looking for work. My friends Pishoy and Viktor, whom many of you know, went with me, but we had a hard time finding jobs or a place to stay, since we had no money, so they came back after a short while.

"I made some friends in Cairo, and they gave me a place to

stay. They helped me find a job, and I started to make a little money. They introduced me to their friends, showed me around, and took me to some of their parties. Before long, I was drinking and having fun with them. I was having more fun than I ever had in my life. It was not like the things we did in our little village. I was happy there, or at least I thought I was.

"They took me to places where there were many different kinds of people—people from different parts of Egypt and from other countries, and from different religions, too. There were many Muslims there, some Jews, and some other types of Christians—not all Copts. I didn't know who was who, but everybody was friendly. It was fun. I thought we were all the same.

"In our little village, everybody we know is a Copt. There are Muslims there too, but we Copts keep to ourselves, as you know. Everybody knows everybody's parents, brothers and sisters, and all. We know where to go and where not to go. We don't go to places where we know there might be problems.

"But in Cairo, I was with these people, and I really didn't know them that well. Things are different in Cairo than they are in our village. The people are different. They think differently, they act differently ... it's just different, a lot different, and it took me time to adjust.

"That was about the time when Egypt was having elections and everybody was talking about who should win and this and that. I didn't know anything about what was going on. I had never voted in an election before. I didn't even vote in that election, I'm sorry to say. But when the Muslim Brotherhood took over, things really changed. I saw several of the Christians I had met lose their jobs. I saw how it was when Morsi became the president. Even on the streets, in bars, in restaurants ... everywhere ... things changed. When my friends and I went to places, if there were Muslims there, we knew there could be trouble. But most of the time, I couldn't tell who was a Muslim and who wasn't. As Copts, most of us wear a cross, but often it's under our clothes, where it can't be seen.

"I'm not one to start trouble, but I said the wrong thing to someone at a party one night, and we got into a fight. My friends broke it up and got me out of there before anything bad happened, but that man didn't like me just because I was a Copt. I had said something to him about how bad things had been since the Brotherhood took over, and he took offense.

"I stayed away from the bars for a while after that, but things kept getting worse. The people I was staying with were Copts, like us, and some of them got angry about the way things were, and they started doing some bad things in response, to retaliate against what was being done to them. I tried to stay out of it, but sometimes I'd get myself in trouble just by being with them.

"One night as I was walking back to the apartment where I was staying after I had had more to drink than I should have, I came across that guy I had been in a fight with. He was walking down one side of the street, and I was walking down the other. He was alone, and so was I. I saw him before he saw me, and I tried to avoid him by ducking into an alley, but he saw me, and when he did, he came after me right away. We got into a fight, and fortunately for me, I won."

Touma hesitated. I could tell he was upset talking about these things.

"But I knew he was hurt pretty badly. I'm sure he had a broken nose, because he was bleeding a lot, and he wasn't conscious. In fact, I'm not sure if he lived or died. I didn't call for help or anything. I just ran off before anyone could catch me.

"The next day, when I woke up, I was afraid the police would come find me and I would be taken to jail, so I decided to leave Cairo right then and there. One of the guys I had become friends with knew some people at Port Said and he had told me, before all this happened, that there were jobs we could get on the docks.

"I left that morning for Port Said. I didn't even tell my friends that I was leaving or where I was going or anything. I just left. I was scared."

"You went to Port Said?" Guirguis asked. "I didn't know that."

"I didn't tell you or anyone else. I knew our parents wouldn't have allowed me to go. I didn't want to go home as a failure, with no money and nothing to show for all the work I had done.

"A guy said that there was plenty of work there because of all the shipping business that goes on at the port. It's the second biggest city in Egypt, next to Cairo, and it's a huge place. When I got there, I couldn't believe all the ships that were there, and all the trucks, cranes, and tractors to move stuff in and out of them. It was enormous.

"I found out pretty quickly that Port Said was a really bad place for Copts. It was supposedly a lot better for us before Morsi took office, but after he became president, everything was being run by the Brotherhood. Most of the workers were Muslims to begin with, and I was told that Copts weren't able to get any of the good jobs after the Brotherhood took over.

"The only job I could find was loading trucks and doing hard manual labor, which was the lowest paying job there was; jobs like that were the ones the Muslims didn't want. I got hired right away, found myself a place to stay, and ended up staying there for almost a year.

"But when the army ousted Morsi, things got worse for us—much worse. The Muslims started attacking Christians, especially Copts. They burned the church I was attending, and many people were beaten badly by mobs of angry men. After that happened several times, some of the young men got guns, knives, and other weapons so we could defend ourselves.

"I was given a gun, and—"

"You got a gun, Touma?" Guirguis asked.

I didn't know anyone who had a gun. They were hard to find, and I thought only the criminals, the police, and the army had guns. The government controlled that. I was as surprised as Guirguis to hear Touma say that.

"Yes," he responded. "I did. It was a small one. I don't know how or where they got them, but I carried it around with me all the time, even when I was at work. I slept with it under my pillow. We were always afraid that something might happen to us.

"One night I was with some other men guarding the church. About midnight, several trucks drove up and men jumped out of them. They lit some torches and started running toward the church.

There were more of them than us, and we knew they were going to destroy our church if they could, but we were ready for them.

"They didn't know we were there. We surprised them, and after several minutes of cross fire, they turned and ran away, leaving the bodies of several men behind.

"Not long after they drove off, we could hear the sirens of the police coming, and we ran off. We were gone by the time they got there. Over the next few days, I found out that the police were looking for me and the others.

Again I was afraid that I would be arrested and taken to jail. That's when I decided to leave Port Said. That's when I went back home. I didn't want to go anywhere else after that. I didn't want to come here, but as you all know, there was no work in our village ... I had no choice."

I could hear my brother crying, and he said, "But I brought two of my younger brothers with me ..." He cried some more, and after several moments, he went on.

"So I have sinned, and I have done little to make me worthy of heaven," he said through his tears.

Demetrius asked him, "Touma, have you told us all that you wish to tell us?"

"No. There is more. I killed at least one of the Muslims that night, and maybe more; I'm not sure. I fired all the bullets I had. I saw men fall and didn't see them get up. They were still lying on the ground when I ran off. If I didn't kill them, I'm sure they were badly wounded."

No one made a noise for some time, and then Abanoub said, "Is it wrong to kill someone who is trying to kill you? Is it wrong to kill someone who wants to destroy our church and kill our people? I say it is not! I don't think you did anything wrong, Touma. I don't!"

No one else spoke, and then Demetrious asked again, "Is there anything else you would like to tell us, Touma?"

"No," he responded.

"Say a good act of contrition to yourself, Touma, and may God have mercy on your soul," Demetrius said solemnly.

CHAPTER 17

Cyril Repents

At that, Cyril spoke up: "I would like to go next. I am a sinner, and I wish to repent my sins to you, my brothers. I am heartily sorry for the sins I have committed and for all the things I have failed to do that I should have done. I ask for your forgiveness and that the Lord, our God, can forgive me as well.

"We are all alike in that most of us come from the same village, and the rest are from villages nearby—except for Omar, that is. Most of us went to the same church, to the same schools, and we know each other's families and friends, like Touma just said. I am younger than Demetrius, Raghib, and Rushdi, but I am older than most of the rest of you, but we are all the same, really. We are Coptic Christians first and foremost. That is what defines us. That is what makes us who and what we are. That is what makes us brothers.

"We are proud of our Egyptian heritage, and I think we're all proud of where we come from, even though it's a small village not famous for much of anything. That's where our fathers and mothers, and their fathers and mothers, and their fathers and mothers before them, came from. That's who we are too. We can trace our families back to the time of Jesus Christ and the time when St. Mark came to Egypt. We are truly blood brothers. There is no doubt we are all related to one another, even though we may not know how.

"I am so deeply saddened to think we are all going to die

tomorrow—as much for you as I am for myself—but I am proud to be with all of you at this time of great sorrow. I love each and every one of you. I do. I will be proud to die with you for our church, for our religion, for our God, and for who we are. I love who you are and what you are. We are going to die tomorrow because of our faith. These men who will kill us are deranged men who believe that what they are doing is what their god wants them to do, but there is only one true God, and our God must have a reason for allowing this to happen.

"Our God wants us to love our neighbors as we love ourselves. Our God wants us to turn the other cheek when we are spit upon. When our God, Jesus Christ, was dying on the cross, He asked our Father in heaven to forgive the men who were killing him because, as he said, 'they know not what they do.'

"That is what our God tells us to do. He doesn't tell us to go out and kill anyone who doesn't believe in Him! He tells us to do our best to bring the good news of Jesus Christ to them, to show that we are Christians by our love. Our God is better than their god. We know that is true.

"My brothers, I want you to know that I look forward to what is going to happen to us tomorrow. I do. I know that sounds crazy. I know how sad you all are that you will never see your loved ones again. I know how sad it is that you, and especially you young men, will never experience things that you should have been able to experience in this lifetime.

"I know how afraid you all must be as to how we are to meet our death. I am just as afraid, but I will not show that fear to these men who are going to kill us in the morning. I will go to my death with a smile on my face. I will.

"I will look these men in the eye, and I will tell them with my eyes that I am not afraid of them. I will let them know that I go to meet my God with joy and gladness. I want them to know that I believe what we preach.

"I believe that all of you are going to heaven tomorrow. I believe that our God will welcome all of you into His loving arms. I believe that you are all going to be martyrs, just as Jesus Christ was a martyr, and just as St. Mark was a martyr, and just as the thousands upon thousands of our Coptic brothers and sisters before us have been martyrs since the time Jesus Christ walked upon this earth and told us how to gain everlasting life.

"In fact, my brothers, in a strange way, we should thank these evil men for what they are going to do to us. They are making martyrs of you all. You are dying because you are followers of Christ. You are going to heaven because of what they are going to do to you. Be proud of that.

"Think what it must have been like for Christ as He carried the cross through the streets of Jerusalem on His way to Golgotha; or what it was like for St. Mark to be dragged through the streets of Alexandria; or of St. Peter, who was crucified on a cross by the emperor Nero. He was hung upside down, at his request, because he told them he was not worthy enough to die as Christ had died.

"And think of all of the other apostles, saints, and followers of Christ who were killed because of their belief that Jesus Christ is the Lord and Savior.

"Yes, my brothers, you should be proud to die as martyrs … proud to die because of your faith in the teachings of Jesus Christ … thankful for it, in fact.

"I believe that what Demetrius has told us is true. I believe that if you make a good act of contrition and repent of your sins, you will be forgiven for your sins and all of us will be welcomed into heaven tomorrow, no matter what you have done in your lives before now.

"Think of the two men who died on the cross with Jesus Christ … remember them? Both of them were surly criminals who deserved to die for their crimes, but one of those men, the man on His right, named Demas, saw that Jesus Christ was innocent, and he recognized Jesus as the Messiah.

"Remember what Jesus said to him? He told the man that he would be in heaven with Him and meet God that very day. He told him, 'Today you will be with me in paradise.' The worst of us here is not as bad as that thief, yet Jesus forgave him. Your sins will be forgiven, and your faith will save you, just as it saved that man.

"I believe that. I believe it with all my heart. I hope that all of you believe it just as I do and that you will all meet in heaven tomorrow. I hope, and I pray, that none of you will be like the other thief, who cried and lamented his bad fortune in being caught and punished for his crimes. That man didn't confess his sins. He didn't repent. He wasn't sorry for what he had done. He was sorry only for being caught and punished.

"I believe that if you are truly sorry for your sins, no matter how bad they are, and if you truly pray for forgiveness, God will grant those prayers. I believe all of that. I believe that with all my heart, and I hope you do too."

Cyril exhaled and was quiet for a few moments. No one spoke, because we knew that he wasn't finished. He had yet to reveal his sins. A few seconds later, he continued.

"Yes, my brothers, I believe all that I have just said, but that was the Deacon in me—the part of me that made me want to become a priest. Now comes the hard part. I must repent of my sins as a fellow human being, just as you have, and I must do so fully and completely, and I must be sincere in doing so. I must be open and honest. I must tell you everything, holding nothing back; and that is not an easy thing to do, but I must. If I want to be saved, and I do, that is what I must do.

"So here goes. I am not who and what you think I am. I'm not the godly man that you all think I am; nor am I the godly man who I wanted to be. I am a sinner who hides in the shadows.

"Yes, I wanted to become a priest, and yes, I studied to become a priest, but as you all know, I didn't succeed. I wasn't able to accomplish that. Many of you probably think that I will someday, but that isn't going to happen, and that is my greatest disappointment in life.

"I truly believe—with all of my mind, heart, and soul—everything I have said to you here tonight, and I believe in our God and everything our religion stands for. So you might wonder why I didn't succeed. Why have I failed? Why didn't I become a priest?

Cyril hesitated for several seconds. "This isn't easy for me. There are very few people in the world who know what I am about to tell you. I am a homosexual."

Several men gasped, while others murmured. Chains rattled, but no one said anything. Cyril continued. "I have been able to hide it from everyone for years, although I'm sure there are some who may have suspected it. My parents don't know. They would never understand. My father still hopes I'll change my mind and become a priest. My mother still hopes I'll find a woman, get married, and give her a grandchild. It would break their hearts if they knew the truth. I'm their only child.

"You all think of me as a devout Christian—one who is always helping at the church and always at whatever functions the church has going on, and you thought that when I wasn't there on Sundays, I was in Alexandria or Cairo, working at our mother church—and I was, occasionally, but most of those weekends when I was away, I was with a man."

Again there were murmurs, but they weren't as loud this time. The initial shock had worn off, apparently.

"My lover is a man much like me. He, too, wanted to be a priest, and he, too, failed. We found each other at the seminary, and we stayed in touch with one another. It wasn't until several years after we both discontinued our studies that we became physically involved with one another.

"Neither one of us was forced to leave, because the church never found out the truth, but we both left for the same reason. We both told the church leaders that we were unable to keep the vow of celibacy. They assumed that was because we were attracted to women and that we wanted to have wives and families.

"As you all know, our priests are invited into the priesthood, and I had been invited. Our church has deacons, priests, and bishops. Our priests must be married before ordination. Our deacons can be either celibate or married, whichever they choose. When I went off to seminary, my dream was to become a bishop. I planned on being celibate, because bishops must be celibate.

"As you all know, there are several kinds of deacons. The first, or lowest, category is that of hymnists, or epsaltos, and I became one of them at a young age. I became an arch-epsaltos, or leader of the hymnists, by the time I was sixteen, as some of you may remember. The next type of deacon is an ognostis, or reader, and I became one of them at a very early age too. The next level is the epideacon, which has more responsibilities.

"So when I returned to our church and told people that my plan was to become an epideacon—which was, and still is, theoretically possible—no one questioned me.

"As all of you now know, that is not possible either, because of what I have told you. Truly, I cannot become more than what I am … an ognostis … and even that is a lie. If we were to live beyond tomorrow, by some miracle, I would have to step down from that position, since my secret is now no longer secret."

"I would not tell anyone of what you have told us," Demetrius said. "A confession is intended to be a private conversation with God, or His representatives, and we are His representatives tonight. I want all of you to know that is how I feel, and I would ask all of you to agree to do the same, if by some miracle we don't die tomorrow."

Before anyone could answer, Cyril continued. "Thank you for saying that, Demetrius, but this is not a confession; it is a repentance. It is not confidential, and we both know I could no longer pretend to be something I am not. You and everyone here would know, even if you didn't tell anyone else, that I was living a lie, and we all know that neither you nor anyone else in this room will ever think of me the same way as you did a few minutes ago. I am now, and will forever be, an outcast from our church.

"Our church, which I love very much, recognizes homosexuality as a sin. There is no hope of redemption for a homosexual. It is a sin against the Holy Bible, against our traditions, and against the teachings of our church. Copts think it is a crime against humanity, as if we are less than human!

"Unless and until our church changes its position on this, and that is not likely to happen in my lifetime, I am doomed. Our church says that I will burn in hell because of what I am. I can only hope that God will see things differently."

The room was silent for several moments, and Cyril's words seemed to echo. Then Demetrius said, "If you were in the United States, you wouldn't have that problem, would you?"

"But we're not in the United States, are we?" Cyril responded. "Besides, the Coptic Church in America is the same as it is here. It is true that some of the other Christian churches have become more tolerant about such things, but not ours; and we're about to die anyway, aren't we? So what am I to do?"

"If you repent of your sin, the sin of homosexuality, God could forgive you, couldn't he, Cyril?" Moghadan asked. "That's what Demetrius just told us, didn't he? That God can forgive all sins, right?"

"But that is part of the problem, Moghadan," Cyril answered. "I don't think that it is a sin."

"If that's true, then you cannot be forgiven, Cyril, can you?" Raghib asked.

"No, I can't," he replied, and he began to cry.

"You are just like me then," Raghib said, "We are both doomed."

Cyril sobbed for several minutes before continuing.

"You see, our church thinks that people who are homosexuals *choose* to be homosexuals, and that is not true! I wish, with all my heart, that I were not what I am. I didn't choose this; this is the way God made me! I swear to you! I do not want to be what I am! I am not proud of what I am!"

And he began to cry more. Several minutes later, he continued.

"No society in the world has accepted homosexuality as normal."

"Except in the United States," Rushdi said. "Such people have the same rights as every other person."

"That's not entirely true, Rushdi," Cyril responded. "Even in the United States, where the laws say that homosexuals have the same rights as all others, they still aren't seen as normal. They are treated differently. They are still discriminated against, despite those laws designed to protect them.

"Ever since Sodom and Gomorra, the act of a man having sex

with another man has been seen as abhorrent—an unnatural and immoral lust. The very word 'sodomy' comes from those days. The Bible is full of references to the punishment homosexuals are to receive at the hand of God for their crimes, and they are seen as crimes," he sobbed.

"Yet knowing that, you cannot change your way of thinking, Cyril?" Demetrius asked.

"I cannot!" Cyril screamed. "Why don't you believe me!"

At that the doors flew open again, and several men rushed in, yelling at us as they came.

"Shut up, you dogs! Shut up! What is going on in here? Are you trying to get away?" one yelled as he walked around the room, kicking men and checking to make sure that the chains were still on all of us. The other two stood at the doorway but didn't say anything.

"Can we have some more water?" Boctor asked.

"No, you can't have any more water!" the man responded. The man kicked Boctor's feet as he said this.

"You will have more water only if I say so, and I say no! I was sleeping, and you woke me up. If you wake me up again, I will beat you … all of you! Do you hear me?"

No one made a sound. After several minutes of stomping around and hitting people on their legs with a large stick, he left, and as he did, he once again yelled at us, saying, "Shut up and go to sleep!"

We were quiet for quite a long time, but I'm sure no one was sleeping. I wasn't. Demetrius then whispered, "Cyril, I must say that I am surprised by what you have told us. I admit that I have believed all of my life that homosexuals choose to be homosexuals. From what you have said, and with the sincerity of your words, I now wonder if that is true."

"I promise you, Demetrius, it is not true," Cyril told him.

"At least for you, Cyril" Abanoub said. "I don't think that is true for most homosexuals. Is it?"

"I doubt that you, or anyone else in here, Abanoub, knows any homosexuals, so how could you know that?" Cyril asked.

No one responded to that comment, probably because it was true. I didn't know any homosexuals.

"Given our circumstances, Cyril has no reason to lie. Truly, he had no reason to confess his sin to us," Raghib said. "I never would have told anyone what I told all of you if I didn't think we would be killed in the morning. I would have gone to my grave with those secrets. To me, he has made a true confession—much more than a repentance. If all sins can be forgiven, then it seems to me that you, too, should be forgiven. Don't you think that is true, Demetrius?"

Demetrius sighed and said, "I am not a priest. Cyril is the closest thing we have to a priest with us here tonight. He should know the law of the church better than anyone else, and I'm sure he does. Cyril, tell us … can all sins be forgiven?"

Cyril responded, "A priest has the power, given to him by Jesus Christ Himself, to forgive sins, but Christ didn't say that all sins were to be forgiven or that some sins could never be forgiven. He said to the apostles, 'If you remit the sins of man on earth, they will be forgiven in heaven as well,' or something like that, so I would say that a priest has the ability to decide what sins are to be forgiven and what sins are not to be forgiven. But there are no priests here with us tonight, so I can't answer your question. Sorry."

Again the men were silent.

Then Theophilos said, "I am taken by the intensity of the feelings and emotions you have shared with us, Cyril. If it were up to me, which it isn't, I would forgive you."

"Would you forgive me, too, Theo?" Raghib asked.

"Absolutely!" Theophilos responded.

"And how about you, Abanoub?" Cyril asked.

"I'm not so sure, Cyril. I will have to think some more about your situation. Our church is firm on such things."

"I thought so," Cyril replied, "and I agree with you. As a matter of fact, our church is quite firm on such matters, isn't it? There is little room for doubt, is there?"

"Did you ever consider becoming a monk?" Asaad asked.

Asaad had been very quiet all night long. I thought that might have been the first time he spoke, but I wasn't sure. Asaad was in the group of men in their late twenties. He kept to himself. He and Sarabamoon were good friends. He was a tall, very thin man—probably the tallest man in our group. He was well over six feet tall. Most of us were nowhere near as tall.

"No, Asaad," Cyril responded, "that was not possible either. Monks struggle with their physical needs, and they try to force their desires to submit to their will, but they are required to be celibate too. That was not an option for me."

"But you could have kept your secret better, perhaps," Asaad persisted.

"Actually, Asaad, I'd say I kept my secret well, wouldn't you agree?" Cyril responded. "I just couldn't keep it from myself, because now I've told all of you."

"So you crave sexual relations with other men?" Boctor asked, "just as we crave sexual relations with women?"

Some of the other young men giggled at that. That was all some of them ever talked about. I had friends who were girls, but I had never had sex with any. I had never thought of having sex with any of my friends who were boys, though. I didn't want to think about them in that way.

"That's right, Boctor," Cyril responded. "I love my partner; I do. Of all the people in the world I will miss seeing, it is him I will be thinking of when I die."

"Even more than your parents, Cyril?" Abanoub asked.

"That's a hard one. Will you who have wives miss your wives more than your parents, brothers, sisters, friends, and other family members? Or your children? I don't know. It's different. I will miss them all, and I will miss all of you, too."

Again everyone was silent, and then Demetrius said, "Let's not discuss this topic any further, please. Let Cyril finish his repentance. We all know it's a sin to have sexual relations before marriage, or to have sexual relations with anyone other than your wife during a marriage, or to have sex with a woman to whom you are not married, even after your wife dies. Those are the laws of our church. If any of us commit those sins, we must confess them. Cyril's problem is that he prefers a man over a woman. It is still a problem involving sex, and that is a problem for all of us, isn't it?"

"But you don't burn in hell for those sins, do you, Demetrius? But I will," Cyril responded bitterly.

"Adultery is a serious offense, Cyril," Demetrius replied.

"But not as serious as mine," Cyril responded.

Then Demetrius asked, "Is there anything else you wanted to tell us, Cyril, before we move on?"

"No. That is the only sin I have to confess. In all other ways, I have lived, or tried to live, an honorable life, but I am ashamed of who I am and what I am. I ask you for your understanding—and for forgiveness, even though it will do no good."

"It took great courage for you to give us your confession, Cyril," Demetrius told him. "I wish there was something we could say or do to lessen your pain, but I'm afraid I can't think of anything to say, other than that your fate will be in God's hands. He will decide what that will be, not us. I wish for you the best that can be, whatever that is. Who would like to go next?" When no one spoke up, he said, "Mekhaeil, what about you? Do you have anything that you wish to tell us?"

I had been silent, listening to every word spoken by the others, and his question hit me like a bullet. I wasn't ready for it. I stuttered and told him that I didn't have anything to say.

CHAPTER 18

The Morning Comes

I don't remember much after that. It was at that point in the night that I fell asleep, overcome by exhaustion. The last words I remember hearing were from Demetrius, who was asking the others who hadn't spoken yet if they wanted some time to repent of their sins to themselves or if they would share their thoughts with the others. Guirguis hadn't said anything yet, and I wish I had been able to stay awake to hear what he had to say.

When I awoke, I heard Omar say, "I would rather die with you than live with these misguided men."

Demetrius said, "Then we are all agreed; that is what we will do. We will die as Copts."

I didn't know exactly what they had decided to do, but I figured they had agreed that no one would convert. I was going to do whatever everybody else did.

A rooster was crowing just outside our building. That was what woke me up. I tried to wipe the sleep from my face, but with my hands chained behind me, I couldn't. I moved my head as far as I could in either direction, but I was unable to get my head to make contact with any part of my body except by bringing my knees up and leaning forward as far as I could.

When I did that, Sarabamoon, who was on my right, said, "Are you ready for the day, Mekhaeil?"

I told him I was still praying to God that we would be saved.

"Keep praying," he told me.

No one was talking, but everybody was stirring. We could hear the sounds of men talking outside our room. Some dogs began to bark.

Moghadan, on my other side, said, "I hope you are right, Mekhaeil. We will soon find out our fate."

Touma, who was across the room from me, said, "And Mekhaeil, remember that I love you very much, and I apologize to you for bringing you with us. I wish I had left you behind as our father urged me to do."

Guirguis added, "And that goes for me, too, Mekhaeil. I am very, very sorry also."

"So have you decided what to do? Are you going to convert, or tell them that you will, if they will allow you to do that?" I asked.

"We will never convert, Mekhaeil," Touma responded, "and we won't lie to them and say that we will. We all agreed to die before doing that."

"Everyone?" I asked.

"Everyone," he confirmed.

The sounds of footsteps alerted us that men were approaching our building. Their voices became louder and louder. At that moment, I felt fear.

Up until then, I didn't think we were going to die. I refused to believe that we were going to be killed, despite what everyone else was saying. At the very least, I didn't think we were going to die that morning. I was sure something good would happen. I had remained hopeful, almost confident, that we would be saved somehow.

But when the door to the building flew open and the light of the morning sun caused me to squint, I was afraid—more afraid than I had ever been in my life. When my eyes adjusted, I looked around the room and was able to clearly see everyone else. Everyone was grim. No one said a word.

Several of the terrorists yelled at us, telling us to get on our feet. It wasn't easy to do without being able to use our hands. Our feet were still chained together. I was struggling to get to my feet when Sarabamoon somehow was able to grab my right elbow and help me stand up.

Once we were on our feet, I watched as one of the men standing in the doorway unhooked one end of the chain that ran through the cuffs on our ankles. He pulled on the other end of the chain, which was still attached to the wall, until the chain came out of the cuffs on Abanoub's feet. He was the first man in line.

I was horrified to watch as another terrorist hooked a pole to the collar around Abanoub's neck and then pulled on it violently, yelling at him as he did so, telling him to walk. I watched as the man led him out of the building.

The man was so mean and so cruel that I started to cry. I had never seen the face of that much hate before in my life. I could hear it in his voice, see it in his actions, and feel it inside of me. This man hated Abanoub and all of the rest of us just because we were Christians.

I felt as if I were going to faint. I was afraid I was about to fall down. My knees were shaking. I began to whimper like a baby.

Sarabamoon was able to get his hand on my arm, and he steadied me, but it didn't stop the tears from running down my cheeks.

As soon as the chain was pulled from Rushdi's ankles, another terrorist hooked a pole to his neck and yanked him out the door.

Next up was Cosmos, then Halim, and Cyril, and then Raghib. When they got to Touma, I couldn't help myself; I started to cry uncontrollably.

Touma looked over and yelled, "Be strong, Mekhaeil. I love you! God loves you!"

At that, the man with the pole hit Touma on the side of his head.

"Shut up and walk!" the man yelled.

"He's just a boy!" Touma yelled back.

At that, the man hit him again. Touma fell to the ground. The man yanked Touma to his feet and yelled at him some more.

Next was Theophilos, and then Magdi, Demetrius, Yousry, Nabir, and Boctor. When they got to Guirguis, I cried all the louder.

"Be strong, Mekhaeil!" he yelled at me. "I love you, my brother!"

A terrorist hit him across his back, causing him to fall, and dragged him off, not waiting for Guirguis to get to his feet.

Then it was Omar. The man with the chain seemed to hesitate a little, probably because Omar was so much darker skinned than the rest of us. When he did, I thought that maybe the man suspected he wasn't one of us, because he didn't look like we did, but then he was led out like the others.

After Omar, it was Clement, Ignatius, and Maurice. When they got to Moghadan, and I was next, I stopped crying. I sniffled and then said, "I am a Christian! I gladly go to meet my God."

Moghadan said, "Good for you, Mekhaeil. I will see you in paradise tonight."

The man holding him slapped him across the face, told him to shut up, and pulled him past me. Then, after the chain was pulled through my ankles, the man pulled it through Sarabamoon's ankles at the same time. A terrorist put a pole on Sarabamoon's neck and took him away, leaving me standing there. My hands were still chained behind me, and the collar was still around my neck, but my feet were free. I said again, "I am a Christian. I gladly go to meet my God!" A man told me to shut up, but that was it. No one hit me or did anything else about it.

The last man after Sarabamoon was Asaad. Once he was taken outside, there was only the one terrorist left in the building with me. He put his hand on my left elbow and told me to walk. He didn't hook a pole to my collar, and he didn't yell at me as all the others had done.

We walked a few feet outside of the building and came to a stop. I stood there next to him and saw my twenty-one comrades standing in a line, two feet apart, with a terrorist holding a pole in front of each. All of the men still had their hands cuffed behind them.

As I stood there, I looked at each of the men, one by one. Each was looking straight back at me. I knew that each and every one of those men was hoping—and praying, probably—that I would be spared. I felt the love that they had for me, even at the darkest hour in their lives.

As I looked back at them, I felt my chest swell with pride. I took a deep breath, and exhaled, sniffling and sobbing as I did. I could see tears in the eyes of Touma and Guirguis. I said nothing.

I glanced over at the man who was holding me, and I saw that it was the same young boy who had captured me. I didn't say anything to him, and he didn't say anything to me.

At that moment, another man—one of the leaders, apparently—walked over to where the men were standing and said, "To the beach!"

The men sprang into action. Other men started yelling commands, and everyone started moving. They led the men right past where I was standing, in reverse order from the way they had been led out of the building, with Asaad being the first one.

"Faster!" They yelled, and the men began to trot. Each and every one of them looked me straight in the eye as he went past me.

If I live to be a thousand, I will never forget the looks on their faces. I saw no fear in their eyes. I saw defiance. I saw strength. I saw courage. Those men were not afraid to die. I felt a strange sensation. Part of me was saying that I should have been running down the road with the others, yet another part of me was glad that I wasn't. I was proud of them. I was overwhelmed with sadness because of what was about to happen to them, but I was still afraid of what was going to happen to me. I wasn't proud of myself at that moment. I was more afraid than courageous. I said nothing.

I followed them with my eyes as they trotted away. In a matter of seconds, all I could see was their backs. I was able to see a large body of water off in the distance. I hadn't seen it the day before. I watched until they reached the water and came to a stop. At that point, I asked, "Where are you taking me?"

He didn't answer my question but grabbed my left elbow and said, "Walk."

We walked several yards over to where a pickup truck was parked. He began taking the shackles off of my feet and from around my neck, but he left the handcuffs on. Then, when I thought he was going to put me in the truck, he turned me around and said, "Watch."

Though it was several hundred yards away from where we stood, I could clearly see all of the men on their knees, bent over. I watched as one man, who must have been the chief executioner, raised a large sword high above his head and struck the first man in line.

At that point, I closed my eyes, unable to watch further. Several minutes later, the boy turned me around and put me in the backseat of the truck. He stayed outside of the vehicle.

A few minutes later, another man, several years older than either of us, walked up and got in on the driver's side as the boy got in the backseat next to me. He was carrying two small black bags with him, which he threw on the floor on the passenger's side. I didn't think anything of it at the time. Just before he started up the truck, The man pulled a hood from his pocket and said,

"Put this on him until I tell you to take it off."

"Yes, sir, Habibah!" the boy replied.

As the boy was putting the hood on me, the driver asked, "What's your name?"

"Mekhaeil," I responded."

"You are a lucky boy, Mekhaeil. Allah has spared you today," he told me.

At that, Habibah started up the truck, an old Ford, and we sped up the hill. He was driving so fast and kicking up so much dirt that, with the windows down and the wind blowing through the truck, conversation was impossible.

An hour later, the truck skidded to a stop. Habibah told the boy to take the hood off me and, after my eyes adjusted to the bright sun, I saw that they had brought me back to the construction site from which we had been taken the day before. It was still at least a mile away. There was no one around and nothing in between.

The boy, whose name I never learned, got out of the truck, walked around to my side, opened the door, and helped me out. Then he took the handcuffs off of me without saying a word.

He threw one of the bags to me and said, "Here are your clothes. Put them on now."

I thanked him. As soon as I did, I wished that I hadn't. I took off the jumpsuit and put on the clothes he had given me. They weren't mine, but they fit.

The boy put the jumpsuit in the bag and got back in the truck. Then he looked at me and said, "Go! Tell the world what you have seen! Allahu Akbar!"

At that, they spun around and sped off back the way we had come. I stood there watching until the truck was out of sight. I was able to see the trail of dust for miles as it climbed the hills.

I didn't know quite what to make of his last words to me at the time, but I understood at that moment why they had let me go. They wanted the world to know what they had done. They weren't ashamed of what they did at all.

I stood there in a daze for several minutes, and then fear returned. The thought entered my mind that they might turn around and come back and get me, so I began to hurriedly walk toward the place where, less than twenty-four hours earlier, my entire life had been changed forever. After a minute or two, I began to run.

CHAPTER 19

My Return to Egypt

Half an hour later, when I was back within the construction site, I sat down, tired from the walking and running but mostly still dazed and very confused. I put my head in my hands and cried. What was I going to do now?

No one was in or around the building where we had been working, and I couldn't see anyone or hear any sounds of work being done anywhere nearby. After what had happened to us the day before, I figured that the job may have been completely shut down, at least for a while, until adequate security could be provided so it wouldn't happen again.

Part of me was thankful that I was alive, that I hadn't been beheaded, but another part of me felt some shame for what had happened. I thought of my brothers, and of Demetrius, Rushdi, Raghib, Cyril, and all the others. I thought of all that had happened within the last twenty-four hours, and it felt like a lifetime ago. I thought of all the things I had heard and all the thoughts that had gone through my mind in the last day, and then I cried some more.

The longer I sat there, and the more I thought about things, the more ashamed of myself I became. Omar's words rang through my brain repeatedly. He had preferred to die with my brothers and my friends than to live with the men that killed them. I wished that I had made the same decision, and then I cried even more.

Minutes later, I forced myself to get up, and I walked aimlessly through the deserted construction site until I came to the road that ran in front of the main entrance to the area. I sat down on a large stone and watched as a few cars passed by. Not long after, I saw a microbus coming down the road toward me. I stuck out my thumb.

The bus stopped within a few feet of where I was sitting, and the side door opened up. My first reaction was one of apprehension, not knowing who was in the vehicle or what they might want from me. I was still traumatized after what had happened the day before.

The driver asked, "You want a ride or not?"

I noticed that the bus was nearly full of passengers, several of whom were women with little children.

I stood up, walked to the vehicle, and said, "Yes, but I don't have any money."

The driver, who was a young man, must have felt sorry for me, as he said, "That's okay. Jump in!"

I heard some women groan, because there wasn't much room left. A young woman in the back row grabbed her young son and moved to her left, leaving some space for me. I squeezed myself in. Once I was seated, the woman moved as far away from me as she could. I'm sure I smelled awful.

"Where are you headed?" the driver asked.

"Where are you going?" I responded.

"This bus is headed for Marsa el Brega," he replied.

"Is that as far as you go?" I asked.

"Yes, but there are other buses that will take you as far as Cairo and beyond, though you'll have to pay to do that. Not all drivers are as nice as I am," he said with a smile.

I thanked him, told him that was where I was going, and then closed my eyes. I was still very tired from the night before and wanted to keep to myself. He tried to engage me in conversation, and I responded with short answers. I didn't tell him anything about what had really happened to me. I was afraid to tell him the truth.

As I sat in the bus, I looked at all the other passengers and wondered if they were Muslims, Christians, or Jews. I wasn't about to ask. Since there were no men on the bus other than the driver and some young boys, I didn't feel threatened, but I was distrustful. I didn't know who or what they were or what they might say or do if they knew what I'd been through.

I'm sure I looked as pitiful as I felt, or worse. One of the younger women, who had two small children with her, must have been able to tell how thirsty I was. She handed me a bottle of water without saying anything to me. I nodded my thanks and drank it slowly, a little at a time.

The bus ride to Marsa el Brega took most of the day. There were a number of stops along the way, with people getting on and off at every stop, it seemed. The woman sitting next to me got off at the very first stop. I wondered if she did that just to get away from me.

I felt ostracized from the world and everyone in it, as though I were an outsider or an unwanted guest. I had never felt anything like that before. Instead of being my normal, friendly self, I became paranoid—afraid of whom I might be talking to. I avoided everyone's glances.

Marsa el Brega had been a small, fishing village many years ago, but now it was Libya's biggest port for the tankers carrying oil and other petroleum products. It was on the Gulf of Sidra, and the coastal highway we were on connected it with Tripoli and Benghazi and went from there on to Cairo. We had passed through it on our way to Sirte from our homes in Egypt months before.

I remembered the conversation that had taken place when some of the older men were telling me and the others all about the city and how it had grown. I remembered how we were all smiling, happy to have a job and to be able to make some money. We had been in a bus much like the one I was in. I remembered where everyone had been sitting. I could see their faces. It brought tears to my eyes.

Once the bus arrived in Marsa el Brega, I found myself at

what had to be the main hub for all the microbuses in the city. There were hundreds of them. I had been told that they were the most common form of transportation in the country, even more so than trains and the larger buses, but I had never seen anything like it; there were so many vehicles in that one place.

The first thing I did was find a bathroom. There were no showers, but I used soap, water, and paper towels to clean myself up as best I could. I brushed my teeth, using the soap, with my finger.

I hadn't had anything to eat in over twenty-four hours. My last meal was lunch the day before. I was starving, and I was still thirsty. The bottle I had been given was long gone. I drank water from the sink.

When I was finished, I wandered around the terminal area, looking at maps on the wall, trying to decide where to go and how to get there. I didn't know what to do or where to go.

I didn't want to go back home. I didn't want to face my parents or the parents, wives, children, and other relatives of all the men who had died that morning. I didn't want to tell anyone what had happened to us. I was still in Libya, and I was still afraid. Also, I didn't want to have to explain why I was still alive and everyone else wasn't.

I had no money, and I had no idea where I was going to find something to eat. I thought about stealing some crackers or candy bars from the store in the terminal, but I was afraid I'd get caught. I drank some more water from a water fountain in the terminal.

I was exhausted. I didn't get much sleep on the bus, and I had slept very little the night before. I thought about just lying down on one of the benches and falling asleep. It was now late in the day and people were coming and going; many of them were just getting off work.

I watched as people crowded into the buses all around me. As one bus filled up and took off, another bus pulled up, and it was filled up and gone immediately. No one paid any attention to me. I was sitting upright, but I kept dozing off. When my head would fall down, I would wake up.

There were televisions scattered all over the terminal, which was quite large. It was much bigger than a soccer field. I was extremely tired and was so hungry that all I could think about was getting something to eat. I wasn't paying any attention to what the people on TV were saying or what anyone else was doing, but then I heard one of the broadcasters mention the killing of twenty-one Coptic Christians by ISIS.

At that moment, it seemed as if everyone in the building stopped talking, stopped walking, stopped whatever they were doing, and listened to what was being said. A video of the men walking to the beach on their way to being beheaded was shown on the television. Within seconds, a loud murmur erupted into a roar.

I could no longer hear what was being said by the announcers, because the people started shouting. Everyone starting pointing at the television, telling others to watch. They were all horrified by what they saw, but no one as much as I was.

The video showed the men as they walked by very close to where I had been standing, and then it showed them on the beach. It was almost as if it were taken exactly where I had been standing. Fortunately it didn't show the actual beheadings, but it did show the men kneeling down with their heads lowered to the ground, as if they were about to have their heads cut off. The announcers said the men had been beheaded.

I couldn't believe my eyes. There, on television for the world to see, were my brothers and my friends. I just sat and watched, mesmerized by what I was seeing. I put my hands over my face. I didn't want to watch it again, but I couldn't help myself. I had to see what the world was seeing of what had happened to them. I didn't say a word or make a sound.

I wondered who had shot the video and where that person had been standing. How was it that I hadn't seen that being done? How was it that the television station was able to get it?

I thought to myself that Habibah had to have been the one to do it. Everyone else was gathered around my friends as they trotted over the hill to the beach moments before they were killed. I had seen those very same things.

A camera or camcorder must have been in the other black bag Habibah had been carrying. He must have been the one to shoot the video, and he must have been the one to have taken it to a television station or to someone who would make sure the video made it to a television station. That was the only explanation I could think of.

The announcer said that ISIS claimed responsibility for the killings. Not only had these people killed my friends, but they were proud of it. They didn't try to hide it. They were bragging about what they had done. It sickened me even more.

So why had they let me go? They had already shown the world what they had done. Did they want me to explain it to people in gory detail? The video was gory enough. I wondered why I wasn't killed too.

My heart and my mind were full of hatred for them—even more so than when I was their prisoner, if that was possible. I'm sure I was still in a state of shock from what I'd been through, and not thinking clearly. Still, I wasn't about to tell anyone that I had been there.

As I considered it, the thought occurred to me that some people might think that I must have converted, and I didn't want them to think that. They would ask how it was that I hadn't been killed. What would I tell them?

I continued to stare at the television set, but I wasn't listening. I kept my head in my hands, with my elbows on my knees, peering through the slits between my fingers. They didn't show any close-ups, but I saw each and every man, especially my two brothers, clearly in my mind.

There were close-ups of Moghadan and Sarabamoon as they walked by the camera. I couldn't believe it. It had been less than twelve hours or so since the killings had occurred, yet there it was, on TV for the world to see. I felt sick to my stomach, as if I were going to throw up.

I was unable to move. It was as though I were frozen or numb. This was clearly the biggest story of the day in Libya—and the world, probably—so every few minutes, the announcers would retell the story for everyone who might have missed it the first time.

At one point, I saw that the video was on every TV throughout the entire terminal, on different channels and in different languages. And there were dozens of television sets sitting high above the floor of the building. Al Jazeera was broadcasting in Arabic. Libya's TV was on, and there was an English-speaking station too.

Some people continued to shout. Other people sat down and cried. I was sure those people must have been Christians. Others went on their way back to their lives. Buses continued to run. Life went on.

By the end of the half-hour telecast, or when the news portion of it was over, other daily-life stories were being told, such as reports on the weather or sports, just as if it were any other day on earth. To me it was as though the sky had fallen and the world would never be the same. To others it was just another story of atrocities that were occurring all across the Middle East.

No matter what show was on, a ticker would appear at the bottom of the television screen saying that twenty-one Coptic Christians had been beheaded by ISIS in Libya. That's when I knew that it had been ISIS who had captured us. The initial shock had worn off, though. People weren't reacting as they had earlier.

Every now and then, there would be a segment in which the announcer would say something like "We interrupt this broadcast to bring you news of a horrifying event that occurred just outside of Sirte, Libya, earlier today …" They would proceed to tell the story and show the video again and again. Occasionally someone who hadn't heard the news already would yell and scream.

Before the news came on, I had been thinking that I might be the only one in the world to know about what happened. I never dreamed that the terrorists would tell the world about it, and I could not have imagined that they would have videotaped it for the world to see. I was stunned by the level of hatred that it took for those men to do those things.

Part of me was relieved to know that the world had found

out what had happened. At least I no longer had to worry about being the one to break the horrible news to family members back in our village. Now I was aware that everyone knew that we had been captured and killed.

I thought to myself that everyone back in al-Aour would be thinking that I died too. They wouldn't have known about Omar. Twenty-one of us had left Egypt to go to Libya, and twenty-one men had been killed.

Raghib was using a different name, so no one would know that he was there. I was pretty sure the terrorists wouldn't return the bodies so that a positive identification of the men could be made, but after seeing the video on TV, I wasn't sure of that. My guess was that families and friends from Egypt would be the ones providing information about the men who had been killed. The more I thought about it, the more convinced I was that everyone thought I was dead too.

It was still Saturday, though Friday seemed so long ago, but the fact that no one had been working at the construction site where I had been hours before told me that our employers would have provided the world with information too. By now the world knew the names of everyone captured, and my name was surely on the list.

The owners of the construction project had undoubtedly provided names to the press and government officials, but they would have given the names of twenty-two men, not twenty-one. The ISIS video showed that twenty-one men had been beheaded. Someone would figure out that something was wrong, but that would take a while.

Some people, especially all Copts, would be wondering whether or not there had been any effort to save us. Everyone from my village would want to know if there had been a ransom offer. Some people might have questions about whether we had been given an opportunity to convert. I wondered about those things too.

Though I was still tired and hungry, the video and the news story breathed life back into me. I was now full of something—or rather a whole lot of things, such as rage, anger, confusion, sadness, and depression—but mostly I felt paralyzed. I had nowhere to go, and I was unable to get up. I had no way of expressing what I was feeling, and I had no one to express those feelings to.

I remained sitting on the bench, staring at the TV, for a long time—a couple of hours, maybe. Later the volume of traffic at the terminal died down dramatically. Buses continued to roll through constantly, but the number of buses and the number of people in and around dwindled. I still had no idea where I was going to go or how I was going to get there.

As I sat there in a stupor, I heard some people speaking Arabic with an Egyptian accent. I turned and saw two people, a man and a woman, looking at one of the maps of the city on the wall. They were trying to find a place to rent a car. They had apparently missed the last bus out for wherever it was they were going.

I walked up to them and asked if I could get a ride with them. I told them that I was trying to get to Alexandria. They looked at each other puzzledly. They were an older couple—married, I thought—and weren't in the habit of taking hitchhikers, I was sure.

The woman must have been able to tell how desperate I was, because she was the first to speak. She said, "We are going to Alexandria too."

She turned to the man and asked, "What do you say, Gabriel?"

As soon as I heard her say his name, my heart jumped. That was my father's name, and Gabriel was the name of nearly a dozen Coptic popes over the centuries, many of whom had been martyrs. I thought that they must be Christians, and Copts at that.

The man had somewhat of a pained expression on his face, and if it had been up to him, I doubt that he would have given me a ride. I know that I looked pathetic, and I'm sure I still smelled bad. He looked at me and then said to his wife, "If it is all right with you, then it is all right with me."

Then he said to me, "We are looking to rent a car. Do you know where we can do that?"

I told him that I didn't, and then he looked back at the map and said, "I believe there is a place several blocks away. Would you mind carrying some of our bags? It is a bit too much for my wife and me. We can't carry them all by ourselves."

That was probably the reason they agreed to give me a ride—they needed help carrying their bags. I gladly agreed and picked up two of the four bags lying next to where they were standing—the two biggest ones. The three of us hurried out of the terminal.

As we walked down the street, moving as fast as we could, the man explained, "Our bus arrived late, and we missed the last bus leaving for Alexandria tonight. It's getting late, and we must hurry, or the place may close."

By the time we got there, it was getting dark and it looked like the rental car place was starting to close up. The front door was still open, though, and Gabriel opened it. I was standing behind the two of them and said, "I'll wait outside and watch the bags."

They looked back at me—thinking that I might run off with the bags, I'm sure—and then dropped their bags and hurried inside.

Ten minutes later, they walked back out with keys in hand. I followed them to the car. They had rented a four-door vehicle, which was probably larger than they would have gotten if I hadn't been going with them.

They put most of the luggage in the trunk and some in the backseat, leaving enough room for me. They asked my name, and I told them my real name, Mekhaeil Zacharias, although after I said it, I wished I hadn't.

They introduced themselves to me. Her name was Sofia, and their last name was Ibrahim, both of which were common Coptic Christian names, but I didn't ask them if they were Coptics at that time. I was afraid to, because I feared that if I offended them, they might tell me to get out of their car.

Gabriel then said to me, "Well, Mekhaeil, make yourself comfortable. We have a long ride. It will take us at least twelve hours to get to Alexandria, and I intend to drive straight through."

We were soon leaving the outskirts of the city and on the road back to Egypt. I don't remember any conversation after that. I was fast asleep within minutes.

The next thing I remember is the sound of cars sounding their horns. I woke up abruptly, brushed the sleep from my eyes, stretched out my arms and legs, and asked, "Where are we?"

"We are back in Alexandria," Sofia told me.

"Thank God," I responded.

"We are glad to be back in Egypt too," she said.

Then Gabriel said, "We are headed to our home, Mekhaeil. Where do you want us to drop you off?"

I hadn't given that any thought up until that moment. I responded, "Are we anywhere near St. Mark's Cathedral?"

At that, smiles came over their faces.

"You are a Copt?" Sofia asked.

"I am," I told her.

"So are we," Gabriel said.

"Do you have family here?" Sofia asked.

"No, I don't," I answered.

"So why do you go to the cathedral, Mekhaeil, if you don't mind me asking?" Gabriel asked me.

"I'm going to become a priest," I told him. I had never thought of becoming a priest in my entire life. I was surprised to hear the words come out of my mouth.

"Good for you!" Sofia told me. "That is a big commitment for a young man like you to make."

"I know," I told her, "but my heart tells me that I must do something to stand up for what is happening to us at this time. It is a very dangerous time to be a Christian these days."

They looked at each other knowingly, and then Gabriel asked, "Did you hear what happened yesterday in Sirte?"

"I saw it on the news last night while I was in the terminal, before I met the two of you," I responded.

"That is why we left Libya," Sofia told me.

"Me, too," I said.

"Things are not good here in Egypt either, but it is nowhere near as bad as things are in other parts of the Middle East,"

Gabriel added. "ISIS will take over Sirte before too long; I am sure of it."

"Is that why you left?" Sofia asked.

"Yes," I told her.

"What were you doing there?" Gabriel asked.

"I was working for a construction company," I answered.

Again they looked at each other, and then Sofia said, "The twenty-one Coptic Christians who were beheaded were taken from a construction site just outside of Sirte. You weren't anywhere near there, were you?"

I was becoming more and more nervous as the questions became more and more personal. I wasn't ready to talk to anyone about what had happened to me over the last twenty-four hours, even them, even though they had been so nice to me.

"No," I told her, "but I was not far away from where they were."

"But you were afraid it could happen to you, weren't you?" Gabriel asked.

Yes," I said, "and they made us all go home after it happened, and that's when I decided to come back to Egypt."

"It's a scary time for all of us," Sofia added.

No one said anything for several minutes, and then Gabriel said, "St. Mark's is not that far from where we live. In fact, that is where we go to church. We will take you there."

Ten minutes later, Gabriel brought the car to a stop directly in front of the church, which was much smaller than I thought it would be, but the complex took up several city blocks. There were buildings that were clearly a part of the church, surrounding the main church, all of which towered over the church itself. I had never been there before, and I was in awe. I had seen pictures, but it was more impressive for me to see it in person.

"Thank you for the ride. It was nice to meet you," I told them.

"It was our pleasure. We barely noticed you were in the car. You slept the whole time," Sofia said. "We are especially pleased to know that we helped a fellow Copt, too."

They must have been able to tell that I had never seen it before, because Sofia asked me, "Do you know where you are going?"

I told her that I didn't.

"The rectory is in that building over there," she said, pointing to a large building on the other side of the street, off to her right."

I thanked her.

"You have no bags? No clothes? Nothing?" Gabriel asked.

Sheepishly, I told him that I didn't.

Do you need any money, Mekhaeil?" Gabriel asked.

When I didn't answer right away, he got out of his car, pulled his wallet from his back pocket and handed me a one-hundred-pound note.

"Here, take this," he said.

At first, I refused, saying, "No, thank you. You have been too kind to me already. Thank you for the ride. It has been a gift from God that I met you last night."

Gabriel insisted, saying, "Mekhaeil, you are welcome. Take this. You will need it." He pushed the note into my hand and said, "You can pay me back later if you'd like. Good luck! Maybe we'll see you in church sometime."

At that he got back into his car, and they drove off. As I stood there, I thought to myself that it was indeed a blessing that those two Coptic Christians had found me and delivered me to this place. I was relieved to be where I was, though I was still uncertain as to why I was there and what I was going to do now that I was there.

I watched them drive away, and when they were out of sight, I turned to admire the cathedral.

CHAPTER 20

Sunday Morning

We had been captured on Friday, less than forty eight hours earlier. Now it was early Sunday morning—too early for the first Mass of the day. I walked inside the cathedral, sat in the last row of pews, and knelt down.

There were a couple of people walking about on the altar, getting things ready for the first Mass of the day, but no one else was in the church except for me. I was dressed in rags, and I'm sure I still smelled badly. These were work clothes, and they weren't even mine. I knew that I would be completely out of place once people began to arrive. I didn't belong there dressed as I was. I planned to leave once worshippers began to file in.

I said a prayer—one all Copts say early in the morning. After making the sign of the cross, I said, to myself, "In the name of the Father, the Son, and the Holy Spirit, one God. Amen. Kyrie eleison, Lord have mercy, Lord have mercy, Lord bless us. Amen. Glory be to the Father, and to the Son, and to the Holy Spirit, both now and ever, and unto the ages. Amen."

I sat down in the pew and thought about the words I had just uttered. They had new meaning after all of the things I had heard on Friday night and into early Saturday morning. It was hard for me to believe that not even twenty-four hours had passed since I had escaped having my head cut off.

The things I had heard that night made me believe those words more so than ever before. I truly believed that Jesus Christ was the son of God, as I had been taught since I was a small child. He was not just a prophet, as the Muslims said, and not a heretical rabbi, as the Jews thought him to be.

Even though I was still exhausted and very confused, I felt differently about who I was. My belief in all that the Coptic Church stood for was now stronger than ever. Now I had faith, not just a belief, that there is only one true God and that Jesus Christ is a part of that Holy Trinity.

I was a different person. I knew it in my brain, but I could now feel it in my heart. In a strange way, I felt as if I were a new convert to the church. I was now a true believer.

I closed my eyes and tilted my head back. I could see Demetrius, Touma, Guirguis, Rushdi, Raghib, Cyril, and all of the others clearly. I could hear their words echoing through my brain. More than anything else, though, I kept seeing the video, again, of them on the beach the day before, even though I had seen it all with my own two eyes.

I shuddered and shook my head back and forth, trying not to break down and cry. I couldn't help it. I leaned forward, put my head in my hands, and began to cry. At first I started to whimper, then I started to sob, and then the tears came streaming down.

I don't know how long I was in that condition, but the next thing I knew, I felt a hand on my shoulder. I sniffled, cleared my throat, and turned to see a priest in a black robe standing next to me. Before he could say anything, I said, "I'm sorry. I was just about to leave."

I'm sure he was able to see that I was in some serious distress. I hadn't had anything to eat in two days, I was thirsty, I was hungry, and I smelled. I was a pitiful creature. However, this man wasn't there to throw me out of the church, as I feared. He was there to help me.

"What's wrong, my son?" he asked.

"I'm thirsty and hungry, Father, but I have some money," I told him as I pulled out the hundred-pound note Gabriel had given me. I don't know why I did that. I should have known that he didn't care about the money.

"And you are a Copt?" he asked.

I thought to myself that vagrants and homeless people must come to the church begging for food and clothing quite frequently, and I answered, "Yes, I am."

"Come with me," he said.

I stood and followed him through the church, into the back, and behind the screen in the haikal, where only the priests, deacons, and altar servers are allowed to go. Then we walked out of the back of the church and headed toward the building that Gabriel and Sofia had told me was the rectory. We walked through the back door, straight into the kitchen.

There I saw several women busily scurrying around, putting things in the oven and preparing meals. He stopped next to a small table and told me to sit down. Then he said to one of the women, "Mrs. Deeb, would you be so kind as to give this young man something to eat? From the looks of him, he hasn't eaten in a week."

The woman responded, "Of course I would, Father Bishoy. I'd be glad to."

I perked up when I heard her name. Deeb is a fairly common Coptic name, and though I doubted she was related to Demetrius and Ignatius, she might have been. I thought she would have been a distant relative at best; I didn't mention to her anything about them.

He then turned to another one of the women and said, "And Mrs. Daoud, when he's finished eating, would you mind seeing if we don't have some clothes that might fit him?"

She responded by saying, "Of course I would, Father Bishoy. It would be my pleasure."

He then added, "And before you give him those clothes, would you show him where the showers are? I think he'll feel much better after he gets cleaned up and fed."

"Of course I will, Father," she responded.

He then turned to me and said, "I am saying the seven o'clock mass, so I have to leave you. If you are still here when I come back, I'd like to talk to you. Would that be all right, son?"

I immediately responded, "I'll be here."

"Good. I look forward to talking to you."

"Thank you, Father," I said.

"If you are finished in time, you might walk back over to the church, if Mass isn't over by then."

"If I'm finished in time, I will," I told him.

Within minutes, Mrs. Deeb brought me a large, round loaf of bread, some butter, and a glass of water.

"Enjoy!" she said.

I drank the water in one long gulp, and as I was beginning to tear open the loaf, she added, "Here. These might help."

She gave me a knife, a fork, and a napkin. I thanked her and cut the bread and began to butter it. Soon after, she brought back a plate of eggs with onion skins in them.

"This is really an old Hebrew recipe, but don't tell anyone," she whispered. "It's called Beid Hamine. It has some olive oil and coffee grounds in it. We like to mix things up for the priests every now and then." She patted me on the shoulder and smiled at me. I'm sure she could tell how famished I was.

The other woman brought me another glass of water. I finished it before she had time to turn around and walk away. She took the glass and said, "I'll be right back with another glass. You are welcome to as much as you want."

I thanked her.

After she brought me the third glass of water, she and the other women were back to what they had been doing before I entered the room, and I was busy devouring the food. They weren't paying any attention to me, which was good, because I was eating the food so fast they might have become concerned. I was eating as if I were afraid someone might come and take it away. I was famished. I ate too fast.

They brought me a second helping of everything. When I was finished, I sat there, stuffed but feeling much better. After a few minutes, one of the women looked over and saw that I had eaten everything but the silverware and the plates. She walked over and said, "Well, that didn't take long. Would you like some more?"

"No, thank you," I answered. "I'm full."

"Are you ready for that shower?" she asked.

"I am," I responded.

"Follow me," she told me.

She led me down a hallway, opened a door, and said, "I'll bring you some clothes that I think might fit you in a few minutes. Soap and towels are on the shelves."

I walked in and saw a large bathroom with several sinks, several toilets and several showers. Towels were stacked in a cabinet against the wall, with bars of soap and bottles of shampoo next to them. She closed the door behind her when she left.

There were mirrors on two of the walls. One was a full-length mirror at the other end of the room. I walked up to it to look at the person I saw in it. I could see a difference in me. I was no longer the boy that I had been a few months earlier, just completing his schooling. I was no longer the boy I had been two days earlier. I was no longer the boy I had been yesterday.

I stopped within a foot of the mirror and looked into my eyes. I ran my fingers through my hair. I was a mess, almost unrecognizable even to myself. I still had no facial hair, though I had some fuzz that was so fine that maybe I was the only person in the world who could see it. There still wasn't enough to shave off. Men had told me that once you shave, the hair grows faster. I wanted a beard to make me look older, but most Copts shave, except for the priests, deacons, and bishops. While we were working in Sirte, we all had beards, except for me.

In all my life, I had never looked worse. My clothes were disgustingly dirty, and my hair, which was black and bushy, was a tangled mess. More than anything else, however, my eyes were different. They were still the same dark black as they had been since I was a child, but they weren't the smiling, happy eyes I was used to seeing. They weren't the same. I had seen and experienced things that changed me. I was no longer a boy.

I didn't look in the mirror, smile, and ask myself how I looked, as I usually did. And I didn't think to myself whether I thought the girls would find me handsome or cute. I looked in the mirror and asked myself who and what I was.

What was I going to do with my life after experiencing the things I had experienced? I didn't know. I took off my clothes, grabbed a bar of soap and some shampoo, and stepped into a shower stall, pulling the curtain behind me. I turned on the hot water and let the water run over my head. I stood there, with the bottle and the soap still in my hand, for several minutes, and then I began to shampoo my hair. After that I began to scrub myself. I scrubbed hard, as if I could rid myself of the evil and terrible things that I had been exposed to over the last two days.

It was still hard for me to believe it hadn't even been forty-eight hours since we had been captured. I had another five hours, or more, until then. I stayed in the shower until my fingers began to prune. It was the longest shower I had ever taken in my life.

When I walked out of the shower, I noticed a pile of clean clothes in the corner, by the door. I reached for a towel and began to dry myself off. There were a couple of chairs at the end of the room, and I walked over and sat in one. I was still feeling exhausted, even though I had slept the whole night in the car.

I think I was more confused than anything else, actually. I heaved a deep sigh and thanked God for Father Bishoy and for what he had done for me. I sat there in silence, not sure what to do.

Several minutes later, another man walked in. He was a young man, about my age, and he had a tonia on. I thought he was probably an aghanostos—or maybe someone like me, without a place to stay. He greeted me and proceeded to use one of the other showers.

While he was showering, I put on the clothes that had been laid out for me. They were plain, they were clean, and they fit. She had also left me a pair of shoes, but they were too small. I put my old shoes back on.

I walked back into the kitchen area with my dirty clothes in hand.

"Would you like for us to wash those for you, young man?" a woman asked.

I told her that they could be thrown away, but I didn't tell her why. I asked if they had shoes a little larger than the ones I had been given, and she led me down another hallway to a room where there were many shoes and clothes of all sizes and colors to choose from.

"Take your pick," she told me.

I picked out a pair of shoes that fit me and asked if I could have a different shirt and pants. I chose a black shirt and pants. They matched my mood.

After that, the woman, who was much older than my mother, asked, "Is there anything else we can do for you, child?"

I asked her if there was any place where I could lie down. I told her I hadn't slept much in the last few days. She led me to a room that had a bed, a dresser, a small table, and a chair in it.

"We won't be needing this today. Make yourself at home. We'll tell Father Bishoy where you are when he finishes saying Mass," she told me.

I fell asleep within minutes.

CHAPTER 21

St. Mark's Cathedral

Some time later, I awoke to the sound of someone knocking on the door to the room I was in. I sprang to my feet, opened the door, and saw Father Bishoy smiling at me.

"Feel better?" he asked.

"Much better. Thank you, Father," I replied.

"Would you like to sleep some more, or are you ready to get up?" he asked.

"I think I've had enough sleep for now. If I don't get up, I won't be able to sleep tonight," I told him.

"Good. Then let's go for a little walk, shall we?"

I started to clean up the bed, and he told me, "Don't worry about that. Leave it for now. You can sleep here tonight if you'd like."

We walked out of the rectory and around the corner, heading to a grassy area where there were a few trees and some benches.

"Let's sit here, where it is quiet and we won't be disturbed— or at least I hope not," Father Bishoy said. "Someone is always looking for me, it seems."

After we sat down, he turned to me and said, "Now, please, tell me your name."

"I am Mekhaeil Samaha," I lied, even though I knew it was a serious sin to lie to a priest. I was afraid to give him any truthful personal information.

"And where are you from?"

"Al-Minya," I said, lying again.

"And what are you doing here, Mekhaeil?"

"I have come to Alexandria to become a priest," I told him.

"Have you?" Father Bishoy asked, in a voice that seemed to question the veracity of what I had said, and then he asked, "And do your parents know you are here?"

"Of course," I lied again.

"And your parish priest … what is his name again?"

At that I felt very uneasy. I didn't know the name of the parish priest in al-Minya, and I think Father Bishoy knew that I wasn't telling the truth. As I was thinking of how to respond, he said to me, "Mekhaeil, entering the priesthood is a very serious decision for a young man to make, and men are chosen to become priests. You know that, right?"

When he said that, I remembered that Cyril had told us about that. I had forgotten about that part of it. Then he asked, "How old are you?"

"I'm sixteen," I told him, as if that were proof that I was a man, well able to make such a serious decision.

"Sixteen," he said. "So you just completed your schoolwork, did you?"

"Yes, I did," I responded in a confident way.

"And have you applied to attend university, or have you sent any of your paperwork to the seminary?"

When I hesitated before responding, he said to me, "Mekhaeil, listen to me … I see many young boys—or boys who are becoming young men, such as yourself—and I have seen many who have lost their way … maybe their parents were killed, maybe they've run away from their parents, maybe they been the victims of abuse or neglect on the part of their parents … and other such things. And when I saw you in church this morning, dressed the way you were and crying as you were, I knew that you were in great distress. The church is here to help you. Even if you were not a Copt, I would help you, and I am happy to have been able to help you this morning as I have, but you must tell me the truth or I won't be able to help you much more than I have already.

"Now, Mekhaeil, let's start over … tell me your name."

"My name is Mekhaeil. That is my real name."

"And your last name? It isn't Samaha, is it?"

"No."

"Why don't you want to tell me your real name, Mekhaeil? I am a priest. What you say to me is confidential. I won't tell the police. I promise. Are you in trouble with the law?"

"No, I'm not in trouble with the law, Father, but there are things that I just can't tell you right now. I can't tell anyone." I covered my eyes and put my head in my hands and put my elbows on my knees.

He gently put his hand on my head and said, "Okay, Mekhaeil, I can see that something has happened in your life that has affected you profoundly, but I can't help you unless you tell me what it is, so here's what we're going to do. I'm going to leave you here for now. I want you to think about whatever it is that is bothering you, and after you have done that, I want you to come find me. I'll either be in the church or in one of the mission rooms today. It is Sunday, and we have many things going on today. Sunday is, as you know, the biggest day of the week for us, but you are very important to me. You are like a lamb who is lost from his flock, and …"

When he said that, I was reminded of what Raghib had said about him being a lost sheep. I hadn't thought about it, but I probably came to St. Mark's because of him and his experience here. Father Bishoy's words reminded me of what Raghib had said that night.

"… today is a particularly busy day, as our church suffered a great loss yesterday," he continued.

"I was a child once, just as you are now, and things happened in my life that caused me to become a priest. I remember how difficult those times were for me, and I know how difficult they are for many young men, especially Coptic Christian young men here in Egypt these days. You are a Coptic Christian, yes? That much is true, yes?"

I straightened up, took a deep breath, and said, "I am, Father."

"But you're not from Al-Minya, are you?"

"No," I admitted.

"I'm sure there is a good reason why you don't want to tell me where you are from, but we won't talk about that now. And Mekhaeil, if you decide that you want to leave and go on your way, that is fine. You don't have to come find me and tell me anything if you don't want to, and you can keep the clothes and shoes if you'd like. Consider them a gift from God.

"I want you to think about what I just said. If you want me to help you, I will, if I can, but you must be honest with me, okay?"

At that he stood, and said, "I'm going now. As I said, you can come find me if you want, when you are ready. And if you haven't come to see me, I might just come back here in an hour or two and check on you to see how you're doing. Would that be all right?"

"Yes, Father," I responded. "And thank you for everything. You might have saved my life. I had nowhere else to turn."

"That's what I'm here for, Mekhaeil. That's why I am a priest— to be here for God's lost sheep, as well as to tend to His flock of sheep who are not lost and do my best to make sure they don't get lost."

"Thank you, Father. I will think about the things you have said," I said, "and I will come find you and let you know what I decide to do."

"Good luck, Mekhaeil, in making the right decision. Ask God to help you make that decision," he told me. "Pray with me." He held my hand, and together we said a prayer. When we were finished, he smiled and walked away.

I didn't know what to do. It had been a little over a day since I had come as close as a human being can get to dying, and I still didn't truly understand how I had avoided being killed, other than that they wanted me to tell everyone about what had happened.

I really didn't understand what it was I was supposed to do now that I was away from the terrorists. I wasn't ready to tell the world what I had seen. Besides, the world had already seen it.

Actually, the more I thought about it, the more afraid I was to tell Father Bishoy what had happened. I didn't want him telling anyone about it, but I knew that he was a priest and that he would have to keep it secret. I was pretty sure that if I told him not to tell anyone, he wouldn't tell anyone. I could make him promise not to tell.

I didn't want to talk about what I had seen. I didn't want to talk about what had happened to my brothers and my friends. I tried not to think about it, but that was all I could think about. How could I think about anything else?

I knew that if people found out that I was one of the ones who had been captured in Sirte, and that I was with those men right up to the time when they were beheaded, I would be besieged by all of my family members and all of the families of the other men who had died; they would want to know all of the details. It was too painful for me to think about, let alone talk about. I didn't know what I would say to them.

Mostly, though, I was still ashamed of myself. I wished I had died with them. I wished that I were as strong in my faith as they had been in theirs. I wished that I could have faced death as they had. I faced it like a little boy, crying and whimpering, not like a man—not like the men they were.

Every time I thought about it, it was worse. I kept replaying every scene in my mind—when we were captured, when we rode in the truck after being captured, when they put the collars and chains on us—all of it. I also remembered how scared we were, and how we didn't really know what was going to happen to us, though everyone else thought we were going to die.

As I looked back, it seemed more gruesome than it had been while I lived through it. Trying to explain to people what it was like would have been impossible. I couldn't begin to describe to people all that I had seen, all that I had heard, and all that had been said by my friends, let alone how I felt.

I sat there trying to think what Demetrius, Cyril, or even Clement and Boctor would have told me to do. Everyone had a different opinion about it. Everyone had a different perspective on it—especially Omar. I had listened to everyone and to everything that had been said, but what did I think of it all? It was too much for me. I didn't know what to think.

Of all the people in that room, I think I learned more from Omar than I did from anyone else. He explained things to me from the perspective of a Muslim—a Shiite, but a Muslim nonetheless. I didn't truly understand the difference between a Sunni and a Shia before that.

I wasn't all that sure that I wanted to become a priest anyway. The thought of becoming a priest had never entered my mind before. I wasn't even a good aghanostos, but I remembered that was what Cyril did. I might have said that just because I thought that would be what Father Bishoy might have wanted to hear.

I have to admit that my faith had been shaken at first on the night of our capture by what happened to us. Like some of the others, I asked God why it had to happen to us. Why were we going to die, and why wasn't He going to come to rescue us? But as I reflected back on it all, what I remembered most was the faith of the men I was with and what those men had decided to do.

How could I even think to ask why He let that happen to us? I could never understand why it was happening, just as I would never understand all that had happened since the days of Jesus Christ. None of us would. We all knew that God worked in mysterious ways. I told myself something good had to come of it. I just couldn't imagine what that might be.

I learned so much about the history of our church and our people that night. I admit that that night, I wondered why our God had basically allowed us to be kept us as slaves and second-class citizens in Egypt for almost two thousand years. I admit that I wondered if maybe the god of the Muslims was stronger than our God. I didn't know what to believe that night.

Just thinking about these things sent a creepy feeling through me, but I couldn't help it. That's what I had thought as I heard all those things. And the Muslims had won during all those years, except during the Crusades for a short period of time, and then again a hundred years ago when the Europeans took over the world. But Muslims still dominated the Middle East—and Egypt, to a large extent—even now.

I had to figure all of those things out for myself. As I sat there, I realized that I couldn't blame God for what happened to us, even though I was so sad about what had happened to my brothers and my friends. I hated, truly hated, the Muslims for what they had done to us. I had never hated anything or anyone in my life.

Hate was a new emotion for me, and I didn't like it. Plus, here I was in Alexandria, and Muslims were still killing Christians in Egypt, let alone in Libya, Syria, Iraq, and other places around the world. If not for the military, Muslims would probably have burned all of our churches and killed all the priests by now, just as Touma and Raghib had told us.

I realized, as I sat there, that I had no choice. There was no doubt about what I had to do. I knew that I was a Copt, and what had happened to me and the others was something that had happened to Copts for almost two thousand years. I didn't want to be afraid anymore. I could not let myself continue to be afraid to do those things.

After a while, I decided I would tell Father Bishoy where I'd been and what had happened to me, but only if he promised not to tell anyone else. Then, after I told him, I could ask him to tell me what he thought I should do. I had no one else to turn to and nowhere else to go. I needed his advice.

I thought about what Touma had done by going to Cairo, and then on to Port Said, but I couldn't do that. He had friends that he was with, but even with those friends, he got himself into a lot of trouble. Plus, when he did it, he was older than I was. I was still a boy, trying to become a man. That wasn't an option.

I also remembered what Raghib did. He asked the priests in Alexandria to help him find a job, and they did. I could ask Father Bishoy to help me find a job. Maybe I could find out how to become a priest, but I wouldn't start doing that just yet. That wasn't really in my heart.

After a long while, I was ready to talk to Father Bishoy, but I still wasn't sure what I was going to tell him. There were some things I wasn't ready to tell him, such as some of the things the men said that night. I was sure he was going to ask some questions I wasn't going to want to answer, and I wasn't sure what I was going to do about that. I decided I would just tell him I wasn't ready to talk about those things yet. He'd understand; at least I hoped he would.

After making that decision, I felt some relief. I knew that I wasn't going to be able to keep all I had been through, and all I had seen, to myself for long. Things were happening fast, though, and I felt like a wounded animal that needed to hide for a while and heal. This seemed like a good place for me to hide.

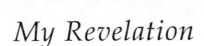

CHAPTER 22

My Revelation

It was now sometime in the middle of the afternoon. Time didn't matter, but I thought about where I had been the day before at this time of day. I was still on the minibus on my way from Sirte to Marsa al Brega, exhausted, starved, filthy, and thirsty. The day before that, I was in the room, chained together with all the others. What was going to happen next, I didn't know, but it couldn't be as bad as the last two days. Things had to get better.

As I sat on a bench in the shade under a tree after a good meal and a long shower, with clean clothes on, I had to admit that I felt fine. I hadn't been injured. No one had beaten me. I had no scars on my body. I was okay, physically, other than a few minor aches and pains. My shoulders still hurt from having my hands chained behind me for so long, and my wrists were sore from the handcuffs; but other than that, I had no physical problems to complain about.

All of my problems were in my head. I wondered if people, such as Father Bishoy, could just look at me and tell what was going through my mind. My eyes might have been glazed over. I might have said inappropriate things. I may have been acting strangely. I didn't know how to act or what I was supposed to say or do after what I'd been through.

I didn't know how others saw me, but I wasn't myself—or at least I wasn't the same sixteen-year-old boy that I had been two days ago. I truly had no idea what I would be doing tonight or tomorrow, let alone next week or next month. I was in a fog.

I just sat there staring at the ground or off into space, though I wasn't sleeping. I don't know how long I was in that condition, but the next thing I knew, Father Bishoy was sitting beside me, telling me that the current church sat on the site of the original church founded by St. Mark. Then he asked, "Did you know that?"

His question startled me, and I mumbled a negative response.

"So have you given some thought to our last conversation?" he asked.

"Of course, Father," I responded. "I have thought of little else."

"And what have you decided, my son?"

I rubbed my eyes, turned to look into his eyes, and asked him, "If I tell you something, do you promise that you won't tell anyone—and I mean no one … not even any of your fellow priests—unless or until I say it is all right for you to do so?"

At that Father Bishoy, who had no idea what I was about to tell him, said some things that he'd probably said a thousand times to people over his years of being a priest.

"Your confession to me—and we'll call it a confession, though I don't know what you're going to tell me—is completely confidential. I have sworn a sacred oath to God and to my fellow priests, and to you and all those like you, to keep those things private. However, there are times, such as when a serious crime either has been committed or is about to be committed, that I am required to break that vow and tell other people what you have told me. I would do my best to try to talk you out of committing a crime or talk you into making appropriate restitution, even if that meant you might have to be punished for whatever it is you said or did.

"For example, if you were to tell me that you had a gun and that you planned to kill someone, I could not allow that to happen. I would be required to do something. There are exceptions, but up to this point in time in my life as a priest, I have never revealed anything that anyone has ever confessed to me to anyone else. Does that answer your question, Mekhaeil?"

"Yes, Father. I don't have a gun, and I don't have any plans to kill anyone, but I must confess that if I had the chance, there are many people I would kill, and I wouldn't hesitate to do it ... I wish I could, but I can't."

At that Father Bishoy sat back a little, still not sure what to make of me and what I was about to tell him. He said, "You have much anger inside you for such a young man, don't you, Mekhaeil? How old are you? Sixteen, you said?"

"Yes, Father. I am sixteen years old," I told him.

"Something very bad must have happened to you to make you feel that way. Are you ready to tell me about it, Mekhaeil?"

"Do you promise not to tell?"

"As I just said, unless it is something I cannot keep to myself, I promise you that I will tell no one what you tell me, unless you allow me to do so, okay?"

I looked into his eyes, hoping to make sure that I could trust him. He had dark black eyes. They were kind eyes. He had a gentle voice and a full black beard that had many gray hairs in it. He had a slight smile on his face—not one of happiness but one of friendliness. I trusted him. After all, he was a priest.

"Okay," I responded, and then I took a deep breath, and asked, "So you heard about the twenty-one men who were beheaded yesterday ..."

"Of course," he said, looking at me as if I had just asked the dumbest question anyone had ever asked him. "We are in great mourning now all across our land. Of course I am aware of it. Why do you ask such a question?"

"I was there," I told him.

He must have thought that I meant that I had been in the vicinity, or in Sirte, or somehow close to the area, because he wasn't immediately impressed.

"You were in Sirte?" he asked.

"Yes," I told him.

"Did you know some of the men who were captured and killed?" he asked.

"I knew them all," I told him.

"How is it that you knew them?" he asked.

"I was working with them when we were captured."

At that he became more interested, and he asked, "You were there when the men were captured? In Sirte?"

"Yes. I was with them when they were captured," I told him.

When I said that, the expression on his face changed. I think he thought I was lying to him again, or that I was crazy, but he moved closer to me, looked squarely into my eyes and asked, "You were with them when they were captured, Mekhaeil?"

"Yes," I told him. "I was taken prisoner too."

At that he leaned back. I knew, or I thought, he must have been thinking I was lying at that point. He sighed and asked in a soft, gentle voice, "Mekhaeil, if you were taken prisoner with the others, how is it that you are here, sitting with me?"

"They let me go," I told him.

"That was when? Yesterday morning? And here you are now? How is that possible?" he asked.

I could tell that Father Bishoy was pretty sure that I wasn't telling him the truth, but he was being as nice as he could about it. He might have been thinking I was mentally ill. That made me stop and think for a few seconds. I hadn't thought about that possibility. I had never thought that people might not believe me and my story.

I was so afraid of people asking me to tell them about it that I never thought people wouldn't believe me. Furthermore, I had lied to him before. No wonder he thought I was lying now. It was still hard for me to believe they let me go, so I could understand why he wouldn't believe me.

"I'm telling you the truth, Father. I know I lied to you before, but I'm telling you the truth now," I told him.

"Really?" he asked. I think he wanted to believe me, but I had to prove it to him; this was hard for him to believe.

"Yes, I am, and I don't know what to do. I have told no one what happened. You are the first person to know."

Father Bishoy began to probe me about my story in a nice way, not calling me a liar, but challenging me nonetheless.

"So tell me again how you knew these men, Mekhaeil—the Copts, that is. And they were all Copts, yes?" he asked.

"Most of us were all from the same village, and two of the men were my brothers," I responded.

"What village is that?" he asked.

"al-Aour," I responded.

"And what were their names?" he asked.

"My brothers? Or the rest of the men?"

"Your brothers," he said.

This was something I thought the news might have reported. I didn't know if the names were in the papers or not. I hadn't heard any names mentioned on the television. He was testing me.

"Touma and Guirguis Zacharias," I told him.

"So your last name is Zacharias and you are from al-Aour," Father Bishoy said, as if he had discovered something. "And the name of your parish priest is what?" he asked.

"Father Ignatius," I answered.

"And I know that is true, Mekhaeil. I know Father Ignatius very well. Will he know you?"

"Yes, of course," I answered. "He has known me since I was a little boy."

At that he asked me, "Are you thirsty? Are you hungry? Is there anything I can get for you?"

I hadn't eaten in hours and hadn't had anything to drink since those three glasses of water, so I responded, "Yes, I am, Father. Could I have a drink of milk?" I asked.

"Stay here. I'll be right back, but we are in mourning now, so no milk, cheese, or meat, Mekhaeil."

I didn't think anything of it at that time, but when I saw him hurrying back with a glass of water and a plateful of Ghorayebah cookies, it occurred to me that what he had really done was go in to the rectory and read the story in the newspaper about the men who had been killed. Or perhaps he might have called Father Ignatius. Whatever the reason, he had a much different look on his face when he came back.

He handed me the plate and the glass of water and asked, "So

Mekhaeil, tell me … how is it that you escaped?" His tone was much different.

"They let me go," I told him.

"They just let you go, Mekhaeil?" he asked. "Why did they do that, do you think?"

"They told me to tell the world what I had seen."

At that Father Bishoy sat back and looked at me in a completely different way. I was sure that, at that moment, he began to believe I was telling him the truth.

"Did they ask you or the others to convert to Islam?" he asked.

"No, they didn't."

"You didn't tell them that you would convert, Mekhaeil, did you?" he asked.

"No, I didn't, Father," I responded, "and neither did any of the others. Even if they had told us our lives would be spared if we converted, none of the men would have done that, but they never asked us, although I wasn't there at the very end, when they were killed."

At that Father Bishoy leaned back and sighed again, but he said nothing.

"I was the last one captured, Father. I had been hiding several hundred yards away. I was the first one to see them coming, and I warned everyone. Touma, my oldest brother, told me to hide, and I did, but they found me."

Father Bishoy must have seen how hard it was for me to tell him these things, because he reached for my hands and grabbed them. He was a big man, much taller than I, and he was large, too. My hands were small inside of his.

"I cannot imagine how difficult that must have been for you, Mekhaeil."

The sincerity of his words surprised me. It took me a few seconds to respond.

"It was," I told him. "I was afraid to die, Father."

"That's understandable," Father Bishoy replied. "I think everyone in the world would have been, Mekhaeil."

"I didn't want to have my head cut off … like my brothers." I took my hands from his and put my head in my hands and began to cry again.

Father Bishoy stroked the back of my head with one hand and said, "It is a terrible thing you've been through, Mekhaeil … a terrible thing."

We didn't talk for several minutes. I continued to cry, but then I sniffled, straightened up, and said, "Now you know, Father."

"You poor boy! You have been through a horrible ordeal," he said, now grasping my hands in his again. "But why did you come here? Why didn't you want to go back to your home, Mekhaeil, to see your family? They must be worried sick about you. You know they are."

"I'm sure they are," I answered, "but I wasn't ready to face them. I'm still not. I wasn't ready to face anyone. I didn't want to talk about it to anyone. I'm ashamed of myself, really, Father."

"Why are you ashamed, Mekhaeil? You did nothing wrong, did you?" he asked.

"I should have died with them, Father. I shouldn't be here," I answered.

"That's why you lied to me—because you feel ashamed?" he asked.

"Yes, Father, and I didn't want to tell anyone, not even you; but you have helped me so much, and I knew I would have to tell someone, so I decided it would be best to tell you."

"I'm glad you did, Mekhaeil," he said.

"I feel better after telling you. Thank you, Father, for listening to me … and for believing me."

"God brought you to me, my son. I am His instrument. Thank God for that," he told me.

I sniffled and then blurted out, "I keep asking myself why He didn't help us! Why He allowed that to happen." I began to cry again, just thinking of us being in that room, talking about Jesus Christ, Muhammad, Moses, and all of the other things we talked about.

Before Father Bishoy could respond, I continued, with tears in my eyes. "But I realize that I can't think that way. I know that our God is the one true God. I know that He has a reason for all that happens. I know that, Father, but it still hurts," I said. Father Bishoy said nothing in response, and then I asked, "Is it wrong to question why God allowed that to happen?"

He said, "God works in mysterious ways, Mekhaeil. We cannot know why He does things or why He doesn't do things, but as you said, our God is the one true God. Don't lose sight of that."

"That night, while we were all chained together, knowing we were going to die in the morning, we talked about God, the Muslims, the Jews, Jesus Christ, St. Mark, and a whole lot of things, and I was confused by all that I heard. I'm still confused, Father, but I know I am a Copt. I knew I would be safe here."

"You are safe here, Mekhaeil," he told me. "I think that's enough for now. I think a good night's sleep will help you. Will you stay here with us tonight, Mekhaeil? You know that you are welcome here."

I had nowhere else to go, and I readily agreed. Then he asked, "How is it you got here, Mekhaeil? It's a long way from Sirte to Alexandria."

I told him that I had taken a minibus to Marsa al Brega, that Mr. and Mrs. Ibrahim had given me a ride from there to St. Marks, and that I had slept in the car the whole way.

"The Ibrahims are very nice people. They went to Libya to make money, too, just as you and the others did. They were working with bankers, as I recall. I didn't know they came back."

"They told me that they left because of what happened to us," I told him.

"But you said nothing to them about how you were involved?"

"No, I didn't, and you promised not to tell anyone, right, Father?" I reminded him.

"I did, and I won't, Mekhaeil, unless you allow me to. I think you have quite a story to tell, and it is one our church will want to hear."

"That's what I'm saying, Father! I'm not ready to tell anyone about it—not yet. I don't want people to ask me about it. All I would do is cry. I don't want to think about it, but it's all I can think about. I have nothing but bad, evil thoughts in my head. As I told you, if I could, I would kill every single one of those men, but I can't. There is nothing I can do."

"Yes, Mekhaeil. Yes, there is. I think God has a plan for you, but let's talk about that tomorrow," he said. "I think you've had enough for today. Let's go for a walk."

CHAPTER 23

Pope Tawadros II and President el-Sisi

W e stood and began to walk back toward the rectory, and then Father Bishoy said, "How about a little tour of the church—your church—Mekhaeil? I have many things to do the rest of the afternoon, so I will be busy, but I have a few minutes now. Would you like that?"

I told him that I would. As we walked toward the church, he said, "This church has been burned down and destroyed several times since St. Mark came here, but what you see sits on top of the original church. This is where St. Mark came to Egypt to spread the good news about Jesus Christ. This is a sacred place for us Copts, Mekhaeil—perhaps our most sacred place."

Minutes after entering the cathedral, as he was just beginning to tell me about a statue of one of the saints at the back of the church, men in uniform, carrying weapons, suddenly came marching in. We immediately turned to watch as dozens of people, including television crews and priests, came in behind them.

"That's Pope Tawadros himself!" Father Bishoy exclaimed. "This must be something very important. It must have something to do with what happened to you and the others in Sirte. I wonder why they are here and not in Cairo. That's unusual."

I didn't say anything. We were standing off to the side. Father

Bishoy stood next to me, watching what was happening along with me.

"Oh my goodness!" he added. "That's Abdel-Fattah el Sisi!"

I knew that he was the president of Egypt, but I'd never seen him before. I said, "I've seen him on TV and in the paper, but never in person."

People continued to pour into the church, including many more soldiers, police officers, and priests. We watched as the pope and the president, and a few of the priests, walked onto the altar. Other priests took seats in the front pews. Soldiers lined the two side walls of the church. A dozen police officers were near the altar, preventing anyone from going any closer. They began directing people where to sit. Cameramen got as close as the police officers allowed them to.

Father Bishoy turned to me and said, "Stay here, Mekhaeil. I'm going to sit with my fellow priests."

I sat down in the last row of pews, off to the side.

When the church was nearly full, the soldiers closed the back doors. When they did, Pope Tawadros II stepped up to the pulpit and said, "This is an extremely sad time for our church, my brothers and my sisters, and for all Egyptians. As you have heard, twenty-one of our fellow Egyptians, all of whom were Coptic Christians, were beheaded yesterday in Sirte, Libya, by Muslim extremists. We, as a nation and as a religion, are in mourning. I ask you all to join me now in a moment of silence,"

He dropped his head, and there was complete silence in the room for over a minute. He then spoke again. "I ask you to join me now in prayer. This is a prayer we Copts say at a time like this, when mankind commits an atrocity of such barbaric proportions that our Christian principles and values are challenged to the extreme. This prayer reminds us of the suffering and death Jesus Christ endured for us, and the compassion He had for us and for all mankind even at the moment of His death."

Again he bowed his head, and he began to pray. "Oh Jesus Christ, our God, who was nailed to the cross and killed sin by the tree and by Your death, You made alive the dead man, whom

You created with Your own hands, and had died in sin. You put to death our pains by Your healing and life-giving passions, and by the nails with which You were nailed to that cross. Rescue our minds from the thoughtlessness of earthly deeds and worldly lusts, to the remembrance of Your heavenly commandments, according to Your compassion. Now and forever and unto the ages of all ages. Amen.

"I confess to you, my brothers and sisters, that I, like you, am so deeply saddened and troubled by what happened to our fellow Christians—who were from the small village of al-Aour, not far from here—that I, like you, must remind myself of the compassion Christ showed us.

"At this time, I ask that you continue to pray for those twenty-one men and for their families, and for our church, because all of us are in danger. These terrorists threaten our lives on a daily basis. We must, however, remain faithful to who we are as a people and to what we believe as followers of Christ.

"It is not in our nature to commit such atrocities; nor is it in our nature to respond in kind when such atrocities are committed against us. Instead we turn to those who protect us from such people. We turn to the leaders of our country at a time like this, and we ask our leaders to help us.

"Abdel Fattah el-Sisi, our president, joins us today to offer his condolences and to let us know what Egypt, our country, is going to do about what happened to those twenty-one men, whom I do hereby officially declare to be martyrs. President el-Sisi ..."

Pope Tawadros II stood back, and the president rose from his chair and walked to the pulpit. The pope stood behind him as he spoke.

"Thank you, Pope Tawadros," he began. "This is my first opportunity to address the people of Egypt about what occurred yesterday in Libya. We have all seen the shocking video of what took place there. I want you all to know how deeply saddened I am by what happened to those men, and I want to tell you that we, as a country, will not stand idly by and watch as these terrorists continue to commit atrocities in this part of the world against Christians and anyone else who does not believe as they do—especially Egyptians.

"Although the men who did this are not in this country, they are not far away. They purposely chose their target. They purposely captured and killed twenty-one Coptic Christians, knowing that they were Egyptians. I assure you that their barbaric acts will not go unpunished."

As I sat there, I was reminded of the many times we asked ourselves that night why our country didn't come to save us. At the time, we blamed Egypt and el-Sisi for not coming to rescue us.

He continued. "When I first heard the news of their capture, and we were told of the event late Friday afternoon, I asked our generals if we knew where the men had been taken. They did not. I asked them to do their best to find them, and they did, but they were unsuccessful. I told them to continue their efforts to locate the men. They did so tirelessly, but without success."

I can't say that I felt any better when I heard that, but I could not blame him as much as I and the others had two nights ago.

"Also, I want you all to know that we received no ransom notes. There were no negotiations regarding the release of these men. I want you all to know that we did not refuse to negotiate with these terrorists; we were not given the opportunity to do so."

That, too, was something I needed to hear. The men had talked about that. We knew that many countries in the world, such as France and Germany, had paid money to rescue people who had been captured by other terrorist groups, and that the United States and England, among others, refused to do so, but we didn't know what, if anything, Egypt would do. Again, it didn't make me feel better to hear him say that no ransom had been refused by Egypt, but it answered another of the questions that the men had asked that awful night.

He went on. "At my direction, last night, planes struck selected targets in Libya where we know terrorist cells are located. I personally ordered our military to bomb the home of Basheer al Darsi, who is a known leader of one of the radical Islamic groups that terrorize this region.

"Our army is on high alert. Our planes are ready to fly. Our soldiers are ready to be deployed at a moment's notice. Our ships are ready to sail. Egypt will not allow these terrorists to continue to purposely terrorize either those Egyptian citizens here in Egypt or those who happen to be in another country at the time.

"Under my leadership, religious diversity is welcome. Our country, and our world, is composed of billions of people, many of whom have differing beliefs regarding God. I will protect all Egyptians, including all of you who are Coptic Christians, as well as any and all religious people and groups that do not condone or perpetrate acts of violence, to the best of my ability.

"I offer you my assurances, and I firmly pledge to you that Egypt will not tolerate acts of violence against its citizens by foreign terrorists, no matter where those acts occur, for as long as I am the president of this country. I promise you that.

"Again I offer you, Pope Tawadros, and all Coptic Christians, my sincere and heartfelt condolences for the loss your community has sustained at the hands of these terrorists."

At that he stepped back a few steps, and Pope Tawadros then moved forward, up to the microphone, and said, "On behalf of all Coptic Christians, I thank you, President el-Sisi, for being with us on this sad occasion as we remember our twenty-one Coptic brothers who were put to death for their belief that Jesus Christ is our Lord and Savior.

"I wish to leave all of you gathered here today with this final thought, which comes to us from Jesus Christ Himself as He spoke to His disciples and others, as found in Matthew 5: 'Blessed are you when they revile you, and persecute you, and say all manner of evil against you for My sake. Rejoice and be exceedingly glad, for great is your reward in heaven, for so they persecuted the prophets before you.'"

I immediately thought of Touma, Raghib, Cyril, Clement, and the others, who feared that they were doomed to eternal damnation for the sins they had committed, though they repented of those sins. I wondered if, in fact, they were in heaven.

Pope Tawadros then said, "Please bow your heads and pray

for God's blessing. Father, we ask that you bless us and keep us safe in this hour of great sorrow we presently endure. We ask that you bless and keep our president, Abdel-Fattah el Sisi, safe and give him the strength and the courage to fight the evil that exists in this world. We ask that you bless and keep our country, Egypt, safe and well. These are difficult times that we live in, and we ask that you take those twenty-one martyrs into heaven with you and give their friends and families consolation so the wounds they have suffered will be healed. And we ask all of this in the name of the Father, the Son, and the Holy Spirit. Amen."

I raised my head and watched as he and the others began to leave the altar. The police stood in the aisles and, after the president and the pope passed by, directed the people out of the church in an orderly fashion, row by row. The last to leave were the soldiers. Fifteen minutes later, I was sitting by myself, alone in the church.

CHAPTER 24

Father Bishoy

I sat there in silence, thinking about all that was taking place in my life and the life of my church and my country. It was hard for me to comprehend. What was going to happen next? How was all of this going to end? Would it ever end?

The faces of my brothers and the others were always with me. The horror of what had happened to them yesterday remained vividly in my thoughts. Father Bishoy was the only one who knew what I had been through, and I hadn't told him much of anything about it, only that I had been there.

Part of me still wanted to keep much of that to myself. It was too graphic, too painful, too raw, and I didn't want anyone to shine a spotlight upon me. What if like-minded terrorists in Egypt saw it? Would they come after me?

I still had no place to stay, no place to work, no money, and nothing other than the clothes on my back, which weren't even mine, and I was completely dependent upon Father Bishoy and the church to help me through this. I knew that I would be telling the whole story to Father Bishoy—and soon.

I began to think of what I would say and how much I would tell him. Would I tell him everything, or would I hold things back, such as what Raghib told us about him killing people, or about my brother Touma and what he had done, or about what Cyril told us? I wasn't sure. Maybe I'd tell him, and maybe I wouldn't.

Half an hour later, the back doors to the church opened. I turned and saw Father Bishoy walking toward me.

"Mekhaeil! I'm glad to see that you are still here."

"I have no place else to go, Father," I responded.

"Come, let's go for a walk. I'll finish with the tour another time. Let's go outside. It's a beautiful day, and now everything has changed around here with the pope and the president having been here, so I have some time to be with you," he said.

It was late afternoon, and the sun was behind the tall buildings that surrounded the cathedral.

"Alexandria is a beautiful city. I'll take you to a special place in it," he said. I readily agreed. I had no place else to go and nothing else to do. "Because it has so many miles of coastline on the Mediterranean Sea, we are the largest seaport, by far, in Egypt. Let's walk down to the water. It is a good place to watch the sun set."

We walked for a while through the streets, which were not too crowded, it being a Sunday afternoon. He pointed things out to me as we went and told me things about the history of Alexandria; I had already learned some of it from Demetrius, Omar, and the others two nights before, but I didn't mention any of that to Father Bishoy.

When we reached a place where I was able to see the water, Father Bishoy pointed to some benches that lined the sea wall for hundreds of yards, and said, "Let's sit there. This is my favorite spot in all of Alexandria. I try to come here every night to watch the sun set. There are days when I am unable to do this, and I miss it when that happens."

We sat in silence for a few moments, and then he turned to me and asked, "Do you want to talk about what happened to you and the others any more today, Mekhaeil, or would you rather wait until tomorrow? I know how tired you must be. It's up to you."

I turned to him and asked him, again, "If I do, do you still promise not to reveal what I tell you to anyone, without my permission, Father, now that you know what it is I am about to tell you?"

"As I told you before, if we consider this to be a confession—and I will do so if you ask me to—I promise you that it will remain confidential. Is this to be a confession, Mekhaeil?" he asked.

"Well, yes," I responded. "If that is what I must do for it to be confidential, Father. I'm not ready to tell the world, or my family, or the families of those who died there what happened, but if I tell you what others said, and things I said or did, will you keep all of that just between the two of us too, as if it's part of my confession?"

"What others said? What are you talking about, Mekhaeil?" Father Bishoy asked.

"Everybody made a confession, not just me, Father," I responded.

"You all made a confession? But there was no priest there. How could you do that?" he asked.

"I'm sorry. You're right. They said that they were repenting of their sins. Demetrius said that the early Christians made their confessions to their fellow Christians and that that was acceptable, since there weren't any priests back then; but Cyril said we couldn't do that, so we didn't, but many of the men told of their sins, just as if it were a confession, and they called it a repentance."

Father Bishoy sat back, thinking about what I had said, and then he asked, "So because they thought they were going to die, the men repented their sins to each other that night?"

"Yes."

"All of them?"

"Most of them did. I fell asleep at some point, so I didn't hear what everyone said, but I heard what many of the men said, Father," I told him.

"And you too?" he asked.

"Actually, I didn't say anything. They asked me if I had anything to repent of, and I told them that I didn't."

"Well, let's start with you, Mekhaeil. Is there anything you want to confess now? If this is to be a confession, you must confess your sins, yes? Why didn't you say anything then?" he asked.

"I was too embarrassed to say anything, Father, especially in comparison to what the others said," I told him.

"What is it that you wish to confess to me now, Mekhaeil?"

I turned away sheepishly and said, "I guess I would tell you about things involving girls and sex … impure thoughts, Father."

"And have you had sex with girls, Mekhaeil?"

"No. I just think about it a lot," I told him.

It was uncomfortable for me to say that to Father Bishoy. I had always made a confessions when I was looking at the priest and the priest was looking at me, but for some reason, this was different. I didn't know him like I knew the priests at home.

"Nothing else, Mekhaeil? No stealing? No mischief, like writing things on walls or breaking things that belong to someone else? No cursing? Or—"

"I never cursed much before I went to work with the men in Sirte, Father, but when working there, I learned how to curse, so I did that too."

At that, Father Bishoy chuckled and said, "I'm sure you did, Mekhaeil. Was there anything else?"

When I told him that there really wasn't much else that I had done in my life to confess, he said, "Mekhaeil, I absolve you from your sins. Go and sin no more, and for your act of contrition, I ask that you tell me what happened to you and all the other men. That should keep everything you say to me safely within the confines of this confessional, I think."

"I trust you, Father."

"On that you have my promise, Mekhaeil," he assured me.

I then proceeded to tell him that we had heard the sounds of gunfire for days and that we had received reports of the terrorists being in the vicinity. I explained that we planned to leave the very next day to go back to our village and that we were just waiting to get our last paycheck before leaving. I told him, again, that I was the first to see them coming and that I yelled out a warning, and I explained how we were captured.

Father Bishoy listened attentively as I went into great detail about how the others were rounded up and put into the truck, how that young Muslim boy was the one to find me, and how I tried to avoid being captured by saying that I wasn't with them. Then I told him about how we were thrown about in the back of the truck, with little air and no water, and how I thought I was going to die right then in that truck.

"That must have been awful for you and the others, Mekhaeil," he said softly.

"It was," I told him.

I became more animated as I relived those moments. I'm sure I rambled and said things that were hard for him to understand, but I was telling him whatever came into my mind. Father Bishoy sat there quietly, listening to my every word, interrupting only to ask me to clarify certain things. Every now and then, people would walk by; whenever they did, I would lower my voice and wait until they passed. I didn't want anyone else to hear any of the things I was saying.

I told him of how they yelled and screamed at us when the truck finally stopped and they let us out, and how they put the collars on our necks and led us into that little building with the poles. He grimaced when I told him about that, and the rest, but he became most interested when I told him about Demetrius and how he was the one who convinced us that we should prepare to meet God by making confessions to each other.

"Demetrius, you say, was the man who did that?"

"Yes, he was. There were several men who spoke at length that night, but Demetrius was our leader. He was the one who prepared us for what happened the next morning," I told him.

"So you all were sure that you were going to die in the morning?" he asked.

"I wasn't. But I was the only one. I thought someone was going to rescue us, but Demetrius and all the others were as sure as they could be that we were going to be killed," I responded.

"So when these men made their repentances, they did so as if it would be their last confession, yes?" he asked.

"Oh, yes," I assured him. "There were many who said things that no one knew or suspected. I'm sure they never would have said those things if it weren't for the fact that they knew they were going to die."

As soon as I told him that, I realized that I had said more than I had planned on saying, but Father Bishoy was more interested in hearing about what was taking place inside the room than he was about what was actually said.

"Remarkable!" he said. "They were true followers of Christ, weren't they?" he asked.

"Not everyone. I heard the pope and the president say that, and it was on the news, too, but it's wrong," I told him. "One of the men wasn't. His name was Omar, though that may not be his real name. He probably told us his last name, but I don't remember it," I told him.

"So that man wasn't a Copt?" he asked, surprised. "Was he a Christian?"

"No. Omar was a Muslim," I said.

"Why did they kill him?" he asked.

"Because they thought he was one of us," I responded. "Actually, he was a Shiite Muslim, and he said that if they knew that, they would have treated him worse than they did us," I told him.

Father Bishoy nodded knowingly. "But everyone else was from that one village—is that correct?"

"No. Most of the men were from al-Aour, my village, but several were from villages nearby. Everyone else was a Copt."

"And did all of them believe that they would be going to heaven after making a confession, even though there was no priest there to absolve them of their sins?" Father Bishoy persisted.

"No, not at all. Some thought that they were doomed and that there was no hope of salvation, and others thought that they weren't worthy," I answered. "I don't know that anyone really believed that he would be going to heaven. They all hoped so, though,"

"But they truly repented of their sins?" he asked.

"Yes, they did, but as I said, I fell asleep at some point during the night," I told him, somewhat ashamedly, "so I didn't hear everything."

"That was a terrible ordeal, Mekhaeil," Father Bishoy said. "Don't be ashamed of that. You're just a young boy. You had probably never stayed up all night once in your whole life before that night, had you?" he asked.

"No, I hadn't," I responded. "I was exhausted. I tried, but I couldn't keep my eyes open," I admitted. "I wanted to stay awake and hear all that the men were saying, but I couldn't."

"You wanted to hear them tell about the sins they had committed during their lives, Mekhaeil?" he asked.

"No, that wasn't it. Although some of the things they said surprised me quite a bit, I was more interested in the things they said about why it was happening to us—why these men wanted to do that to us. The men talked about the history of our people and our church, and about the history of the Muslims and the Jews, Muhammad, Moses, and all the rest."

"The men talked about those things?" Father Bishoy asked, clearly surprised to hear that, too.

"Yes. That is what Demetrius said we should do. He said the others should do it for the young men, like me, because it would help us understand why we were being killed and who these men were who were going to kill us."

"Hmm ... interesting," he said. "So tell me, what did you learn from that?" he asked.

I told him that Omar, who was actually from Afghanistan, told us all about Muhammad and Islam; that Cyril, who had studied to become a priest and was a deacon in our church, told us all about the history of the Coptic religion; and that Rushdi, who had been a history professor at a university, told us all about the Crusades and explained that Christians, Muslims, and Jews have done terrible things to each other for centuries; and so forth.

"And this was before any of the men made their repentances?" Father Bishoy asked.

"Yes, Father," I told him. "Many of the men didn't want to tell the others their sins. They wanted to confess to themselves or not at all. Also, many of the younger men said that they might be willing to convert if given a chance, but Demetrius convinced everyone that it was worthwhile to talk about those things and maybe change the minds of some of them. At least, I think that was the main reason why he had us do that."

"Hmm … amazing," he said. "Demetrius thought that if the younger men, like you, knew more about our history, the history of Muslims, and the rest, it would help you all decide not to convert if given the opportunity, and to face death if you weren't given that opportunity?"

"I think that's right. And apparently it worked, because no one converted. Everyone else was sure we were going to die in the morning. I think I was the only one who believed that, somehow, we would be saved. One of the men wanted us to kill ourselves, like some ancient Jews did long ago, but we couldn't figure out a way to do it because of the way we were chained. And besides, not everyone thought that was a good idea."

"You thought you would live, Mekhaeil? Why?"

"I believed that my father and the others from our village would find a way to save us. Others thought maybe the Egyptian army would rescue us. Some thought that the United States or some other countries in the world would come to our aid. A couple of men thought fellow Christians would help us, but in the end, I think I was the only one who thought God would save us. I was wrong."

"But He saved you, Mekhaeil, didn't He?" Father Bishoy asked.

I looked at him blankly and said, "Maybe He did … I hadn't thought of it like that. But why me and not someone else, Father? Why me and not any of the others?"

I lowered my head and put my elbows on my knees and my head in my hands. Father Bishoy put his hand on the back of my head and said, "Mekhaeil, I think it was God who saved you, but I have no idea why. You are still a boy, though after what you've been through, I think you have become a man in a matter of days. Those men were true Copts! They were true martyrs. They were willing to go to their death for their church and for their belief in Jesus Christ. I am so happy to hear that, Mekhaeil!"

I was puzzled. I was still so depressed and so saddened by

what had happened that I couldn't understand why Father Bishoy was so happy about what I was telling him.

"Many people converted over the centuries to avoid being killed, but never a true Copt … never a true Copt! Those men were true Copts!" Father Bishoy exclaimed, almost gleefully.

"Cyril told us that what was happening to us was just like what Christians had done to Muslims and Jews did during the Spanish Inquisition," I said. "Or it might have been Rushdi who said that; I'm not sure."

"You learned a lot that night, didn't you, Mekhaeil?" he asked.

"I did. I heard many, many things I had never heard before," I acknowledged.

"And what are you going to do, Mekhaeil, now that you have learned those things, been through what you have been through, and been saved by God?"

"I don't know, Father … I don't know …" I responded. "I'm hoping that maybe you can help me with that."

At that, Father Bishoy stood and said, "I have some thoughts, but we've been here for hours now. It's getting late, and we must be getting back before it gets dark. I think you've had enough for one day, don't you, Mekhaeil?"

I hadn't told him much of what really took place yet, but I was tired, and I was hungry again, so I readily agreed. Together we walked back to the rectory. Not much was said on the way.

When we arrived, we found two places set in the kitchen, with food and drink ready for us. Father Bishoy heated up the bread and the food, and after saying a prayer, we ate our dinner in silence. When we were finished, he said, "Mekhaeil, when you wake up, come back here and someone will serve you breakfast. I have some responsibilities I must attend to in the morning, but I would like to continue our conversation sometime midmorning if you don't mind. Would that be acceptable to you?"

I told him that it would be. We said good night to each other, and I found my way back to my room. It was hard for me to believe all that had happened over the two days since we were captured.

Even today, so much had happened. I had seen Pope Tawadros II and the president of my country, but the most important thing that had happened that day was that I had met Father Bishoy. He had helped me a lot.

As I put my head on the pillow and pulled the blanket over me, I felt a need to see my mother and my father for the first time in a long time. Now I was alone, and I had never been so alone before in my life. I missed my family. I was asleep within minutes.

CHAPTER 25

More Revelations

The next morning, I awoke with a start and looked around the room, wondering where I was for a few seconds. I lingered in bed, pondering what today would bring. I could tell from the amount of sunlight in the room that it was late—much later than I was used to waking up.

For months the men and I had woken up before dawn and been ready to go to work at first light. We worked long, hard hours, and we usually worked seven days a week. Although the days were lengthening, they were still much shorter than during the summer months. On a normal workday, we would work from about seven in the morning until five in the afternoon.

I had gone to bed early the night before, right after dinner, and I thought to myself that I must have slept a long time—maybe twelve hours. I rolled out of bed and noticed some clothes in the corner, by the door, with a towel on top. After making the bed, I took a shower, dressed, and went down to the kitchen.

The women there made a big fuss over me, calling me a sleepyhead and asking me how I could sleep so long. It was almost nine. I hadn't slept that late since I was a little boy. I was never allowed to sleep that long. There was always something to be done, whether it was school, church, or helping my parents with chores around the house.

I just smiled and said that I must have been very tired. They had no idea what I had been through. Apparently Father

Bishoy hadn't told them anything; otherwise, they would have understood.

They put plates of food in front of me, just as they had done the day before. I hadn't had such meals since I was in my home many months before. I ate the food much slower today than I had the day before, when I was famished.

While I was eating, the women were all talking about the visit by President el-Sisi and Pope Tawadros to St. Mark's the day before. Since there had been so many cameras there, I knew it was something the whole country knew about. I didn't mention to them that I had been there.

Father Bishoy was the only person who knew what I had been through. He was getting the news before anyone else. I was the only one in the world, other than the terrorists, who knew what had really happened.

Just as I was finishing, Father Bishoy walked into the room and asked, "Sleep well, Mekhaeil?"

"I did, Father. Thank you," I responded.

"And these nice women have taken good care of you, have they?"

"They have. Thank you for that, too," I said.

"Thank them, not me," he said.

After I thanked all of the women and finished the last drop of milk in my glass, he asked, "Would you like to go for another walk, Mekhaeil?"

I knew he was anxious to learn more about what had happened three days earlier. Although I hadn't watched television or seen a newspaper, I was sure the whole country wanted to know what Egypt was going to do about what had happened to me and the others in Sirte.

It was then that I realized my story was going to be of great interest to many people, not just the families in al-Aour. Father Bishoy was undoubtedly as interested as anyone else to find out. Up until then, it had been all about me and my feelings.

Ever since I decided to tell him about what happened, I had started to feel more like I wanted to tell him. It seemed as if I needed to tell him about what happened. I agreed to the walk.

On our walk back to the bench where we had sat the previous day, Father Bishoy asked me about my family, my church, and the community where I was from. He had never been to al-Aour before. He was genuinely concerned about how the parishioners would deal with the loss of so many of our family members. It wasn't just about me.

February is the coldest month of the year, although January isn't much warmer, but even then, it's not too cold. The average temperature is twelve degrees Celsius, and on this day it was about that. It was a beautiful winter day for Alexandria.

I was glad the women had given me a sweatshirt with hand pockets in front and a hood just before we left. I had the hood over my head and my hands in the pockets. We chose a bench in the sun, with no one else close by.

Once we sat down, Father Bishoy said, "Thank you, Mekhaeil, for sharing with me what you and the others went through a few nights ago. I've given a lot of thought to what you have told me so far. Is there anything else you would like to tell me about what you and the others discussed that night, believing that you all were going to die?"

I hesitated before answering, trying to remember exactly what Boctor, Clement, and the others said, as well as what Omar told us about what Muslims think of life after death, and then I said, "Everyone believed in God, and all, except for Omar, were firm in all of the things we Copts believe in, but as I mentioned yesterday, there were some who were so unhappy with what was happening to us that they said some things I really don't think they meant. Those were the younger men. I think they said those things because they were just so afraid of dying and didn't want to die. I don't want anyone to know about any of that, okay?"

"As you wish, Mekhaeil," he responded. "I won't say a word about any of that. But the men were hoping to cleanse themselves before what we call the last day. Is that accurate? Even those who were considering converting to Islam, yes?"

I thought about it again before answering, and then said, "Yes, Father. I think everyone in that room thought he was going to meet God the very next morning, and everyone was preparing for that; but there were differences between the older men and the younger men, as I said before."

"So everyone, except for the Muslim, was a true believer? They all believed in the message of Jesus Christ?" he asked, solemnly. It was more of a statement than a question.

"Yes, Father. I think that is definitely true—especially by the time morning came." I remembered all the things Clement had said, but even he believed in Jesus Christ and His message. I didn't mention any of that.

"And even though they knew that they couldn't be absolved of their sins, because there was no priest there to absolve them, they repented of their sins openly to one another, yes?"

"I think that's true, Father, though, as I said before, I didn't hear what everyone had to say. Everybody I heard was as honest as he could be," I replied. "Actually, I was surprised by how honest they all were."

"I find that remarkable, Mekhaeil. It strengthens my faith as a priest to hear you tell of it. It makes me feel good about our religion and our people to hear your story. I think there is an extremely good lesson to be learned from what you and the others went through. They died knowing that they were going to meet our God … and they would rather have died than converted."

I looked at him, and when I did, I thought I saw some wetness in his eyes, as if he had been brought to tears. I didn't say anything, but then I thought of all that I had heard from Boctor and I wondered if I should tell him about what he and Clement had said, and I thought of my brother Touma, and of Raghib and all the things the two of them had done, and of Cyril. I decided not to say anything about them at that time.

"Actually, Father, even the best man in the room, Demetrius— at least I thought he was the best man—thought he wasn't worthy, and the worst were sure they were doomed."

"Why is that, Mekhaeil? Why did they feel that way?" he asked.

I looked at him and asked, "Do you want me to tell you what some of them said, Father?"

"Only if you want to, Mekhaeil."

Without naming anyone, I told him that two of the men had killed Muslims who had attacked them, and I explained that Demetrius had said he had done nothing with his life and felt that he would be seen as a failure in the eyes of God.

When I was finished, Father Bishoy leaned back, sighed, and said, "They are all martyrs, Mekhaeil. They are all in heaven as I speak. You heard Pope Tawadros say so. Trust me on that. Is there anything else you want to tell me?"

I asked him about Demetrius. I asked him if he thought that God would judge men for not using the gifts they had been given as harshly as He would judge men for what they had done with their lives, and he told me, "No one is worthy, Mekhaeil. We are chosen by God. From what you told me, Demetrius was a wonderful man, but when God gives someone a gift, a special thing, I think He expects the person to whom such a gift is given to do something with it, don't you?"

I didn't say anything. I knew he was talking about me. I didn't know what to say. Then he continued.

"I read in the paper what I could about all of the men, and I saw that most of them were in their early twenties. Your name is in there, Mekhaeil, but you knew that it would be, yes?"

"I was pretty sure that it would be. Actually I expected it to say there were twenty-two men. There were twenty-one Copts there, but then there was Omar, so I figured it would take some time for people to figure that out. There were twenty-one men shown on television, though, so that's why it said twenty-one people died, which is true. It probably didn't mention Omar, did it?"

"I didn't notice. Many of the men were still in their teens, but you were by far the youngest, weren't you, Mekhaeil?" he asked.

"Yes, Father, I was. I think that is part of the reason why they let me go. I don't have a beard, and I look like a little boy. Most of them had beards to make them look older, but I couldn't grow one. I have this scraggly little thing. I wanted to look older too," I responded.

"Anything else you want to tell me, Mekhaeil?"

I thought about it, and then I said, "I would like to ask you about what one of the older men said to us. I am curious as to what you will say about him. His name is Raghib Sarraf."

"Raghib Sarraf from Alexandria? The vice president of the Egyptian Rug Company?" Father Bishoy asked.

"Yes, Father. That's him," I replied.

"I thought he was dead. I have not seen him or heard of him in quite some time. He was with you?" Father Bishoy asked, noticeably surprised. "His name wasn't in the paper."

"He said he was using a different name," I told him.

"What did Raghib say that you would like to discuss, Mekhaeil?"

"He told us many things, Father. In fact, what he said was one of the most powerful things I heard all night," I said.

"Really? Why is that?" he asked.

"He was one of the two men who killed some people," I replied.

"He was? What did he do?" Father Bishoy asked, clearly interested in Raghib because he knew him.

"He told us of how he came to Alexandria as a young boy, much like I did, Father. In fact, I think I might have come here because Raghib told us that's what he did when he was a young boy like me. He left home right after completing his schooling in our village, and he came to St. Mark's, just as I did yesterday, and the church helped him get that job with the rug company. I can't say that is exactly why I came here, Father—looking for a job, that is—but in the back of my mind, I think that what Raghib said that night influenced me more than I realized."

"He was from al-Aour; I didn't remember that," Father Bishoy said softly. "Yes, I knew him, Mekhaeil. I knew him when he was a young boy, about your age. We were about the same age, actually, but we were very different. I may be a year or two older.

"I watched him as he grew up and became so powerful … Raghib Sarraf … he was a powerful man, Mekhaeil, a very powerful man. My, oh my. To think that he was with you and the others in Sirte … isn't that something!"

I didn't say anything in response, and then he continued. "So tell me, what did Raghib say, Mekhaeil?"

I told him Raghib had killed some people who broke into the rug company late one night, and I went on to explain that that was why he had run away and that he regretted the life that he had led, in some ways. But I also noted that he was proud of what he had accomplished in other ways, and all the rest.

"None of us had any idea of the things he had done," I told him. "I was shocked. He was one of the men who thought that they were doomed to die and go to hell, Father. He didn't think he could be forgiven for all of the sins he committed during his lifetime."

"Hmm," Father Bishoy mused, apparently thinking of how to respond. Then he said, "Once he began to make all that money, buy those expensive cars, and travel all over the world, we never saw him in church again. I haven't seen him in years, but he died as a martyr, Mekhaeil, just like the others. Remember that. He is in heaven with Demetrius and everyone else."

"He said he never would have told anyone any of those things if he hadn't thought he was going to die the next day, Father, so I think he was honest and truly regretted his sinful life, if that helps."

"I'm sure that it did, and I'm gladdened to hear it. Thank you for sharing that with me. Anything else, Mekhaeil?"

The only ones I could think of were Cyril, Boctor, and Clement, but I didn't want to talk about them, so I said, "Well, as I said before, there were several young men who basically said the same thing, Father."

"And who were they, Mekhaeil?" he asked.

"Yousrey Maalouf, Nabir Yassa, Magdi Wassef, Moghaddan Ramzy, Maurice Sarraf, Cosmos Nazir … I think those were all of the younger men, Father," I replied. "Plus my brothers, Touma and Guirguis."

"And they all said the same things? Girls, sex, impure thoughts, some minor bad deeds—things like that?" he asked.

"Yes, Father," I told him. "I don't remember anything bad

about any of them, except they all cursed, but I told you that already."

"All right. I have heard such confessions thousands upon thousands of times. I think I could make the confession for all of them, since I have heard the same things so many times," he said. "Such things are normal."

I thought of Abanoub, and I said, "I think you'll be glad to hear about Abanoub Samaha, Father."

"And what did Abanoub say, Mekhaeil?"

"Father, out of everyone in the room, even Demetrius, he was, I think, the most devout of any of us. He was older than most of us but not as old as Demetrius or Raghib or some of the others, but he had a wife and five children, and he was as good as a man could be, I think. He didn't want to die and leave his family alone, without him, but he was the most ready and the most willing to die, Father."

"Five children … that's so sad. So what did he repent of, Mekhaeil?"

"He was much like Demetrius. He just said he wasn't worthy. I don't remember anything bad … maybe impure thoughts … I'm not sure. I don't remember anything. But he, more than anyone else, told us that we should die as martyrs and be proud of who we are."

"You are right, Mekhaeil. Such a man is clearly a true martyr, dying for his religious beliefs."

"Anything else?" he asked.

"There was Ignatius, Demetrius's son, and he was just like Demetrius. They looked alike, acted alike, and were always together … and they didn't curse—neither one of them. I never heard either one say a curse word. I even heard Abanoub curse when he hit his finger with a hammer by accident one day, but never Demetrius or Ignatius," I said.

"And I'm sure they left many children behind too, didn't they, Mekhaeil?"

"Oh, yes. Most of the men had wives and several children," I told him. "Except for the younger men. Most of them weren't even married yet."

"So sad, but Abanoub and the others are in a better place. Next?" he asked.

"There was Theophilos Aziz and his brother Halim. They were in the middle, as far as ages go. They weren't as old as some, but they were much older than the younger men we've already talked about," I told him.

"And what did they say, Mekhaeil?" he asked.

"Again, I don't remember them doing anything wrong, other than impure thoughts, cursing … and that was it. They were good men. Both had wives and children."

At that, Father Bishoy said, "They were all simple men, weren't they, Mekhaeil? And good Copts. Mekhaeil, I was as sure as I could be, before hearing you tell me what actually happened, that the men killed were good men who were killed for no good reason, but I can't tell you how pleased I am to hear you confirm these things about them that I and the rest of the world would never know otherwise. It reinforces all that I believe.

"Keep in mind that people are killed for no reason all the time, but a martyr is one who dies for a cause or a belief, and in this case that belief is in Jesus Christ, our lord and savior. Those are true martyrs."

"There was Rushdi, too. He was one of the elders of our church, like Demetrius, and he was also a professor at Cairo University. He taught history, and he's the one who told us all about the Crusades. He—"

"You talked about the Crusades, too?" Father Bishoy asked, obviously surprised.

"Yes. That was part of it. Demetrius, or maybe it was someone else, wanted to know why the Muslims were doing these things to us, and Omar said that Christians had done these same things to Muslims in the past," I told him.

"Interesting," he said, "I can't tell you how surprised I am to hear that on the night before you were to die, you talked about why the Muslims were going to kill you and those other things. Tell me again, please. Why did the men do that, Mekhaeil?"

"Demetrius thought it was important for us to understand them better. No one could really understand why they were going to kill us. We hadn't done anything to them. We had no money … we had nothing they wanted. I learned many things that night that I didn't know, and so did many of the other young people. I think we all learned something. Not everyone wanted to do that, though."

"Did the men think about Jesus and what He would have done?" Father Bishoy asked.

"We talked about that, and how Jesus forgave the men who crucified Him, and how He turned the other cheek, but no one in the room that night could forgive those people for what they were going to do to us. No one wanted to die, Father. Everyone was crying, saying prayers, and singing our music. They were good Copts, Father, but none of us was that good."

"You all said prayers and sang songs, Mekhaeil?

"We did," I answered.

"That is wonderful. Anything else?" he asked.

At that point, the only people left I could think of were Cyril, Clement, and Boctor. I was going around the room in my head, trying to think of anything else we discussed that might be of interest to him. Those were the only ones left, so I chose to tell him about some of the things Boctor had said.

"Boctor Daoud was one of the younger men, and like many of the other young men, he had no wife and no children, but he was one who would have killed himself, if he could, rather than let them kill him."

"It is not permitted, as you know," Father Bishoy said.

"We knew, Father, but that's how he felt, and he, more than anyone else, I think, was really upset that God would allow this to happen to us," I told him.

Father Bishoy nodded. "I see."

"And he was trying to figure out a way for us to escape. At first, I think he would have converted in a heartbeat if they would have let him, as he was so distraught about everything. But in the end, he and everyone else agreed to accept their fate and die as good Copts. He said his mother would kill him if he converted, even if they didn't."

We both laughed.

"I am so happy to hear that, Mekhaeil," Father Bishoy said. "Thank you for sharing that with me. His mother will be glad to hear that too; I assure you of that. But I won't tell her. You will have to do that if you choose to do so."

"Then there was Clement ... Clement Barakat. He, too, was a very unhappy man ... unhappy with his life, unhappy with everything. He, more than anyone else, was ready to die," I told him.

"Why was he so unhappy?" Father Bishoy asked.

When I told him about how his wife and children had been killed, and how he might have lost some of his faith in God, Father Bishoy said, "I hope he reconciled with God prior to his death, but he, too, is a martyr. Anyone else?"

"The last one is Cyril ... Cyril Bahgoury," I said.

"I know Cyril. I saw his name in the paper. I remember him from his days at the seminary. I was sad to see that he was among those who were killed. What were his sins? What did he confess?" he asked.

"Well, this one was the most shocking of all," I said.

"Shocking? Why is that, Mekhaeil? He was a deacon in your church, wasn't he? Some of us, including me, expected that he would become a priest, or maybe even a bishop, eventually, once he decided whether or not he wished to be married."

"That's true, Father," I responded, "but this is one where you really have to promise me that you won't tell anyone about what I'm going to tell you."

"I won't. I promise," he said.

"Cyril was a homosexual," I told him.

Father Bishoy was obviously taken aback. He leaned back away from me with his eyes wide open and said, "No! Really! I never would have expected that!"

"Neither did anyone else, Father," I told him. "Everyone was surprised."

It took Father Bishoy a few moments to regain his composure, and then he asked, "Was there anything else he repented of?"

"No, that was it. He was a true believer. He and Abanoub stood by the church and our beliefs through all the doubts and questions, although Demetrius was just as strong. But Cyril was sure he was going to hell because of his sexuality."

"That is a sin, and it's a big one; that's true," he said.

"Can he be forgiven, Father?"

"That is up to God, Mekhaeil, not me," he told me.

"And the most shocking thing, Father, for me, was that he really didn't want to be that way. He hated being that way. He hated himself for being that way. He told us that was the way God made him, not that he chose to commit sin. He was so sincere about it, Father. Nobody knew quite what to say to him."

"It is a sin, Mekhaeil, and people who have those tendencies must fight hard to avoid those carnal temptations. It is the same way for women; they must fight the temptations too. It's not just men. That is their cross to bear in this lifetime. It is still a choice that they make."

"So they can't be forgiven, Father?"

"That's not what I said, Mekhaeil. It is a sin for men to lust after women or women to lust after men, just as it is a sin for men to lust after men or for women to lust after women. All of that is wrong in the eyes of God except during marriage, as you know. Was there anything else?"

When I told him that was all I could think of, he said, "Good. It's getting late, and I have an appointment to meet with someone at noon, so I need to get back. Thank you for sharing all of that with me, Mekhaeil. Let's talk again after lunch, shall we? When we do, I want to talk about you and what will become of you after all that you've been through."

CHAPTER 26

Malala

After lunch, I sat outside the rectory, under the same tree, on the same bench, waiting for Father Bishoy to join me. Half an hour later, he came running toward me, saying, "Sorry, sorry, sorry, Mekhaeil. I've been extremely busy since we talked, and I'm afraid I won't be able to meet with you this afternoon, but I have a favor to ask of you."

"What is it?" I asked.

"I want you to read this," he said as he handed me a book. "I think you'll find it very interesting."

The book was titled *I Am Malala*, and on the cover was a picture of a young girl with a veil over her head.

"Who is she?" I asked.

"You don't know?" Father Bishoy asked.

"No," I replied.

"You'll see. Will you agree to read it?" he asked.

I had nothing else to do, and I couldn't refuse him, so I agreed.

"Good. I'll come find you when I get free. Will you be on the benches down by the water, or will you be here?"

I told him that I would rather go back to the bench by the water. I hadn't read anything, not even a newspaper, since my school days ended. I wasn't looking forward to reading a book.

Once I was back on the same bench where we had sat before, I began reading. I quickly discovered why Father Bishoy wanted me to read this particular book.

Malala was a Pakistani Muslim girl, just a year older than I, who had been shot in the head at point-blank range by the Taliban because she refused to follow sharia law. She went to school despite being ordered not to, and she openly spoke out on behalf of girls like herself. She wasn't afraid to speak her mind, and the Taliban didn't like that, so they shot her.

Even though the Pakistani Taliban openly declared that they would try again to kill her again when she recovered, she continued to defy them. Her message was that all boys and girls—especially all of the girls in the world, not just in Pakistan—have the right to receive an education. She was an inspiration for all girls in Pakistan and in the whole world. She went to many countries to tell her story.

I knew little of the Nobel Prize, though I had heard of it, but I was impressed to read that she had won it the year before. I remembered clearly what Omar had told us about what the Taliban had done to him and to his family in Afghanistan. I remembered that he blamed the Taliban and its leader, Mullah Omar, for many of the problems that Muslim extremists were now causing around the world, including what ISIS had done to us.

Hours later, I was startled when Father Bishoy came up and put his hand on my shoulder. I had been deep in thought.

"You are enjoying it, it seems," he said.

"Very much so," I replied.

"I thought you would. She is a lot like you in many ways, isn't she?"

"No," I responded, chuckling as I did. "I am not like her at all, Father. She started writing things when she was eleven years old about what it was like to be a young girl living under Taliban rule. I never did anything like that. She's a very brave girl. I'm not like her."

"But you could be, Mekhaeil," he said.

I was surprised when he said that.

"The last thing in the world that I want to do is talk to people about what I went through a few days ago," I told him, "and I certainly don't want to be shot in the head. I am lucky to have a head at all, as you know, Father. I am not like her at all."

"Mekhaeil, I think God saved you from being killed for a reason, don't you?"

"If he did, Father, I don't know what it is. Do you?" I asked.

"Well, I'd rather that you figure it out for yourself, Mekhaeil, but since you asked, I'll tell you what I think. I think you're supposed to tell the world about what happened to you."

That stopped me for several seconds. The thought of what the young Muslim had said to me when I was released immediately came to mind.

"That's what the terrorist boy told me, Father," I acknowledged.

"That's what who said? What are you talking about, Mekhaeil?" he asked.

"When they decided not to kill me along with the others, they put a hood over my head so I couldn't see where they had taken us, and I was taken in a truck back to where we had been captured. They released me about a mile from the construction site.

"When the young Muslim boy, the one who had captured me, took the hood off of my head and the cuffs off of my hands, he said, 'Go and tell the world what you have seen.' Those were his exact words."

"That's remarkable, Mekhaeil," Father Bishoy replied. "Those are the words he used? 'Go and tell the world what you have seen.' I'd say that is more than a coincidence; that is the hand of God at work, Mekhaeil."

"I admit, Father, that when that boy said that to me, I wondered why he said that and what he meant by that, especially after I saw the video on television later that day. But I'm not like Malala, Father; I think you're mistaken about that."

"But, Mekhaeil, those men hate us because of our religious beliefs, and for no other reason whatsoever. What have you ever done to make those men hate you? Nothing! So just as Malala fought against the hatred those Muslim extremists had for her just because she was a woman, or a girl, which caused them to shoot her in the head, you must fight against the hatred these people have for us. And I'm not talking just about you; I'm talking about your family, your people—all of us right here in Egypt! … not in Libya, Syria, Iraq, Afghanistan, Pakistan, or anywhere else, but right here at home, Mekhaeil … right here at home!" He raised his voice and put his face closer to mine as he said those things to me. I was unconvinced. I had no desire whatsoever to do what he was asking of me, and I told him so. I was afraid to talk in class, let alone talk to people I didn't know.

"Mekhaeil, how much more do you have to read of her book?" he asked.

"I'm about halfway through," I told him.

"Why don't you keep reading. Let's talk tonight, when you're finished. Come find me, and maybe we can have dinner together. How's that?"

I agreed. When he left, I returned to Malala's book. It was hard for me to believe that she started doing what she did when she was only eleven years old. Clearly her parents had influenced her greatly. Her father was one who talked in front of large crowds and was very active in community affairs. Still, she was the one who was shot in the head, and she was the one to stand in front of a microphone and tell people what she believed in.

I could not deny that I was impressed by what she had done and what she was continuing to do. I admired her, but it didn't make me think I should try to do what she had done. I still had no desire to talk to anyone about it. It was hard enough for me to talk to Father Bishoy about all of this.

However, as I read about Malala and about what she and her family had been through, my thoughts began to turn to my family. I missed my mother and my father, and my younger brother and sister. Thoughts of them kept coming into my head. I didn't know why I was so resistant to going back home, but I just didn't feel ready.

Several hours later, I finished reading her book. It was now nearing sunset, and I was thinking I may have missed dinner, but I had to finish the book. I couldn't put it down. I had never read a book that had captured me as much as her book did. I was able to relate to what she had been through, though I had experienced none of the physical pain, surgeries, or medical issues that she had to deal with.

I went straight to the kitchen, and women were there cleaning it up. I was late, but they had saved dinner for me. I was told that Father Bishoy was going to join me. One went running off to find him. Minutes later, he appeared and sat down across from me at the table.

"So what did you think, Mekhaeil?" he asked. "Good book, wasn't it?"

I handed it back to him and thanked him for giving it to me to read. He refused to accept it and said, "No, no! You keep it. I want you to have it. In fact, I will sign it for you, as a gift!"

He took the book from my hands, pulled a pen from his pocket, and wrote on the title page of the book, "To Mekhaeil, a very courageous young man!" And he signed it as well.

When he handed it back to me, I read what he wrote and said, "I'm not a courageous young man, Father. I am a coward."

"No, Mekhaeil, you are wrong! You did what any man, young or old, would have done," he whispered, apparently so the few women who were still in the room wouldn't hear what he was saying. "You did nothing wrong!" he insisted. "What should you have done that you didn't do, Mekhaeil?"

"I should have died with all the others; then I would be a martyr too. Those men were courageous—not me."

"Let's finish our dinners and talk later, more privately," he said.

We chatted about Malala and the book over dinner.

"Did you notice that she is now in school in England?" Father Bishoy asked.

"I did," I replied.

"Do you have any desire to continue your schooling?" he asked. "Or are you going to want to go back to being a carpenter?"

"I don't know, Father. I have never thought of any of this before, but I have given some thought to it after reading about her. I need more time to think about things. It's still hard for me to believe that I'm sitting here with you in Alexandria, at St. Mark's Cathedral, having dinner with you, when three nights ago, about this same time, I was chained in a room with twenty-one men who are now dead. When I think of my brothers, I cry. I'm not ready yet, Father. I can't make sense out of any of this, and I don't understand why it happened." I started to cry again.

"I'm sorry, Mekhaeil," he said. "You have sustained wounds that will take a long time to heal. I'm sorry if I have said anything to cause you more pain. In fact, let's not talk of this anymore tonight. How about you think about what I have said and what you have read, get a good night of sleep, and let's talk again tomorrow morning. Would that be okay?"

I agreed, and we finished our dinners in silence. Again I was asleep within minutes of putting my head on the pillow.

The next morning, after showering and putting on another new set of clothes, I had another wonderful breakfast. I was being treated like a king. I knew this wouldn't last forever, but I appreciated it, and I knew I had Father Bishoy to thank for it. I knew that the reality of life would come back into play sometime soon. I still had no idea what that would involve.

After breakfast, I walked outside and sat on the bench, underneath the same tree where I had sat for days now. Father Bishoy joined me not long after.

"So how are you feeling today, Mekhaeil?" he asked.

"Fine, thank you, Father. I have never been treated so well in my life," I told him. "Not even my mother would treat me this way."

"I'm glad to hear it. You are welcome here as long as you like," he said.

"What do the others think of me?" I asked. "You haven't told them, have you?"

"No, no, no … I promised you that I wouldn't, and I haven't. I just told them that you were a Copt who was without a home. We do this for people all the time. No one has said anything about it. They think you are a nice young boy, and they are right.

After a while, some will ask questions, but I won't tell them anything unless and until you allow me to do so. I promise you that, Mekhaeil."

"Thank you, Father," I said.

"So what are you thinking of doing today? Do you have any plans? Is there anything you want to do? Or is it still too soon?" he asked.

"I miss my family, Father," I admitted. The words just popped out from my mouth.

"Are you ready to go home, Mekhaeil?" he asked.

I thought about it a little and then said, "I think so."

"That is a good sign, Mekhaeil. You can only imagine how they are feeling now—and not just them. Think about all of the other families and how they are feeling. You cannot imagine the grief they are experiencing, I'm sure," he said.

I lowered my head and said, "I know."

Father Bishoy waited for a few moments and then asked, "So what do you want to do about it, Mekhaeil?"

I turned to him and said, "I guess I've got to go home."

"Yes. Yes, Mekhaeil, I agree. I think you do. Do you know when you'd like to do that? Are you ready now?"

I sighed and said, "I guess so, but I don't know how to do that. I don't have the money to catch a bus, and I don't want to just show up. The shock might kill them."

"That's true, Mekhaeil. Everyone thinks you are dead. You're listed as being among the dead. No one has any idea that you are still alive," he said.

"That's true," I acknowledged. "So what should I do, Father?"

"I will help … if you let me," he answered.

"How?" I asked.

"If you will allow me to do so, I can call your parish priest and let him know that you are alive and well. I will ask him to contact your family, and the families of all of the other men killed, and let them know. Together we can arrange a time for us to return," he said.

"Us?" I asked.

"Yes. I will go with you," he answered.

"You will? Really, Father?" I asked.

"Yes, Mekhaeil. What happened to you is a terrible tragedy not just for you and the other men but also for our entire church. Many people in the world who were unfamiliar with us, or did not know much about us, now know who we are. But more importantly, we, as a people, have been deeply hurt by what took place a few short days ago.

"We, as a church and as a family, must heal," he said. "I would welcome the opportunity to be a part of that. That is my mission on this earth. That is what God wants me to do. God brought you to me, Mekhaeil. I believe that."

I thought about that for a while, and I understood what he was saying. I agreed, in part.

"I don't want to have them make a big thing of me, Father. I am not proud of myself for this. I did nothing brave or courageous. I know that you say I shouldn't feel that way, but I do. I don't want to be in the spotlight."

"I understand, Mekhaeil," he said, "but some of that is unavoidable. You are in the spotlight whether you like it or not. You cannot hide from it. You must face it, just as Malala faced the Taliban, and just as she continues to face the Taliban to this day. You have a great opportunity to do some good for our church, for your family, for your slain brothers and friends … and for yourself, Mekhaeil."

I still wasn't ready to accept that, and I told him so; but I was ready to go home, and I told him that.

"Do I have to tell them everything, Father?" I asked.

"You will be the one to decide what to tell them and what not to tell them, Mekhaeil. I will only tell people what you allow me to tell them. At the very least, I think I must tell them that you are alive and well and that you will be coming home. You know that you will be asked many questions upon your arrival there, and you can decide how you will answer those questions later, before you get there. How's that?"

I thought about it and said, "Okay."

"May I say that you escaped from them? Nothing more—just that you escaped?"

I thought about that, too. I knew that, eventually, the story would come out. I would decide how to answer all those questions later. For now Father Bishoy was going to let my family know that I was alive and that I was coming home. I agreed to allow him to do so.

"I guess that would be the best way to say it, Father. I did escape," I answered.

"When would you like to go, Mekhaeil?"

"Whenever you say, Father. I have nowhere else to go," I replied.

"I will call your priest now," he said. "Mekhaeil, trust me; they will all be very happy to get the news. And they need some good news; they are all stricken with grief, as you know. We all are."

At that he stood and said, "Stay here. I will be back as soon as I have news." With that he hurried away.

An hour or so later, he came running back and said, "Okay, Mekhaeil, we are leaving this afternoon!"

"This afternoon! That was fast. Really?" I said.

"Oh, yes! They are very excited at the news. The priests and deacons are overjoyed. They are expecting us by six o'clock tonight. They are going to spread the news now. We must hurry!" he told me.

"I have nothing but the clothes I am wearing, and you gave them to me. I can leave now," I said.

"No, we can't leave now. Several other priests want to go with us. Pope Tawadros himself wants to go," he told me.

"Pope Tawadros! What did you do, Father? Did you tell the whole world already?" I asked. "I thought you were only going to tell Father Ignatius."

"No, no, no, but I had to tell my superiors, and they told the pope, and when they all heard, they all got excited, especially him, and now everyone is very excited. I hope you don't mind, Mekhaeil. Pope Tawadros can't make it today, but he will go there sometime soon. You must understand that this is still a time of great sorrow, and we, as the shepherds, must be there to minister to our flock. All of the priests and deacons wanted to go, but the archdeacon will only allow a few to go with us. Is that all right?"

I could hardly refuse Father Bishoy, and the news was already out. There was nothing I could do or say to stop or undo what had been done. The die had been cast. I had passed the point of no return.

When I consented, he said, "Stay here; we should be ready shortly."

Not long after, two big black Volvo station wagons with tinted windows pulled up next to the curb a hundred feet or so from where I was sitting. Father Bishoy stepped out of one of the cars and motioned for me to come.

I sat in the back with two other priests, who were decked out in their finest Sunday attire, including the distinctive black robes and caps. They held their caps in their hands. Everyone was quite excited, and I was the center of attention. I had a sick feeling about what was going to happen when I got there.

CHAPTER 27

The Return Home

One of the priests said that the drive from Alexandria to al-Aour was about 350 kilometers and that it would take over four hours. The two priests I was sitting between were as nice as they could be, but I wasn't comfortable. I was squished in between them. They talked to me and tried their best to engage me in conversation, but I didn't have much to say. The men mostly chatted between themselves.

Father Bishoy was driving, and he would look in the rearview mirror at me every so often to see how I was doing. Several times he asked me if I was okay. I told him that I was, though he knew I wasn't, I'm sure. I was trusting him on all of this.

I was wondering if I had made a mistake. When I woke up that morning, I had no idea that I'd be going back to my village, let alone with two cars full of priests. Father Bishoy talked on his cell phone many times along the way, telling people where we were and what time he expected us to arrive.

Al-Aour is a small village. It may have six thousand people in it, most of whom are Copts, but there is a large number of Muslims there too. Growing up, we went to the same schools and lived in the same communities, for the most part. There weren't many problems between us—at least not as far as I could tell as a child. But there were some, and my family wasn't close friends with any Muslim families. I had few Muslim friends, and those were from school.

I wondered how the village had been affected by what happened and whether Copts were angry at the Muslims because of it. I expected that they would be, but I didn't know. I wasn't sure how I felt about that situation or how I would act when I met Muslims—especially the Sunni Muslims, now that I knew the difference.

As we got closer and closer to al-Aour, I became more apprehensive. I was nervous, actually. My palms began to sweat.

I was looking forward to seeing my mother and father, mostly, and my younger brother and sister, too. I had no idea what to expect as far as everything else was concerned. This wasn't going to be a happy occasion. I expected everyone to be sad and in mourning.

When we reached the outskirts of town, I was surprised to see a sign that said, "Welcome home, Mekhaeil!" At that my stomach muscles tightened up. It was the first of many such signs I would see.

Father Bishoy pointed it out to me and said, "They are happy to see you, Mekhaeil!"

As we got closer and closer to my church, there were more and more people standing on the sides of the streets. They waved at us when they recognized who we were. It was obvious that many people knew we were coming. I was surprised to see them smiling and waving their hands at me. I didn't know what to make of it.

When we got to the point where I could see the church, I leaned forward and saw hundreds of people in the street in front of it. It was blocked off. Police officers were rerouting the traffic. They had barricades up to control the crowd and prevent cars from passing.

"They are here to see you, Mekhaeil!" Father Bishoy told me. "They are happy to see you. I told you so, Mekhaeil! This is a good thing!"

Two police officers moved a barricade so our two vehicles could drive right up to the curb in front of the church. As I sat there, I was able to see my mother and father standing on the top

244 • Pierce Kelley

steps of the church, with my younger brother and sister standing right behind them.

I started to cry. I couldn't help it. I had been thinking about how I was going to react when I saw them, and I had asked myself what the others would act like if they were in my shoes.

I was sixteen years old, and I wanted to act the way a man would act under the circumstances. I didn't want to cry like a little boy, but I couldn't stop. When the doors opened, I ran to be with my family. I heard the people cheering as I emerged from the car. Everybody was smiling. My mother almost choked me to death, she squeezed me so hard. She wouldn't let go. My father had his arms around both of us.

After several minutes, when my mother finally let go of me, I turned and saw that our priest, Father Ignatius, was on the top step with us, a few feet away, with a microphone. Father Bishoy and the others were standing beside him. Father Ignatius began to speak.

"Thank you all for coming here tonight to be with us as we welcome home Mekhaeil Zacharias."

That was all I heard before the people began cheering again.

My father put his hand on my shoulder and said, "Mekhaeil, go and stand next to Father Ignatius."

I did as he told me to do. He shook my hand and then embraced me, as did all of the other priests and deacons. There must have been two dozen of them, including Father Bishoy and his group.

After everyone had shaken my hand, hugged me, and kissed me on both cheeks, Father Ignatius said, "Welcome home, Mekhaeil!" The crowd cheered even more. I waved my hand, and they cheered all the louder. They didn't stop for several minutes, it seemed.

I had thought about what was going to happen when I got home, and how I would react, but I had no idea it would be anything like this. I was numb. I didn't hear much of what Father Ignatius said after that. It was all I could do not to cry. As he talked, I looked around at all the people, and I smiled and waved whenever I saw someone I knew.

I knew most everyone standing inside the barricades, but I saw Muslims there too. They were standing on the other side of the street, behind the barricades. There were many people I had never seen before.

At some point, Father Ignatius handed me the microphone, and asked me to say a few words.

I had never spoken in front of a group like that before. I had never spoken into a microphone before either. I didn't know what to say, but I had to say something. I fumbled with the microphone and then said, "Three nights ago I was sitting with my brothers, Touma and Guirguis, along with nineteen other men, and we were chained together, expecting to die the next morning."

Everyone was silent as I spoke. I looked out and saw that all eyes were on me. I was nervous, but I thought of Malala at that moment, and it helped me. I took a deep breath and then said, "The next morning, they were all killed. But, for some reason, I was spared. God saved my life. I don't know why He did that, but I'm glad to be home."

And then I started to cry.

The crowd began to cheer again. Then I mumbled, "I wish they were all here with me now."

At that point, Father Ignatius took the microphone from my hand and spoke again.

"They are, Mekhaeil … they are all here with us now, I assure you."

Again the crowd cheered.

My mother and father were just a few feet below where I was standing, and I stepped down to be with them. My mother wrapped her arms around me again.

I didn't hear too much of what was said from that point on. Father Bishoy spoke, and I heard him tell everyone that I had gone to St. Mark's and that he had found me sitting in a pew in the back, all by myself, just two days ago. He told them all about how the men had been true Copts right to the end; he said they were true martyrs.

One of the leaders of the Muslim community spoke too. I

heard him say that the men who captured us didn't represent what Islam was all about. He offered his condolences to the families of those who were killed, and his gratitude for my safe return home. He asked that the people of al-Aour continue to treat each other with respect, as we always had, despite what had happened in Sirte.

After what seemed like hours, though I know it wasn't anywhere near that long, Father Ignatius thanked everyone for coming out to welcome me home and said there would be a service in the morning, though it would only be for the families and close friends of the men who had been killed. He also said there would be a ceremony later in the week for the whole community, at a time to be announced. He said Pope Tawadros would be here then.

I knew I was going to have to say something to all of those people the next day, but I was relieved I wasn't going to have to do it right then. I knew most of those families of the men who had been killed. I knew it would be as difficult for them to listen to as it would be for me to speak. Everyone would want to know all about what had happened to us.

I wasn't sure what to tell them and what not to tell them. I would figure out how to handle that later. At the moment, I just wanted to go home.

The priests and my family walked into the church. Nobody else was allowed in. We stayed there for at least an hour, waiting for the people outside to leave.

Father Ignatius and the others had set up some tables with some food and drinks. Father Bishoy talked for quite a while with my father. My mother didn't leave my side. My brother and sister, who were all dressed up in their Sunday finest, stood off in the corner, not sure what they were supposed to do. Nobody paid much attention to them, though I saw Father Bishoy go up and talk to them once or twice.

Everyone in the room came up to me to talk and offer condolences. I didn't say much other than to thank them all for their good wishes and say how sorry I was for what had happened to all of the families and friends of the men killed—especially for my parents, who lost two sons. I was thinking more about them than I was about myself.

When we finally arrived back at our house, I was surprised to see a huge array of flowers and things in the main room. We lived in a small house. My father wasn't a wealthy man. We never had much money. He had worked his whole life as the janitor at our school. He was good at fixing things, and that is where we all learned the skills we needed to get jobs in construction.

Before I had left home, I had been sharing a room with my younger brother. Now I would have a room to myself. I remembered how I had wished I would get the room to myself. Now I wished it wasn't mine.

The main room had pictures of Touma and Guirguis on a table in the center of the room. There were candles on the tables too, as well as some of their favorite things, such as a soccer ball, some hats, and old clothes—things that reminded my parents of them. When we walked in, the first thing my mother did was light the candles.

There was an empty spot on the table too. I knew pictures of me and things of mine had been there earlier. I didn't say anything about that.

I felt awkward at first, even though this was my home—the only home I had ever known. It was obvious that the family was in mourning and there was great sadness in our home. I was still feeling a little strange about me being alive and them not being there.

I sat down on the couch, as I had thousands of times before, and my mother made a big fuss over me. I wasn't hungry or thirsty, but she insisted that I eat and drink. I was tired from all that had taken place that day. More than anything else, though, I wanted to be by myself for a while. I was home.

When my mother and father finished showering me with love and affection, I went into what was to be my bedroom. I was glad to be home, but I wasn't looking forward to tomorrow. I was still shaken by what had happened at the church hours earlier, and many thoughts were running through my head. I was having many different feelings, too, but mostly I was nervous about what was going to happen in the morning.

I knew my father wanted to know all about what happened to Touma and Guirguis and the others, but I heard my mother tell him not to ask. He would have to wait, like the others. She could tell that I needed some time before talking about it.

When I lay down in Touma's bed, which had become Guirguis's bed, I could feel the two of them there with me. It was a strange feeling, but I knew, in my heart that they were glad I was home. I was too young to go off with them as I had, but I had begged them to take me with them, and they had agreed, reluctantly. They had helped me convince our father to let me go, too.

I wasn't able to go to sleep, though I was weary from the long car ride and all of the excitement at the church. I tossed and turned for a long time. The events of the day kept playing through my mind.

I kept seeing the faces of people. The looks on the faces of all of those people who came out to welcome me made me feel good. They truly were glad to see me. I knew how sad they really were and how much they missed all of their families and friends, but they were happy to see me. I felt it. Father Bishoy had been right about that.

I thought about all that had happened in the last few days, since my arrival at St. Mark's. I thought a lot about Malala and what she had done after being shot in the head and going through all of those surgeries. I thought about how brave she had been. I was nervous about what I would say. I didn't want to be the center of attention, but I was, whether I liked it or not.

But then I thought about what Father Bishoy had told me. God had saved me, and He had done so for a reason. I didn't know what the reason was, but I remembered what the Muslim boy had told me and what Father Bishoy had said to me too: "Go and tell the world what you have seen."

At that moment, I realized what I had to do. I had to tell the world what had happened to us. I had to tell the world what those men had done to us in the name of religion. I had to tell the world how those brave men I was with had faced death.

I realized that I might have to go to school, like Malala did, and make myself smarter and better able to do what else I might have to do with my life. I still didn't want to do it. I was happy working with my brothers, being the young boy that I was. I wanted my life back. I wanted my brothers and the others back.

Since that wasn't possible, I didn't have a choice. After what I'd been through, I couldn't go back to being what I was and just pretend it hadn't happened. I had to do what God wanted me to do. That was all there was to it.

Once I figured that out, I fell asleep not long thereafter. I still didn't know what I would say in the morning, but I knew that I would not be ashamed of myself to say it. God had saved me for a reason, and that reason was so I would tell the world about what had happened to us.

Although I was still nervous, I was ready for the morning. I didn't know what would happen after that, and I would worry about that later. I wasn't going to change the world. God would have to do that. I was His instrument.

CHAPTER 28

Telling the World

The next morning, I awoke early. My parents were already awake—and so were my brother and sister, which surprised me, because they didn't usually get up this early. They were still kids and were allowed to sleep late—but not today. My family was excited about what was to take place in a few hours.

My mother was making breakfast. Everyone was seated at the table, waiting for me to get up. I sat down somewhat sheepishly. I wasn't used to all of this attention—especially from my younger brother and sister.

"What are you looking at?" I asked them jokingly.

They laughed nervously. They were both unsure of what to say or do. Maryam was ten, and Sami was twelve. They were both dressed in their church clothes again—the same ones as the day before. I noticed my mother had laid out clothes on the couch for me to wear.

My mother was chirping away while she cooked, keeping things from being too quiet. My father sat there, not saying a word, observing all that was going on. I knew he wanted to ask me about what had happened to his two oldest sons, but he would have to wait too. One time, though, he couldn't help himself. He asked, "You were there, Mekhaeil, right up to the end?"

My mother scolded him. "Gabriel!" she said. That was all that she needed to say, and he stopped.

I answered, "Yes, Papa."

He nodded, lowered his eyes, and said no more.

I talked to Sami and Maryam, asking them about what they had been doing since I'd been gone. Maryam was the first to open up some, and she began to tell me about how she and her girlfriends had been learning how to dance, play music, and do other things. I remembered how Omar had told us girls her age couldn't do such things under Taliban rule, but I didn't say anything about that to her. She had grown in the several months that I had been gone, but she was still a little girl. She didn't understand all that was going on.

I wasn't sure how much she or Sami knew about what those men had done to us, and I wasn't going to ask. I didn't know how much they knew about the problems between Muslims and Christians that were going on in the world. I hadn't known much of our history before Cyril, Omar, Rushdi, Demetrius, and the others explained it to me. I was sure that neither she nor Sami had any idea of any of that. I figured all they knew was that Touma and Guirguis wouldn't be coming home anymore. I wasn't going to tell them anything more than that. If they were going to be in church that morning, they'd hear about it then. That would be soon enough.

I smiled and laughed with the two of them, but my stomach was churning inside. I knew I was going to be the center of attention. I tried to think about what to say and how to say it, but the words weren't coming easily to me.

The hours passed surprisingly quickly. Before I knew it, I was showered and dressed and we were entering the church. When we walked in, the church was already nearly full. My family was ushered up to the front and seated in the first row. We never sat in the first row. That was a first.

As I walked along the aisle to where we were seated, I noticed that the looks on the faces around me weren't the happy ones I had seen the day before. They were solemn. These were the family members of those who had been slain. Their sons, husbands, brothers, or fathers wouldn't be coming home, as I had.

Father Bishoy came from behind the altar to welcome us.

He asked how I was feeling and greeted my family warmly. I thanked him for all he had done for me and told him how happy I was to be at home. He asked if I was ready for what was about to happen, and I told him I was as ready as I would ever be, though I was nervous about what I would say.

All of the priests and deacons, who were all dressed in white with black sashes turned to the side to reflect that they were in mourning, came out shortly after that. Father Ignatius said Mass. Father Ignatius gave a very short homily, saying little more than that this Mass was being offered for the souls of our dearly departed brothers. And then, after Communion and after the Mass ended, he said, "Now we will hear from Mekhaeil Zacharias, the only survivor of the horrific event we all saw on television four days ago." He then motioned to me and said, "Mekhaeil, if you would, please."

I stood and walked to the pulpit. I felt uncomfortable in the suit and tie I was wearing. I hadn't been dressed like that for many months, ever since we left Egypt. I was nervous, but I felt good about what I was going to say. I took a deep breath, and then I began.

"Last Friday I was working with my brothers and the others in Sirte, Libya, when we were captured by men who I later learned were from ISIS. We were herded, like cattle, into a truck and driven away. We were then put into a barn, with our hands cuffed behind us and our legs chained together, where we spent the night."

For the next hour, I told them of every detail I could remember about what had happened to us and how we had spent that last night together. I explained that because we all knew we would likely be killed in the morning, Demetrius had told us that we should prepare ourselves for death and had said that if we were to die, we would become martyrs, like the many Copts before us who had been persecuted and killed for being followers of Jesus Christ. I told them about how we all repented our sins to each other, hoping God would find us worthy of acceptance into heaven should that happen.

As I spoke, I looked out at the hundreds of people sitting before me, but I wasn't as afraid to talk to them as I had thought I was going to be, and I didn't cry. Everyone in the church, all of whom were dressed in black, was crying. The women held black handkerchiefs in their hands and were using them to wipe tears away. The men allowed the tears to run freely down their cheeks.

When I told them about how we said prayers, sang hymns, and talked about Jesus Christ; St. Mark, our founder and patron saint; the fundamental beliefs of our Coptic religion and the history of our church; Christianity, Judaism, and Islam; and about the Crusades, Constantine, the Bible, the Torah, the Koran and all the rest, the crying briefly subsided.

I'm sure everyone was surprised to hear about that, but when I told them that the men vowed to go willingly to their deaths rather than allow those evil people to take dignity from them, or to give the terrorists any reason to think that they would ever deny Jesus Christ and convert to Islam, the people stood and clapped their hands. The priests clapped the loudest.

I told them how, when morning came, I was taken out of line as the men were led, like animals going to slaughter, to a beach and made to kneel down. There were groans and moans throughout the whole time I was talking, but the most wailing came when I told them about how I was forced to watch as the terrorists cut off the head of every one of the men, one by one.

I told them that I expected to die with the others right up to the very last minute and that I had no idea why I was spared. I told them that I was then driven back to the place where we had been captured. Then I paused, found the eyes of my parents, and told them that the last words from the terrorists to me when they released me were "Go and tell the world what you have seen."

Then I said, "That is exactly what I intend to do with my life from now until the day I die."

When I said that, the people stood and clapped—even louder than before, it seemed. When they sat back down, I added, "But I will do so not out of anger or to avenge the deaths of my two brothers or the deaths of your fathers, sons, brothers, relatives, or friends, but to try to help the world find a way not to kill each other in the name of religion. That is not what God wants us to do on this earth. That is not the way Jesus Christ taught us to behave. I forgive those men for what they did to us, and I pray that God will forgive them too."

EPILOGUE

Since the event about which this book was written took place, the Middle East, and the world, has changed dramatically. ISIS went on to capture Sirte, and it continues to control that city to this day. Libya remains a volatile country, and no one has been able to restore order there yet. ISIS has spawned more terrorist organizations, and there have been acts of terror perpetrated in Paris, the Netherlands, the United States, and other countries.

Even more worrisome, perhaps, is that millions of people are fleeing Syria, Iraq, Afghanistan, and other countries, most of whom are refugees from those war-torn areas. Others are fleeing for economic reasons, seeking a better life. Regardless, Europe is besieged with hordes of men, women, and children who have arrived, uninvited, to Turkey, Greece, Macedonia, and Italy, primarily. From there they migrate north, to Hungary, Germany, the Netherlands, Denmark, Sweden, and elsewhere. The European Economic Union hasn't been able to satisfactorily come to grips with the refugee problem, which threatens the very existence of the EEU, as well as several of its individual members.

The Arab Spring, which is said to have begun in Tunisia in early 2011, was initially viewed by many observers with hope and optimism for much-needed change in many countries of the Middle East. Several kings and rulers were thrown from their high positions in a wave of what was thought at the time to be an undeniable and unstoppable movement on the part of the people of that part of the world to establish new democratic governments. Those rulers who were able to weather the storms and remain in power did so either by responding in some satisfactory way to the demands of their people or by crushing their opposition with force.

Other leaders left, abdicating their positions and leaving their countries to those who rebelled. Virtually every country in the

Middle East experienced some kind of uprising or unrest. As of the date of this book's publication, that unrest is worsening in many countries. There are few reasons to be optimistic that a peaceful resolution of the many conflicts in the region is near.

In December of 2010, a Tunisian street vendor, Mohamed Bouazizi, set himself on fire to protest the way he and others like him were being treated by government officials. His death is now considered by many to have been the spark that ignited the region. By January, flames of revolt were burning brightly. National elections took place in Tunisia not long thereafter, but revolt and rebellion had already spread to countries all over the region, and there was no stopping the insurrection.

The hope and optimism of those early days that democratic reforms were about to take place in those countries was short-lived. Over the span of the next five years, debate and diplomacy have all but disappeared. Armed warfare, violence, and the perpetration of abominable atrocities have become the norm. Innocent civilians have been the primary casualties of all that is occurring, which is why so many are fleeing the area.

In Jordan, King Abdullah dismissed the government, and two prime ministers resigned shortly thereafter in response to protests by the Jordanian people. Through the use of a strong and loyal military, he weathered the storm. He remains in power to this day. Because of its proximity to Israel, stability in Jordan is seen to be an extremely important component to peace in the region. It has taken in many refugees.

The situation in Jordan is reasonably stable, and it, more than any other country, is undertaking some positive action to address the refugee problem. In fact, Jordan joined the fight against ISIS and participated in the aerial bombing campaign. However, when one of its pilots was captured, placed in a cage, and then burned to death, the world mourned another tragedy.

In Oman, Sultan Qaboos, who was installed as the leader of the country in a military coup orchestrated by the British in 1970, remains in power, but in 2011 he dismissed his ministers in answer to the protests of his people, who wanted more jobs, better jobs, and higher wages, among other things. He is a monarch, the prime minister, and the leader of the military, and he is also in control of the finances of the country. He, too, survived the storm, owing to the support of a strong and loyal military.

In Yemen, Ali Abdullah Saleh stepped down in 2012 after thirty-three years of rule. That decision helped to reduce tensions for a while, but the country then became a haven for terrorists, in large part because members of the military were part of the opposition movement, so the government was in a divided and weakened condition.

The current leader, Abd Rabbuh Mansur al-Hadi, who was Saleh's right-hand man, hasn't been able to quell the problems. With no strong central government to control the rebels, the situation has deteriorated. One of the worst of the terrorist groups, al-Qaeda of the Arabian Peninsula, is headquartered there. Yemen is considered to be one of the least stable countries on earth, and home for several terrorist organizations.

In Bahrain, protests against the way the country was being governed began as early as February of 2011. Those protests against the king of Bahrain continue to this day. The country has been ruled by the Al Khalifa dynasty since 1793.

The military of Bahrain has been able to suppress the revolt, though there were many months during which a state of national emergency existed and civil liberties were greatly curtailed. The United States has a large military base in the country, and it wants to maintain its presence in the region. The country is actually a collection of islands in the Gulf of Bahrain, which connects to the Persian Gulf, so it provides a safe haven for the many naval ships harbored there.

In Saudi Arabia, there was no change in power in direct response to the tension throughout the region, and that was largely because King Abdullah bin Abdulaziz al Saud, who became the ruler in 2005, responded to those who criticized him by opening the door to reform. He succeeded in implementing many progressive changes. He also made great efforts to allow women more rights, and for the first time, women were allowed to vote last year. The majority of people in Saudi Arabia continue to embrace a strong fundamentalist Islamic ideology, and many opposed such changes. Saudi Arabia, which is a predominantly Sunni state, is deeply involved in the struggles for power throughout the region. It is seen by the world community to be in opposition to those governments led by Shiites.

King Abdullah died in January of 2015. His brother, King Salmon bin Abdulaziz al Saud, replaced him. With his departure, the political climate began changing. A high-profile Shiite leader was executed, along with forty-six other opponents of the government, in January of 2016. Tensions between Saudi Arabia and Iran are extremely high at the moment.

In Egypt, former president Mubarek resigned in 2011 amid loud and vocal opposition on many fronts. National elections were held soon thereafter to elect his successor. When Muhammad Morsi won and his Muslim Brotherhood party took control of the country, problems soon arose. The Egyptian Army took control of the country by military coup. The chief justice of the supreme court was installed as the interim leader. That move was supported by most non-Muslim groups, which allegedly included Pope Tawadros II, head of the Coptic Church.

The military restored government functions and wants the world to think that Egypt is a democracy undergoing some temporary difficulties, not a military regime. The army continues to control the country. The Muslim community is openly hostile to what has taken place, and many Copts and other Christians have been killed in retaliation for their assumed support of the military ouster of Morsi and the Muslim Brotherhood.

In Syria, President Bashar-al-Assad is still the leader, but he is under intense fire. Syria is in the midst of a complicated civil war in which many countries—including the United States, Iran, Turkey, Iraq, Jordan, Russia, and many others—are deeply involved in some fashion. There is a United States–led coalition whose objective is to destroy ISIS.

Bashar-al-Assad has been president of Syria for fifteen years. He succeeded his father, who had been president of the country for thirty years before that. His alleged use of chemical weapons against his own people caused him to be the source of much criticism and condemnation by the United Nations.

Assad's entire cabinet resigned in 2011, on the eve of the revolution against him. While much of the opposition centers around pleas for reform and progress, religion remains the single most divisive issue, which pits Sunnis against Shiites. Assad is a Sunni.

The United States and many other countries continue to call for his resignation. Peace talks began in February of 2016 with the goal of ending the civil war and eliminating ISIS by the combined military force of all concerned parties. There are rebel forces fighting for regime change, in addition to the terrorists.

However, with the rise of ISIS, it seems as if the United States may prefer Assad's leadership over a weak central government, because it fears that the lack of a strong leader could allow other terrorist groups to thrive, even if ISIS is destroyed. That is what happened in Iraq. ISIS, whose goal is to establish an Islamic state in Iraq and Syria, is seen as the greater evil.

The outcome of that war is very much in doubt at this time. The aerial campaign continues, but no ground troops from other countries have been sent in yet, except for those from Iran, which is a Shia country. The United States has thousands of soldiers in the area who are reportedly advisers—not combat troops.

In Sudan, the southern part of the country seceded from the north in 2011. The country of South Sudan now has a seat at the United Nations. In the north, Omar Hassan al-Bashir remains in power, despite enormous pressure for him to resign. He has remained in control through the use of military force that many have described as brutal. Hundreds of thousands of people have died in the Darfur area in recent years as a result of his actions.

In Morocco, which is the westernmost country in the Arab world, at the tip of the African continent, Muhammad VI is king. He inherited the throne from his father in 1999. His father ruled the country for thirty-eight years. His grandfather ruled the country for over fifty years. There are many who protest, calling for democratic reforms, but so far the protests have been peaceful.

Muhammad VI's rule began with much fanfare as he sought to implement many democratic ideas, which some say he learned while attending law school in France. Many of his actions angered

Muslim fundamentalists and traditionalists. His government was not spared during the Arab Spring.

He was the subject of much criticism due to allegations of widespread corruption. He responded by calling for a new constitution and even more progressive changes. So far he has succeeded in preventing any serious threats to his leadership.

In Kuwait, Sheik Sabah Al Sabah is the emir. He succeeded his father and his brother in office. He was the prime minister of the country for forty years before becoming one of what are called the royal rulers, in 2004. He, too, dealt with protests during the Arab Spring.

His cabinet resigned in 2011 amid protests. Al Sabah scheduled elections to pacify the protesters, but they boycotted those elections. At one point, Al-Sabah dissolved the parliament to reduce tension in his country. While he remains in control, his country is in turmoil because of continued hostility between the government and the national assembly to this date.

Lebanon is in turmoil, and as of this moment, there is no president and many are vying for that position. Because of its proximity to Syria, it is receiving hundreds of thousands of refugees. Because of its proximity to Israel, it has received hundreds of thousands of Palestinians, who fled the country because of the bloodshed that was occurring. They were not allowed to return to Israel after the fighting subsided, yet they are not allowed citizenship in Lebanon.

In Iraq, civil war erupted in 2011 as the United States withdrew its combat troops. It was called an insurgency. It has become much more than that. For a while, ISIS posed a serious threat to capture Baghdad itself, despite the efforts of the United States and its allies to prevent that from happening. Iraqi forces, together with their allies, have retaken Ramadi and hope to wrest control of Mosul from ISIS in the months ahead.

The outcome is uncertain, as the underlying basis for the unrest stems from the religious divide between the Sunnis and the Shias in that country, just as in virtually all other countries in the region. It would appear that until that matter is resolved the unrest will continue in some fashion. The trouble began with the death of Saddam Hussein, a Sunni, at the hands of the United States, in 2003.

Nouri al-Maliki, a Shiite, became the prime minister in 2004, with the blessing of the United States. He was replaced in 2014, with the approval of the United States, in response to a decade of continuous protests by a Sunni majority against his regime. The United States withdrew the last of its combat troops in December of 2011, but it is now putting soldiers back in the country as "advisers," for the stated purpose of destroying ISIS and restoring stability to the country.

Afghanistan—which is not considered to be part of the Middle East, though it borders Iran—is in turmoil, and daily attacks by the Taliban remain a constant threat to the stability of the newly elected government. Mullah Omar died of natural causes not long ago, but nothing has changed as a result. Mullah Omar created the Taliban in 1994 or thereabouts, and he was its undisputed leader. He was responsible for implementing sharia law and for directing the military takeover of Afghanistan.

The United States pulled out all combat troops in 2014, as President Barack Obama pledged to do by the end of his presidency. However, in October of 2015, he decided to reverse course and leave thousands of support troops in the country for the time being. Violence and bloodshed remain a part of daily life in that country, because the Taliban, who are Sunnis, allow for no religious diversity—and that includes Shia Muslims. Most observers fear that the Taliban will be back in power before long.

The Palestinian issue remains a source of conflict, and it may be, despite all the bloodshed and turmoil in the region, the single most contentious issue in the Middle East. Israel is surrounded by countries that are overwhelmingly Islamic by faith, some of which openly seek the ouster of the Jewish state from the region. Diplomatic efforts to provide for a two-state solution have failed repeatedly. Fighting between the Israelis and the Palestinians continued during the Arab Spring, and in 2014, there were lengthy and deadly battles in the Gaza strip that drew much attention from the world community, including the United Nations.

There is no diplomatic end in sight for Israel as the current prime minister, Benjamin Netanyahu, is opposed to a two-state solution. Israel's superior military, which has the full support of the United States government, has prevented any serious challenge to its sovereignty. Over 75 percent of the citizens of Israel are Jewish, but the Muslim minority, which is almost 20 percent of the population, are unhappy and openly defiant.

Residents of various countries in Northern Africa are also experiencing horrific acts of inhumanity and violence as terrorists seemingly control the area. At the very least, it is fair to say that leaders of countries like Nigeria, where Boko Haram has captured and enslaved young Christian girls on more than one occasion, are unable to stop them and prevent further atrocities. The United States recently sent in ground troops to help the government deal with the terrorists.

As is evident, that entire region of the world was in tumult after the Arab Spring came into being, and it remains in tumult as of the date of publication of this book. No country was spared. The problems were, to some extent, political, but it appears abundantly clear to most observers that the underlying differences in religious ideology are causing most of the problems.

Without question, the region has seen many wars and much conflict for thousands of years. The Arab Spring and its aftermath are the most recent hostilities that have occurred over two millennia. History truly is repeating itself.

While this book was in production, a mass exodus of people from Syria, Iraq, Afghanistan and other places in the Middle East has caused enormous problems for Europe and all neighboring countries. Terrorist acts have occurred in the United States. Our political leaders claim that ISIS is being defeated on the battlefield, but our military leaders tell us that victory will take many months, if not years, to achieve. Prospects for a peaceful resolution of the various conflicts throughout the Middle East are dismal.

What happened in Sirte, Libya, in February of 2015 was an atrocity of enormous proportions. Since then, other atrocities have occurred and the situation there and throughout the entire Middle East has worsened dramatically. The question of when it will end, and how, remains unanswered. There is no end in sight.

AFTERWORD

The idea to write this book first entered my mind while watching a Sunday-morning news show in December of 2014, on which talking heads were looking back and analyzing what had occurred during the year just ending. When asked to identify the most significant story in the world that was being neglected or underreported, one of the panelists said it was the slaughter of Christians in the Middle East. I was deep into my previous novel, *To Valhalla*, which was about Afghanistan and the Taliban, and I had become aware of how radical the Islamic movement had become, to the peril of Christians, Jews, and others.

ISIS had appeared on the world scene months earlier, raising its ugly head and its black flag. I wanted to learn more about who and what the Christians mentioned on the show were. I wondered whether they were Catholics, Protestants, or some variety thereof. The seed for this book was planted at that time.

The full extent of the truly disturbing plight of Christians in the Middle East became more fully realized by the world when, in mid-2014, ISIS began beheading people and doing more and more incredibly heinous things in Iraq and Syria. While I was still conducting my research, twenty-one Coptic Christians were beheaded by ISIS in Libya in early 2015.

I have watched the video of those men marching to their deaths many times. What struck me the most then—and it still sends a shiver up my spine to this very day—is the attitude those men displayed as they marched, literally, to the beach where they were beheaded. They showed no fear; they were not afraid to die.

It seemed to me that they willingly accepted their fate. There is little doubt in my mind but that those men went to their deaths with the firm conviction that they would be meeting their God that very day. At that point, the focus of the book I was to write became clear.

As I began writing the book, it seemed as if the number of Islamic extremist groups was growing on a daily basis. The situation was getting worse and worse, never better. Despite assurances from our government that we were "winning" the war and that ISIS would be destroyed, it never seemed that way. There was never any good news, never any promising developments.

In Nigeria, teenage schoolgirls were kidnapped and raped by Boko Haram. Not long after that, 148 innocent students were massacred in Kenya by a group that calls itself al-Shabaab. ISIS was killing Christians and destroying ancient religious churches and relics while capturing more cities and more territory in Iraq and continuing the fight in Syria.

The most perplexing part of the problem is, of course, that the despicable and indefensible inhumane acts are being done in the name of religion by zealots who believe their god commands them to do so as part of a worldwide jihad. Christians and others who had committed no crimes and done nothing to bring carnage upon themselves were dying simply because of their beliefs. At every opportunity, Sunnis were slaughtering Shiites, and Shiites were slaughtering Sunnis, and both groups were slaughtering Christians and others who held religious beliefs different from theirs.

For those of us who live in the United States, we take our religious freedoms for granted. Although school-sponsored prayer is restricted in many of our public schools and the words "In God We Trust" are no longer used as frequently in public discourse as they once were, we remain a predominantly Christian nation. *Wikipedia* tells us that over 80 percent of Americans are Christians, but that number is decreasing. In the early 1960s, over 90 percent of Americans were Christians.

Our laws and our legal system prohibit discrimination based upon religion. Prospective employers are not allowed to inquire about religious beliefs. We, as a country, separate church matters from matters of state as best we can, as a matter of law—not policy.

However, many Americans, even those who are devout

followers of Christ, now question the teachings of the various Christian denominations on issues such as same-sex marriage, abortion, contraception, the place of women in the church, the celibacy of priests, the fact that divorced Catholics are not allowed to receive sacraments, pedophiles in the priesthood, divorce in general, whether or not gays or lesbians can be ministers, and other such things.

Many other Americans are moving away from traditional Christianity. They no longer attend church and now call themselves "spiritual but not religious." There are now many more agnostics, who doubt the existence of God, in our country. There are also many more atheists in our country, who deny the existence of God.

The definition of the word *heresy* is "to have an opinion or engage in a practice contrary to church dogma." The word *dogma* refers to a set of principles that are incontrovertibly true. Most people who question their church's teachings on various issues probably wouldn't consider themselves to be heretics. Most people probably wouldn't consider themselves to be dogmatic either.

Americans, by and large, want to exercise their own free will and their own independent judgment. They want to decide for themselves what it is they truly believe. That is the American way—independent, and fiercely so—yet we respect the rights of others who hold differing beliefs.

Since it is extremely unlikely that Christians will convince Muslims, Jews, or any other religious groups that they are wrong and Christianity is the right answer, or vice versa, the real issue to be addressed is how to find a way to prevent men from killing other men in the name of their god in the future. No one has been able to successfully resolve that issue over the last two thousand years, if not more, and innocent people continue to die. How do we prevent history from continuing to repeat itself?

Can there be reconciliation between the three religious communities that dominate the Middle East? Are the beliefs so deeply seated that no change is possible? Are the beliefs so intrinsically inconsistent that a reconciliation of the fundamental issues is unthinkable? Are continued killings inevitable? What will it take to eliminate, or at least diminish, the prospects of future horrific acts?

The most pressing question—and it truly is an urgent matter—is, How can the world stop ISIS, the Taliban, and all of the other terrorist groups from killing innocent people in the name of their religion, as they continue to do as this book goes into print? But the larger question is, How can the world prevent such atrocities from occurring in the future, so that a lasting tolerance of varying religious beliefs can be achieved, and history doesn't repeat itself again?

Pierce Kelley

ABOUT THE AUTHOR

Pierce Kelley received his bachelor of arts degree from Tulane University, New Orleans, Louisiana. He earned his doctor of jurisprudence degree from George Washington University, Washington, D.C. He lives and practices law in Fort White, Florida.

FURTHER READING

Works that I read in researching the topics involved in this book include the following:

Grant, Michael. *Constantine the Great.* Scribner & Sons, Inc., 1993.

Ibrahim, Raymond. *Crucified Again: Exposing Islam's New War on Christianity.* Washington, DC: Regnery Publishing, 2013.

Isbouts, Jean-Pierre. *The Story of Christianity.* National Geographic, 2014.

Lutzer, Erwin W. *The Cross in the Shadow of the Crescent.* Eugene, OR: Harvest House, 2013.

Marshall, Paul, Lela Gilbert, and Nina Shea. *Persecuted: The Global Assault on Christians.* Nashville, TN: Thomas Nelson, 2013.

Meinardus, Otto F. A. *Two Thousand Years of Coptic Christianity.* Cairo: the American University in Cairo Press, 1999.

Rollings, Willard H. *Great Religions.* Columbia, MO: University of Missouri Press, 1992.

For those who don't understand why terrorist acts happen, Massacre at Sirte is a most illuminating read.

There aren't many subjects tougher to tackle than the continuing threat of terrorism and the religious beliefs that fuel it, but Pierce Kelley triumphs with Massacre at Sirte, a simple but searing tale of "what if."

Kelley set out to write about the persecution of Christians, he explains in the book's epilogue, so when twenty-one Coptic Christian migrant workers from Egypt were kidnapped and executed by ISIS in Sirte, Libya, in February 2015, he had the event to pin his tale upon. The "what if" in this scenario: What if one of the men had survived? What story would he tell? So, in Kelley's reimagining of this real-life event, twenty-one men captured becomes twenty-two, as the youngest of the group, a character he names Mekhaeil Zacharias, is drawn into the action but is spared rather than executed. "Go and tell the world what you have seen," his young ISIS captor says upon his release, and this statement takes on great meaning for young Mekhaeil.

For such a simple writing style, Kelley's prose is effective and vivid. You're there, uncomfortably chained with the others on the floor in this pitch-dark, dingy, smelly building with no food or water, no toilet. You're hearing each voice sound out into the darkness in an organized and respectful hypothetical discussion among the men about their lives and their beliefs. One at a time they speak, and Mekhaeil only listens, not feeling he has anything to contribute at such a young age, only wanting to learn from the others. And learn he does. Kelley guides the teen Copt through a gentle evolution of thought pattern and confidence. His growing sense of purpose in the kidnapping's aftermath is predictable but is sweet and satisfying nonetheless.

These men are fully convinced, as they're all trapped there together, that they're going to die, so they confess their sins and reaffirm their beliefs. As it gets down to brass tacks in these moments, their most treasured items are each other's thoughts. Kelley shows them embracing their humanity by sharing and valuing their views. The goal of the more self-assured among them is to prepare each man to meet his maker in the morning with a greater understanding of history and why they have been captured. Questions are confronted: Why do these Muslims hate Christians so much? Should they convert to Islam to live, if given the choice, or die for Christ as he died for them?

Kelley uses the captives' respectful discussion to parallel an overarching point, which he then sums up in his afterword: "Since it is extremely unlikely that Christians will convince Muslims, Jews, or any other religious groups that they are wrong and Christianity is the right answer, or vice versa, the real issue to be addressed is how to find a way to prevent men from killing other men in the name of their god."

There is a strong sense of despair during the captivity part of the story, and one of Kelley's most effective tools is when the men wonder if their country, or another country like the United States, will come to save them. That's a "no," and it's a painful one from this perspective. For those who don't understand why these sorts of terrorist acts happen, Massacre at Sirte—particularly with its extensive history lesson—is a most illuminating read.

-CLARION REVIEW